No Ifs, Ands, or BEARS About It

CELIA KYLE

NEW YORK TIMES BESTSELLING AUTHOR

The first day of Mia's new life in Grayslake, Georgia is not going as planned. The house her grandfather left her looks ready to crumble, boxes cover every inch of the floor and—oh—there's a bear cub in her pantry. It gets worse when the cub's uncle comes by and busts out his fur and claws while on her front porch. Then it gets loads better because suddenly there's a hot hunk of badge-wearing werebear on her lawn ready to rescue her. Yum. Of course, he has to ruin things by trying to take the cub out of her hands. Ha! The cub is hers… No ifs, ands, or bears about it.

Werebear Ty can't seem to get the curvaceous, delectable Mia to understand that, even if she is one-quarter werebear, she isn't keeping the cub. Ty is the Grayslake Itan, the clan's leader, and the little werebear is going home with him… Unless it isn't. It's her smile. If she'd stop smiling and being gorgeous, his inner-bear would support him and Ty would get his way. But the beast wants to make their woman happy, so it's perfectly content to let her do as she pleases. Then things change. Threats arise, danger comes close, and Ty demands she return to his den. No ifs, ands, or *mates* about that.

chapter one

A bear cub sat in her pantry.

Mia squinted and peered into the dim interior. Yup, a bear cub. The small ball of fur shifted, reflective black eyes settling on her with interest.

Heck no, she was not being mauled by a bear.

She slammed the door shut and counted to five, sure it'd been a figment of her imagination. Her mind had been playing tricks on her ever since she'd walked through the door of her deceased grandfather's home. Part of her wondered if he'd decided to haunt her as he'd always threatened. A familiar pang of grief speared her heart. That fleeting thought brought back the memory of standing at the old man's graveside less than a week ago, clutching her dad's hand as her grandfather was lowered into the ground.

Her eyes stung, tears forming and clouding her vision, and she wiped away the moisture as it trailed down her cheeks. He was gone. She needed to push past the grief and live her life. He'd whoop her from one end of the house to the other if he caught her crying over him. The man had lived to a hundred, and he'd been ready for a break already.

1

A low, barking whine came from the pantry, the solid wood muffling the sound but that didn't negate the source's existence.

She had a bear cub. In her pantry.

Gripping the knob, she eased the door open and peeked inside. Yup, still there. Huddled in a tiny ball, little eyes trained on her. Every inch of his fur stood on end.

"Hey, little guy." Mia kept her voice low, hopefully soothing to the cub. She was either dealing with a wild young one or a baby werebear. She was in Grayslake, Georgia. All werebears, all the time. She glanced at the cub. Mia voted for werebear. Like, really, really voted for werebear.

She hadn't inherited the ability to shift but her dad easily transformed from man to bear and back. So, she'd grown up knowing about shifters. And he'd told her, and proved to her, over and over again that *weres* in their animal form still held onto their human thoughts.

She extended a hand toward the cub and kept her voice pitched low. "Hey, sweetheart. Did you get stuck in here? You ready to come out?"

The little cub shook its head and scrambled deeper into the corner.

Crap. Well, crap on one hand and woo-hoo on the other. She was fairly sure she was dealing with a *were*, but he remained in her pantry.

"Okay," she sighed. "The thing about it is, you probably belong to someone who is a heck of a lot bigger than you and me put together. Your momma is going to be angry her cub is missing, and I don't wanna get between you and her."

Like, really, really didn't want to get between a cub and its mother. While a werebear had human love in its heart, there was also the bear's possessiveness and insane drive to kill anything, or anyone, who came between it and its young.

2

The cub shook its head, and its eyes glistened, shining with moisture that hadn't been there before. This had to happen on her first day in Grayslake.

"Okay, well, I'm gonna leave the door open. So, when you're ready to come out—" More trembling and an actual tear escaped the cub's eye.

Darn it.

"Listen, little guy, or girl, I'm sure you belong to someone and they're going to be so worried." She took a chance, and sought to confirm her beliefs. "Why don't you shift for me and tell me where you live? I'll take you home—"

The cub whined and clawed the ground, nails digging furrows into the hundred year old wood floors.

"Hey," she snapped. Cub or not, common courtesy spanned species barriers. "No scratching the floors." The little bear immediately stopped. "Thank you. Now—"

A harsh, heavy pounding on her front door yanked her attention from the cub. The wood rattled in its frame, reminding her she needed to hunt up a repairman to replace it. The door was original to the house, and she hated to swap it out with something modern, but in a town filled with bears… She'd rather have an extra layer of protection in case one of the residents turned cranky at having a mostly-human in their midst.

The hammering came again, followed by a rough yell, and she sighed. Was everyone in Grayslake intent on disrupting Mia's move? First the cub and now this guy. She'd only been in town a freakin' day.

"Answer." *Thud.* "This." *Pound.* "Door." *Crack.*

Aw, the *crack* did it. She'd buried her grandfather less than a week ago and was moving into his home at his bequest. Now some stranger decided to damage a piece of her memories. She didn't think so.

Mia looked to the cub once again. "I'll be right back, little one. Let me..." Her words trailed off as the pungent scent of urine hit her, and a widening puddle emerged from beneath the cub. She didn't need her father's shifter senses. The small bear's stark fear was unmistakable. There was a reason the cub was hiding, cowering, in her pantry, and she guessed it had everything to do with the man darn near breaking down her door.

She held a hand out, palm facing the small one. "Stay."

The only response she received was a tiny shudder.

More pounding from the front of the house echoed down the hallway, the man's increasing growls easily reaching her through the old walls. If this guy had anything to do with the cub, like she suspected, then she'd be facing a werebear pretty darned soon.

Which really sucked.

Her visitor pounded on the door so hard the windows rattled, shaking in their ancient casings and the floor trembled from the vibrations. The closer she padded to the front of her house, the more her fear increased. Her heart thumped, sending blood thundering through her body. It assaulted her, attacking her with unseen hands, and she fought against the growing panic. The shifter would scent her terror and feed on it. Heck, it'd probably turn her into a nice, crunchy snack.

And then where would her little cub be?

Darn, she'd already gone and claimed him as her own. Her father was going to laugh his rear-end off and then remind her she couldn't keep a shifter as a pet.

Ten feet separated her from the entryway, then five.

4

Okay, she had to get her poop in a group. Taking a deep breath, she dug deep within herself and sought out a good dose of anger. Anger trumped fear any day of the week. A shifter had a hard time getting past the scent of rage. She couldn't let the bear on the other side of the door know she was very close to crying for her daddy.

The man slammed his fist against the door, cracking the front window. The jagged line sliced through the glass in the bay window. Her favorite window. The one place she coveted when she visited her grandfather. How many nights had they spent sharing the window seat as she read to him?

Okay, she didn't have to hunt up anger any longer.

Without second guessing herself, Mia turned the knob and wrenched the door open. The move caught the snarling man by surprise, his fist nearly colliding with her face. Had she not ducked, she would have been one dead mostly-human.

The stranger pulled his punch and glared at her. He curled his lip to bare a fang.

But did he apologize? No!

His exposed canine thickened and lengthened, pushing past his lower lip. She should have—would have—been scared, but she glanced at the window seat, the crack in the glass now longer than before, and her anger renewed.

"Can I help you?" Her words were clipped.

"I want my cub." The male took a step closer and straightened, chest puffing out in an attempt to intimidate her. The sweet, heavy smell of alcohol wafted to her on the gentle breeze, and she wrinkled her nose.

He towered over her, but Mia stood her ground. If the baby bear in her pantry was this drunk guy's kid, she wasn't about to let him in. "I have no idea what you're talking about."

"I know he's in there." A low growl surrounded her and her pulse quickened.

"Did you see him come into my home?"

He narrowed his eyes. "Everyone knows better than to hide someone's young—"

"I wouldn't ever hide someone's young." She crossed her fingers as she lied.

He pointed at her. "*Human*, you got my nephew in there, and I want him back."

Mia tightened her grip on the edge of the door. A lot of *weres* thought of humans as less than dirt and it seemed this man was the same. "I'm only three-quarters human." Her father was a halfer, but could still shift, while her mother was fully human. "Like I asked, did you see him come in here?"

"I smell him in this house."

Oh, that was rich. She smirked and crossed her arms over her chest. "Really? Your nephew has hit puberty then?"

She knew the answer, but the snarky angel on her shoulder nudged her into being a butthead.

"I know that kid's scent."

"So, he *has* hit puberty then? Because if he has, calling him a cub has to annoy him." She glanced behind her, noting the boxes scattered through her home and taking up very spare inch. There was no way for her to hide a four hundred pound shifted teen in her house. "I'm not sure where you think I'd hide an adolescent bear."

"He's four." The werebear swayed in her doorway and more of that sweet stench of alcohol drifted toward her. Blech.

"So, he's still holding the scent of the forest. I thought males couldn't scent young before they hit their teens and they had to rely on sight until then. Only mamas recognized their cubs by their smell." Mia shifted her weight. She sensed the bear getting more pissed as time passed. "At least that's what Granddaddy told me." She tapped her chin with a finger. "Maybe he was wrong."

"He also shoulda told you that you don't keep a bear from its cub. It's dangerous. You need to send the boy out here or else you'll end up dead like—" He snapped his teeth together, and another growl came from him, this time deeper and filled with the man's beast. Dark brown hair sprouted from his pores, and his mouth began its shift from human male to deadly grizzly.

Aw, crap on a cracker.

She took a step back, putting at least another foot between her and the psycho shifting into a bear in the middle of her small neighborhood. She glanced across the street and met Mrs. Laurie's gaze. The woman held a cordless phone pressed to her ear. Okay, the ancient woman was either gossiping with Edna at the post office or calling the police. Mia really, really hoped she was getting the cops.

A snarl from her visitor snared her attention. Darn it, his features had taken on more of the beast. His forehead flattened, the distance between his eyes increasing, and his mouth became a fur covered snout. He opened his mouth, exposing two rows of deadly yellowed teeth, and fear rose fast and hot once again.

The man took a step forward, and she had no choice but to back up. Adrenalin filled her veins, pumping fast, and boiling through her body. She had to keep him away from the cub. Fight or flight battled inside her, and she realized she had only one option: fight.

The little cub was terrified of this male, and after meeting him, she easily saw why. He was a drunk and a bully. Based on the way he was trying to physically intimidate her, she didn't doubt he had abused the cub in some way. Women and children were cherished by *weres*. This guy seemed to cherish whisky more than anything.

7

"Sir, I think—"

The jarring whine of a police siren blasted through the air, and some of Mia's fear fled. Since Grayslake was a shifter town, the cop heading her way probably had some fur hidden beneath the uniform. There was no way the bears would put a human in that position.

The guy on Mia's porch spun and snarled at the approaching vehicle. If the whirring noise hurt her ears, she couldn't imagine what it did to the sensitive hearing of the *were*. Good.

The car screeched to a stop in the street, sliding sideways and making the tires squeal with the sudden halt. The male inside the vehicle flung the door wide and jumped onto the asphalt.

"Griss," the massive police officer stepped around the car door and Mia gulped. The cop gripped a handgun with both hands. Shooting him wouldn't put the bear shifter down, but it would hinder his destructive capabilities. "What's going on here?"

"Skin's got my nephew. His parents died and left him to me. Told you last week. He's mine, damn it."

Skin. She hated the derogatory name prejudiced *weres* had given humans. She bit her tongue on the need to correct him.

"Uh-huh." The gun-toting male kept coming, moving in slow, even steps.

As inappropriate as it was, Mia drooled over the guy. Just a tiny bit. What else could she do? The cop was tall, topping six feet, with wide shoulders and she could only imagine the muscles hidden by his uniform. His brown hair shined in the day's bright sunlight, the rays dancing over the strands. Even from the great distance, she was caught by his vivid blue eyes. At the moment, they were hard and angry, but she didn't doubt they could reflect kindness just as easily. His strong, square jaw elicited feelings of safety within her. His entire, overwhelming presence made her think of... being naked. She was really feeling her dry spell.

8

Then the stranger—*Griss*—growled and the sound snapped her out of her lusty haze. Right. A man trying to get through her to get at that poor cub took precedence over the hot cop.

The really hot cop.

"It's my damn boy, Ty." Griss's voice was deeper, more of a roaring snarl than anything.

"She might not have him." Twenty feet separated the cop, Ty, from the half-shifted bear. "Either way, I can't have you wearing your fur on the street. Come on down, now."

Griss swayed and stumbled toward the steps. "You gonna get that boy back? He's mine."

"Uh-huh." Ty nodded. "We'll talk about it, Griss."

Mia snorted. They weren't talking about anything if it involved giving the terrorized cub to the man before her.

Then she realized snorting had been a mistake.

Especially when Griss, even larger than before, spun on her and roared. It wasn't a low snarl or the wall shaking roar of before. Nope, the male was so loud her bay window splintered and shattered into a million pieces.

"Griss, damn it!" The echoing pop from the cop's handgun reached her a split second before a bullet plowed into the frame of her door.

The collision splintered the aged wood and slivers punctured her cheek and temple. She flinched, the stinging pain of the cuts slicing through her. Reacting to the ache, she placed her hand over the wounds and winced. Wetness lay beneath her palm, and the liquid spread more with every second.

But the shot did its job. The lumbering *were* spun back to the officer and snarled, advancing on the gorgeous man. She really hoped the

9

guy had another dozen bullets or so. Otherwise, he was just gonna end up with a face full of pissed off werebear.

The angry male plodded down the creaking wooden steps and headed straight for the cop. The officer could start shooting any time now.

Only a split second later, she realized why he hadn't. Another cop crept around the corner of her house, bent low as he stalked the half-shifted bear. The moment he was behind the distracted male he shot at the man's back. Two metal probes burst from the gun and launched across the distance, firmly embedding in the shifter's back. *Ah, a Taser.* The angry man jerked and twitched, screaming with the pain of fifty thousand volts bursting through his muscles. He spasmed and jolted, finally falling to the ground in a trembling heap. As he lay there, disoriented by the electricity blasting through him, the features of his bear receded.

"Damn it, Ty." Another round of jerks wracked the man's body.

"Don't blame me. Van is the one that got ya." The officer holstered his weapon and slowly approached Griss. His attention was split between the trembling man and the other cop still firmly holding the butt of the Taser, finger near the trigger. Ty squatted by Griss and stared down at the prone man. "Now, if you'd done as I said, you wouldn't be eating Miss..."

The officer looked to her. Mia took a few tentative steps onto the worn porch and stuttered out her name. "B-B-Baker. Mia Baker."

"You wouldn't be eating Miss Baker's front lawn."

"She's got my—"

"Uh-huh." Ty nodded. "I hear ya. Why don't we head to the station and we can talk about it? Maybe have a cup of coffee."

"Damn it." Griss struggled to get his hands and knees beneath him, but the other officer was quicker. Van had a set of cuffs on the bear so fast, Mia hadn't seen him move.

The second Griss realized he was captured he struggled anew, snarling and yanking at the cuffs.

"Come on. You don't want me to hit you again, do ya?" Van sounded like he wouldn't have minded one bit, but the threat quieted the drunken werebear and eventually the two men wrangled Griss into the backseat of the car.

Through it all, Mia watched the way Ty's uniform clung to him, outlined his muscles and nicely framed his ass. Darn, she wanted to nibble it.

"Miss Baker?" Lost in her thoughts, she hadn't noticed Van's approach. Standing on the ground while she remained on the porch, she noted he was eye level. He stared at her with eyes eerily familiar and very much like Ty's.

"What?" She shook her head and grimaced. "Sorry."

"No problem, ma'am." He gestured behind him. "We're gonna get Griss back to the station." He grinned, a wicked smile that crept into her and slithered over her nerves. A hint of arousal unfurled, but it had nothing—nothing—on what happened to her body when she'd first seen Ty. Van leaned forward, propped his forearm on the porch rail, and gave her a wink. "Then I'll be back to take your statement."

A low growl was preceded by a barked order from Ty. "Get your car. We've got a job to do."

The officer's sharp words pulled her attention to him, and her heart stuttered. Yeah, Van was attractive but Ty... Dang.

Giving her another wink and flashing a seductive smile, the officer wandered away, disappearing around the corner of her home. His departure had her turning back to a glaring, definitely angry, Ty. Angry or not, the man was gorgeous.

The car rocked, Griss fighting his captivity and causing the vehicle's springs to creak and squeak. Ty glanced back at the werebear and then to her again. "We'll take him and keep him overnight. Get him sobered up. I'll come back for your statement just as soon as we get him settled in a cell."

He spun on his heel, heading back to the rocking car. In moments, he was traveling down the street, roars following him.

The second he was out of sight, Mia bolted for the house, slamming the door behind her.

"Baby boy?" She crept toward the back of the house, hoping the cub was where she'd left him. After meeting who she figured was the bear's uncle, she prayed she could figure out a way to keep him out of the drunken jerk's hands. "Here, sweet cub."

The pantry door's hinge creaked, the aged panel easing open and then a small brown nose peeked into the kitchen. The snout was followed by the cub's dark brown eyes and furry head. A few flares of his nostrils preceded him fully emerging from the pantry.

Mia dropped to her knees, putting herself at eye-level with the frightened child. "Hey, little guy. He's gone now and we need to figure out what I'm gonna do with you."

The cub eased closer, the pungent scent of urine coming along with him. He whimpered and whined, pressing against her and nudging until she plopped onto the dirty floor. The little bear crawled into her lap, wet fur and all, and she didn't hesitate to cuddle him close. Okay, there was a teensy hesitation, but then those eyes…

"All right, sweet stuff." She pushed her fingers into his thick fur, savoring his warmth.

Mia dug into her jean's pocket and yanked out her cell phone. She'd programmed the small town's important numbers when she'd arrived. Including the grocery store.

The call was answered on the second ring. "Miller Grocery. This is Emily."

"Hey, Emily, I need to place an order for," she glanced at the cub. The *growing* cub. "I need fifty pounds of salmon and maybe seven honeydew melons." The small bear chuffed and she glanced at him, at his begging eyes. "Actually, make it ten."

Minutes later, she ended the call and focused on the child on her lap. "You had to crawl into *my* pantry, huh?"

chapter two

Sporting a few new nicks and cuts, including a nice five inch slice on his forearm courtesy of Griss, Ty Abrams trudged up Mia Baker's stairs. He'd done a little research on the woman before leaving the station. Griss had ranted and raved about her stealing his nephew, and while he didn't really believe the man, he'd still wanted to be prepared when questioning her.

Her stats hadn't told him much. Mia Marie Baker. Single. Thirty-three. Five foot four inches. Brown hair, brown eyes. One hundred seventy pounds. Granddaughter of werebear Eli Baker, but she couldn't shift.

What his research didn't reveal was the way the sun brought out a hundred different shades of brown in her hair or the fact that there were brown eyes and then there were *brown eyes*. Then there was her weight. One hundred seventy was simply a number. It didn't state that her breasts were round and full, or that her waist tapered and then flared to a set of wide hips. Nor did it reveal she had a sweet, heart-shaped face or an adorable, pert nose. And those lips… Damn, he couldn't think about her lips without thinking about them wrapped around a certain part of his body.

The woman was temptation personified. The crazy thing was, his bear agreed. No, "agree" was too tame a word. The beast roared in approval the first time Ty laid eyes on the woman. It pushed and prodded him to get closer and then went berserk when it looked like Griss was gonna hurt her. It'd taken everything inside him to keep his beast at bay while dealing with the drunken bear. Good thing his brother had appeared when he did. Otherwise, Ty's animal would have burst free and taken the half-shifted male down, by any means necessary.

His bear had never been that edgy or close to snapping Ty's control. There were more than a few bears living in Grayslake who had a hair trigger when it came to shifting and fighting due to a perceived slight. It was to be expected since wild bears, in general, weren't the type of animals to happily live together.

Ty stomped up Mia's steps, shaking off any loose dirt that clung to his boots while also announcing his presence. He raised his fist to knock on the damaged door. Damn, he'd have to fix that. Between his gun and Griss's raging, it was kinda crooked. And splintered.

Her whispers had him freezing.

"Hush." A low whine followed the word. A sound that definitely came from a cub. *Aw, damn.* "No, you get in there right now, mister." Another grumbling whine with a squeak on its tail and then the click of a door closing.

He knocked on the door, noting how it trembled within the worn frame. Whether the woman was breaking the law or not, he'd get it fixed.

The door swung wide to reveal a disheveled, but no less gorgeous, Mia Baker. She'd changed clothes, this new shirt clinging a little tighter, her shorts a little more snug, and his cock twitched in appreciation.

"Miss Baker, I'm Sheriff Abrams and I'm also the Grayslake clan's leader, their Itan. I took over for my father about six years ago. Your granddaddy was one of the clan's bears so I'm assuming you know what that is?" At her jerky nod, he continued. "I'm here to talk about Griss Holmes. Mind if I come inside?"

Ty took a step forward, expecting her to move aside so they could continue their discussion in privacy and air conditioning. He was gonna ignore that she smelled delicious, like sweet honeydew, woman, and sugar. Except she didn't move. Not an inch.

"Miss Baker?" He raised his eyebrows and instead of stepping aside, she moved forward. He quickly back tracked and jerked in surprise when she yanked the door closed behind her.

"No, thank you, Sheriff. We can discuss the incident here on the porch." Her words were polite, but her resolve was unmistakable. The woman wasn't letting him in the house.

"I see." Ty stepped back farther, putting space between them. He had to, even if he didn't want to. What he *wanted* was to stay put and let her curvaceous body rub against him. Instead, he gestured to a nearby set of chairs. "Should we sit then?"

Mia gave him a rueful smile. "If you'd like to end up on your rear end." She shook her head. "Granddaddy was a lot of things, including a pinchpenny. I doubt those chairs are anything less than thirty years old."

"All right then." He'd play it her way. For now. Ty dug into his back pocket and pulled out a pen and notepad. "Why don't you tell me what happened."

And she did. Well, mostly, it seemed. Ty was sure he'd heard a cub inside her home. Except she skipped over finding a little bear anywhere near her house and picked up the story with Griss's arrival.

"So, you don't know anything about his cub? The little boy's parents died recently." They'd been on their way to pick up their cub after a night out and had gone off the edge of the road into a ravine. Werebears could recover from a lot, but not a broken neck. "He's only four and probably missing them something fierce. Maybe he went looking for them and got lost. Maybe he hid in someone's house because he didn't want to get into trouble."

Mia looked toward her front door, quiet for a moment, and then returned her attention to him. "If I was positive I had that man's nephew in my home, I assure you I'd give him into your care." She shook her head. "And then I'd pray you didn't hand him over to his uncle. Did you notice how drunk he was? How quick he was to shift and try to take apart my house? I'm sorry, Sheriff. I can't help you."

"Can't or won't?"

"As I said, Sheriff, if I was *positive* I had—"

"Uh-huh. Why don't you tell me who that one belongs to, then?" Ty spied the small cub, its tiny nose peeking through the yellowed curtains, slowly followed by sweet brown eyes.

Mia froze and jerked her attention from him, to the cub, and back again. "Um…"

"Why don't we head inside?"

Her shoulders slumped, and a heavy sigh escaped her lips. She led the way to the front door and then into the home. The entryway was as he recalled, a little worn, but still welcoming even if every inch was packed with boxes. The familiar tattered rugs covered the aged wood floors and the sagging, frilly wallpaper with its peeled corners still decorated the walls.

He followed her deeper into the crowded home, watched her curvy frame navigate around piles of boxes until they entered the living room. The old man's drooping couch still held its place of honor against the wall, but the rest of the furniture was new.

Movement to his left drew his attention and his gaze clashed with the little cub's once again. He removed his hat and squatted down, making sure the kid recognized him.

"Hey, Parker. Causing a bit of trouble today?" Ty kept his voice low and soothing.

Suddenly a pair of tempting, entirely human, legs blocked his vision. "I'd appreciate it if you left my pet bear alone. His name is Randall," the cub whined, and she spun away from Ty. He figured the protective Mia Baker was glaring at the poor boy. "*Randall*," she returned her attention to Ty, "is a very sweet *pet*. Now, you've seen what you need to see and—"

A low knock at the front door preceded the young Rick Miller's deep voice. The teen still had some growing to do, but he sounded like a mature bear. "Miss Baker? I've got your order." The boy stuck his head into the living room. "Oh, hey, Itan." Rick grinned, and Ty smiled in return. Being approachable to the young ones was one thing he'd worked toward when he'd taken over the clan. His father was a stern man who held tight to ceremony while Ty was low key and wanted his people happy and relaxed. "Miss Baker, Mom said to tell you it's real good of you to take care of Parker this way. She put in some strawberries because the cubs really like them. I'll drop everything here in the entry. Y'all have a good day!" Rick disappeared from sight.

Ty slowly panned back to Mia and grinned at her obvious discomfort.

She huffed. "Son of a cracker jack."

Realizing the jig was up, Parker came bounding from behind the boxes. He hopped and tripped his way to Ty and cuddled close. The young boy's scents surrounded him, and his bear helped him wade past the flavors of the forest that clung to every cub.

Fear. He understood its presence since he figured the boy had run away plus his uncle had been Tasered and hauled to jail in cuffs. Except pain lingered as well as...urine. He wrinkled his nose.

She must have seen his expression. "Yeah, he hasn't wanted to take a bath."

"Well, we'll need to get him cleaned up before we give him back to his uncle. That probably won't be until tomorrow so…"

Mia reached down and plucked the fifty pound cub away from him as if Parker weighed no more than a newborn kitten. The boy made it easier by wrapping around her like a spider monkey. "Over my dead and decaying body."

"Now, Mia…"

"Miss Baker," she snapped. "Why don't you stop and ask me why he smells like he had an accident? Ask, Sheriff. Or do I need to call you Itan, too? Will that get you to listen to me?" Mia bent down and eased Parker to the ground then nudged him toward his original hiding spot.

Ty rolled his eyes. He didn't care if she was the most beautiful woman he'd ever laid eyes on, she was feisty and annoying. Damn his bear for finding both of those traits attractive. "Why—"

"Because that boy's uncle came to my door." She leaned close and dropped her voice. He should have told her whispering didn't matter since the boy could hear her anyway. "Parker pissed himself with his uncle's first word. That boy was hiding in my pantry, scared and crying, and he had an accident the very second he heard Griss's voice." She stepped away and nudged the cub back even more. "Sheriff, if you or that man try to take him from me, you'll both get a rear end full of buckshot and I won't send you a get well card."

Ty couldn't help but admire the woman, even if she was making his job a hell of a lot harder than it had to be. He scrubbed his face, thinking through his options. Here was a human woman—he inhaled and sifted through her scent—or mostly human woman his bear wanted to please at all costs. Apparently, keeping Parker would make her happy.

He rubbed the back of his neck. "All right. Let's get him cleaned up, and I'll head over to his house and grab him some clothes." Mia smiled, probably realizing she was getting her way for the most part,

20

and he was quick to squash her hopes a little. "He's only here for one night. One. Griss is in lock up overnight, so that means you can take care of him until then."

Ty stepped nearer and stopped merely inches from her. Her scent wrapped around him again, overpowering those from the small cub. "I'm trusting you, Mia Baker. Your granddaddy was a good man, and he loved you like a daughter. Grayslake doesn't really have child services because bears wouldn't hurt their young." He ignored her snort. "And Parker doesn't have any other family. One night, Miss Baker. One night and then he goes back to his uncle."

Ty ignored the whimper that came from Parker. As soon as the cub shifted back, he could talk with the child and figure out what happened. Because on the floor behind Mia Baker, was a growing puddle beneath little Parker Holmes.

* * *

Two hours later, Ty shook with rage. Unadulterated, pure molten rage. Dear God in Heaven, what he'd seen nearly tore his bear through his skin. The beast clawed and roared and seethed with the need for blood.

It hadn't taken him long to head to the Holmes's home and pack a couple of things for Parker. He'd even swung by his house to shower and change, anxious to be comfortable and clean the next time he saw Mia. His beast wanted the lush woman, and he'd figured his chances were better if he smelled good and wore something other than a wrinkled uniform.

He'd returned to the Baker house to find Mia whining, cajoling, and outright bribing Parker with strawberries in an effort to get him to take a bath.

It took Ty one order to get Parker into the tub and a single glare to get him to shift back into his human shape. Then the fury hit him. Fucking bruises lined the kid's body. Bruises. From head to toe, the child was black and blue. Considering *weres* healed a hell of a lot quicker than a human, he could only imagine what they had looked like when fresh.

Ty held his tongue while the boy splashed in the tub, giggling at the bubbles and whining when he'd been forced to wash his hair with "girl" shampoo. Before long the bath was done, and Parker was eating a big 'ol salmon steak for dinner with berries and honeydew for dessert.

It wasn't until after they'd settled Parker in Mia's bed with cartoons playing on the TV that the two of them got a chance to talk.

She jumped into the conversation with both feet. "He's not going back to that man. Ever. I know you said one night, but I changed my mind. I may not be a werebear, but I care for children just as much as you all pretend to." She waved her hand. "No ifs, ands, or bears about it, his furry butt is staying right here. Possession is nine tenths of the law and all that."

Ty's bear bristled. He was pissed, too, damn it. If he'd known what was happening to Parker, he would have stepped in right away. He took his jobs as Sheriff and Itan of the town's bear population seriously. "Mia—"

"No." She held up her hand to forestall him. "Just... no. You don't get it, and you haven't seen what can happen..." Tears glistened in her eyes, the moisture growing until one snaked its way down her cheek.

Aw, hell. How was he supposed to lay down the law when she cried?

Before she could object, he snared her wrist and tugged her close, wrapping her in his arms. From the moment he saw her, he'd wanted to get his hands on the delectable Mia. He wished their embrace wasn't because she was upset. His bear chuffed and barked in approval, urging him to keep her close and never let go.

Never?

Never.

Ty would think on that later. For now, he had a weepy woman in his arms and a battered kid resting in another room. He held her tight, one arm across her shoulders while he rubbed her back in soft, soothing strokes with his free hand. He tried to pretend the scent of her skin didn't drive him wild. Or the feel of her curves aligned with his body didn't excite him and send arousal thrumming through his veins.

"Don't cry now." He tightened his hold and pressed his face to her neck. "Hush."

As wrong as it probably was, he enjoyed the feel of his skin against hers, the smoothness beneath his rough cheek. The bear rumbled in approval and stretched before padding toward the mental wall that kept it captive. It rubbed and scraped against the barrier, but didn't press for release. It merely wanted to be closer to her.

With her first snuffle, his heart broke. His mind spun, trying to figure out how the hell he could do his job as Sheriff, make Mia quit crying, and be the Itan the little cub deserved, all at once. His bears were tolerant of a lot of things, but leaving a battered clan cub in the hands of a lone female—a lone *human* female—wouldn't fly. Even if she happened to be Eli Baker's granddaughter and one-quarter werebear.

"I'll take him with me and—"

"No…" Mia struggled against his hold.

He refused to release her, and he tightened the hug, making his decision in an instant. His choice would raise more than a few eyebrows, but it was better than dealing with leaving a wounded Parker in her hands. "All right. If you want to stay with Parker, then get some stuff together, and we'll go to my place. You two can stay there. No one can object to the boy staying with the town's Itan for a night."

"I don't know you from Adam. What makes you think…" She fought harder, and he forced himself to release her. His body screamed to keep her close, but he couldn't—wouldn't—hold her against her will. "My parents didn't raise an idiot. You think I'm gonna just—"

Ty shrugged. She had a point; he did have an ulterior motive. His bear wanted Mia in their den. Badly. Which was probably a mistake since his beast had naked ideas about Mia Baker.

"You can come with me, stay in my guest room, and keep an eye on Parker *or* you can stay here while I take Parker with me. He's a cub in my clan, and I'm not leaving him in your care. Choose."

There. Easy.

"Earlier you said he could stay and I'm pretty sure I've already said this once, but I'll repeat it for the slow people in the class and in a way that a bear can understand: mine."

chapter three

Admittedly it was quite creepy, but Mia watched Ty sleep. He'd put up a good fight the night before, arguing about whether Parker would be better off in his home or hers. Ultimately, it was the cub who decided… by falling asleep in her bed. Kids were too cute when conked out, and neither of them had the heart to move him.

So, she'd spent the night with a bear in her bed and another on her grandfather's couch. His very short, very old, very saggy couch. Ty's body was twisted and scrunched in an attempt to fit his six foot frame on the piece of furniture, and she couldn't imagine he'd spent the night in sleepy comfort. Well, she'd told him to leave Parker with her and go home, but did he listen? No. In a sort of peace offering, she'd brought him a cup of steaming coffee to go along with his wake up call.

The man in question snuffled and groaned, lingering between half awake and sleep.

"Ty?" She poked his shoulder and then quickly darted away. When her touch didn't elicit a response, she did it again. "Ty?" Dang it, bears were hard to wake. Her grandfather said it stemmed from their desire to hibernate. Once a werebear crashed, it took a bit to stir them before they were ready to go. And they often awoke cranky.

Okay, one last poke and then she was breaking out the water guns. "Ty Abrams."

Ty exploded in a tangle of limbs. His body sprang from relaxed and prone to upright and snarling in an instant, and Mia jumped back. Coffee sloshed over the edge of the mug and onto her hand and she winced at the burning sting. The sheriff shifted and twitched, his bear shoving past his human features and forcing his head to widen and mouth elongate into the beginnings of his snout. Dark brown fur pushed through his pores while his nails thickened and lengthened. His chest rapidly expanded and contracted, and Mia could only imagine the rapid thump of his heart.

Saying bears disliked being awakened early was an understatement.

Mia held out her uninjured hand in what she hoped was a calming gesture. "Easy. I brought you coffee." The half bear shook its head as if to clear sleep away. "You know, coffee."

Carefully she extended the cup, the initial wave of pain from the burn now a dull, throbbing ache. Ty's huffing and puffing continued, that massive chest teasing her with every rise and fall. The very naughty part of her wondered if the move would look any different after she exhausted him with sex. Which caused her body to respond to him. She'd kept her desire at bay for all of five minutes in his company, but now her traitorous pussy decided to say "hello." That part of her grew heavy, achy, and needy. Her clit twitched as she imagined his fingers and tongue torturing her, and her very heat clenched while she thought of him filling and stretching her.

Bad body, bad.

Ty breathed deep and a matching heat filled his eyes.

I am not going to look down, I am not going to look down, I am not going to…

Aw, crap on a cracker, she looked down. Down at the thick ridge filling his now tattered jeans and the long, hard length that pushed against the zipper of his pants. The material barely clung to his hips—the fabric torn from his partial shift—but there was no mistaking the proof of his arousal.

Because of her as a person, or the scent of her desire?

Mia cleared her throat and held out the half empty mug. "I brought you coffee."

Seconds ticked past, the old cuckoo clock in the hallway squeaking with every flick from one moment to the next. Eventually, the hair receded, sliding beneath Ty's skin as if it'd never emerged. The blackened claws disappeared, quickly followed by the narrowing and retreating of his bear-like muzzle.

That change, those shifts of the human body from man to animal and back again, always fascinated her. When she was younger, her dad hadn't appreciated her demands that he shift every five minutes. So, each time she saw her grandfather, she'd beg him to transform, held captive by the impressive beauty of the shift.

At thirty-three, she still hadn't outgrown the fascination.

Ty took one last heaving breath and then reached for the mug, capturing it with his large hand. It wasn't until he removed it from her hold that she really felt the result of the burn. The ache blossomed into agony, and she quickly cradled it to her chest.

"Sugar, sugar, sugar, sugar…" She spun and fled, intent on high-tailing it to the kitchen. His heavy, thumping stomps indicated he followed her, but she was too focused on her destination.

"Mia?"

She wrenched open the freezer and grabbed a handful of ice, pressing it to the back of her hand. The damage was done, there was no getting around the healing process to come, but at least some of the pain could be iced away.

"What do you need?" Ty's barked question startled her, but she was used to her grandfather's behavior. *Weres* made harsh demands and issued orders, but always with the best intentions.

Cradling her hand to her chest, she kept the ice in place and gestured with her chin to the other side of the kitchen. "A towel from the drawer to the left of the sink. Dampen it, please."

Mia shifted her touch, sliding the freezing blocks over her damaged hand.

He went into action, doing as she asked and presenting her with the wet cloth in moments.

"Ice?" She winced with the next slide of cubes over her skin.

Again he was quick to respond, returning to her in less than a blink. She handed over the melting blocks, taking his compress in return and pressing it to her injury. She spared a moment to glance at the redness and winced again. It was already swelling, and some parts were lighter than others.

Dang.

The clang of ice hitting the bottom of her stainless steel sink preceded Ty's reappearance at her side.

"Lemme see." He kept his voice low, but the order was unmistakable. And one did *not* disregard an order from the Itan. Bend and poke at the words—massage 'em a little—yes. Dismiss? No.

Mia peeled away the icepack and exposed the injury to his gaze. The first glance had him drawing in a sharp breath through his teeth and releasing it on a grumbling sigh. "Damn it, didn't your grandfather—"

"Ever teach me not to wake a sleeping bear? Yeah," she huffed. "Apparently the lesson didn't stick. I tried poking you, but—"

"I'm a deep sleeper. There's not too many that will risk bothering a bear, so we've never had to be on guard over the years." His gaze shifted to her face. "I'll have to make sure my bear knows to rein it in with you."

She didn't want to think about the possibility of waking him ever again. She especially didn't want to consider her waking him while they were both naked, tangled in sheets, and she would kiss—

Mia licked her lips, mouth suddenly dry, and she internally smiled when he focused on the action. Seconds ticked past and silence wrapped around them in a welcoming cocoon.

Heat filled Ty's gaze, and those brown eyes bled black, his bear peeking from behind his human guise. Her breath caught with what she saw. His desire was unmistakable as he stared at her. A low, rumble filled the air, so close to a growl but not quite foreboding enough to send fear through her. He wanted her. Her, Mia Baker of the big butt and jiggly thighs.

Yeah, sometimes she was slow on the uptake, but a hard-on in the living room when the bear came roaring to the surface in a blink was very, very different from what she was experiencing now. Now it was a deep mixture of man and beast staring at her as if she were the tastiest treat. Mia wanted to be eaten.

Ty continued to rub the wet, cold, ice-filled towel across her injury over and over.

"Ty," she whispered and tugged against his hold. The man simply smirked, flashing her a sexy grin, but didn't release her. "Ty," this time it was a whine.

Finally, he removed the icepack, but instead of letting her go, he brought her hand to his mouth. Gentle, chaste kisses were brushed across her burnt skin and what should have hurt, didn't. His gaze locked with hers and sincerity along with something else filled his eyes. "I'm sorry."

Surprise overtook Mia. Men, werebears in particular, didn't like to admit they were wrong and definitely didn't apologize. A sort of dick-ish way to behave, but it was part of the beast.

He brought one hand to her face, fingers ghosting over her skin. "I'm so sorry."

A loud *pop* and *sizzle* behind her elevated his gentle rumbling to a snarl, Ty shoving her behind him as he inspected the room. If he hadn't looked so deadly, she would have laughed.

Instead, she gasped and nudged him out of the way. "Sugar, sugar, sugar... The bacon!"

She bolted past him and ran to the stove, watching said bacon dance in its grease.

The big, bad Grayslake Itan nudged her out of the way. He scooped up the fork and deftly flipped the strips of meat then lowered the heat of the eye. He did the same with eggs she'd forgotten about, turning them over without missing a beat.

Gorgeous *and* he cooked. Heck, he was more gorgeous the more he cooked. Nothing was sexier than the way he flipped an egg or slipped a slice of bacon onto a paper towel lined plate. It made her knees weak. And then there was the toast...

A nudge from Ty tore her away from her breakfast-induced fantasies. "Go sit down." He gestured toward the kitchen table that looked older than her dead grandpa.

"But..."

"Sit, Mia. I scared the crap out of you and hurt you, so lemme feed you." Worry and a hint of... something... tinged his expression.

"I... the coffee... living room floor..." She gestured toward the front of the house with her unharmed hand, dripping water on the linoleum floor. Coffee was soaking into the wood and ancient carpet as they spoke.

"I'll have your floors redone and get your carpet cleaned. Sit." He pointed at a rickety, unreliable looking chair. She paused, deciding on whether to listen, but another wave of the spatula got her moving.

Mia sat and watched. It was like food-laced porn. It took him no time, and very little mess, to slide a plate filled with eggs, bacon, toast, and pancakes before her. She still hadn't figured out where he hunted up the ingredients for pancakes—or the syrup—but it didn't matter. Nope, the Grayslake Itan was sitting at her condemned kitchen table with an all-too-sexy grin in place.

Once again her body reacted to his closeness, her pussy heating and nipples pebbling. When his gaze darted to her chest and then back to her face, his grin broadened into a smile. Darn it, he knew what he did to her. She shoved a bite of eggs into her mouth before she could beg him to throw her on the table and have his wicked way with her curvy body.

Ty took a bite as well and then pointed is fork at her. The man did a lot of pointing. "Tell me about you, Mia Baker."

She wrinkled her nose. "Not much to say. You know—*knew*—my grandfather, right?" At his nod, she shrugged and continued. "I'm sure he regaled you with stories, so there's nothing to tell. Thirty-three, single, graphic designer and wannabe web programmer. I know just enough about coding to be dangerous and tend to break things just as much as I fix them."

Ty quirked a brow. "Does single mean unattached?"

"Um…" She cleared her throat and blinked back the tears quickly filling her eyes. "Yes, recently."

That topic was so far off the table, it was ridiculous. There was no way she wanted to revisit her time with Justin. Zero.

A deep rumbling growl vibrated through the room, and she realized Ty's bear had come out to play. "Did he hurt you?"

"I... He... It wasn't..." A ripple slid over his features and dark brown fur immediately followed. Oh, crap on a cracker. "Not the way you think." She rushed out the words, anxious to calm him. The last thing she needed was a half-ton bear in her kitchen. For some reason, she seemed to push his bear's buttons. Funny thing was, he pushed hers, too.

Ty reached for her, his movements slow and deliberate, giving her a chance to withdraw. She didn't. Why would she? She craved his skin against hers more than her next breath.

A shiver overtook her at the first touch of his palm against her cheek, and he rubbed her skin, the callused pad of his thumb tracing circles. "How?"

"It wasn't..." She leaned into his touch and nuzzled his hand. "In the end, I wasn't what he wanted." She wasn't tall. Or thin. Or, or, or... Or so many things. "He thought I could be, but I'm me and that was a disappointment."

"That's not surprising," a feminine voice dripped with sarcasm and Mia jolted, jerking free of Ty's hold.

His gaze never wavered from hers, and he dropped his hand to pet and stroke her forearm. "Sarah, forget how to knock?"

The words seemed innocuous. The tone was anything but. No, the Itan was pissed. She'd been dealing with the man—even when he'd neared bear shaped—until now. At the moment, Ty was all clan leader.

The woman whimpered but didn't say another word.

Ty's gentle expression vanished, and he slid his palm from her skin. In a single, fluid movement, he rose from his chair and spun to face the stranger in her kitchen. The action gave Mia her first look at the woman. Then she wished she hadn't. Because, really, if the male werebears were hot, this woman was smoking.

While Mia woke with bedraggled hair that stuck up in a half-dozen directions, this chick's 'do was flawless. The dark tresses laid in perfect, soft ringlets, framing her perfect face with its perfect nose and perfectly pouty lips. Then there was the woman's body. It was trim and toned with small curves in all the right places. Mia sported pajamas, and her visitor wore a dress that clung to her. Oh, and her legs. Those suckers went on for miles and the woman easily had six inches on Mia.

She wanted to scratch out the stranger's eyes. A bad thing considering there was little doubt the woman had a bear lurking beneath the surface.

Dang it.

"Well?" This time, the question wasn't barked, but it was a near thing.

"I wanted to check on you. Isaac said you were staying with some *human* and I needed to make sure you were okay." The last bit of her statement held such a simpering tone that Mia wanted to puke. Plus, the idea of scratching her eyes out returned. Especially considering the familiarity she used with Ty. Like the woman had a right to worry.

Ty looked at Mia over his shoulder and smirked, as if he'd read her mind. "You don't think I can handle one little human?"

Sarah glared at Mia, but the expression fled when Ty looked back to her. "Of course you can." The woman approached, hips swaying and a sweet smile gracing her lips. She sidled up to Ty's stiff body and placed her palm on his chest, rubbing it softly. "It's just, you usually spend your nights at the den and—"

A low, grumbling growl came from behind Sarah and a streak of dark fur blurred into the kitchen. It wrapped around Sarah's leg and slid its teeth deep into her calf.

Mia identified the snarling ball of fluff right before the woman kicked him off. Blood dripping from his mouth, Parker went sailing across the room, beneath the table and then collided with the aged kitchen cabinets. A low whine came from his tiny chest and rage boiled up inside Mia.

How dare she? A cub! A mostly-defenseless cub!

She was torn between tending to Parker and kicking Sarah's witchy rear end, but Ty took her choice away. He was on the woman in less than a second, his hand wrapped around her throat while he backed her out of the room. Which left Mia with the little one.

She approached slowly, holding her breath with each step. Werebears, when shifted, could be as unpredictable as their natural counterparts. Cubs in particular. True, they still retained their human thoughts, but the animalistic side of them always waited for a chance to take control. He'd been a sweetheart before, but there was no telling now.

"Parker, honey?" Mia eased down to her knees and half-crawled toward the small, fur covered boy. "Sweetheart?"

A low growl was her only warning before her arms were suddenly filled with squirming, wiggling, and very bloody werebear cub. Parker buried his head under her arm and whined, pressing as close to her body as he could. She fell back with an *oomph* but didn't fight the child's presence.

Screeching from the other room filtered through the walls, but Mia couldn't have cared less. The cub's aggressiveness would have to be addressed, but the woman was a werebear, she should have been able to handle the pain of a child's bite without flinging him across the room.

The shrieks grew louder and louder while Parker seemed to get more and more upset until all sound was silenced by a wall-shaking roar. The air stilled and even the birds outside ceased their songs. Then the rapid click of high-heeled shoes across the wood floors broke into the quiet, immediately followed by the slam of her front door. And the tinkling of more glass. Dang it, sounded like the woman shattered *another* window. They'd boarded up the few windows broken by Griss yesterday, but now…

It was times like this Mia wished *she* was a bear.

Before long, Ty's now-familiar tread signaled his approach and then he was there, squatting beside them. "Mia? You should hand him over before he hurts…" Parker whimpered and burrowed closer, drawing a sigh from Ty.

"He's fine. Bloody, but fine. I think."

"Parker." The cub whimpered. "*Parker*, look at me right now." The child sniffled, but finally pulled his head away from Mia. "We're going to talk about this. I don't know what your parents taught you," Parker whined, and Ty kept going, "but we don't bite people for no reason."

"Ty, I'm sure…" She wasn't sure *what* she was sure of, precisely, but she couldn't imagine the kid doing something like that without cause. Ty shook his head, and Mia turned her attention to the cub in her arms, soulful eyes met her gaze and she snuggled the child even closer. "Look, he's sorry. I'll ground him and—"

"No."

"But—"

Ty placed two fingers over her lips. "He's a bear cub, Mia. Sarah will be healed in half an hour. A full hour, tops. What if he did that to you?" She turned her attention to the whimpering bundle in her arms and sighed. "His uncle gets out today."

Mia immediately jerked away from his touch and opened her mouth to reply, only to have him cut her off. "But he's not going back to Griss until facts are straightened out, and a call is put in to child services. There are several werebear foster families in Grayslake. I want everything in the system."

The "in case I need to take Parker away from Griss" went unsaid.

"You have two choices. You can get cleaned up, help me grab his handful of things, and go to the clan's den. Or you can help me pack his things, and I'll take him to the clan's den without you."

Mia knew she was beaten, but figured she'd give it a shot anyway. Pushing out her lower lip the tiniest bit, she sniffled and drooped her shoulders.

"Nope." Ty shook his head. "Not buying it this time. You're not gonna get me with those sad sexy—" He coughed. "It's not gonna work. Pick your poison because my car is leaving in thirty minutes."

chapter four

Ty tried to look at the trip to the clan's den through Mia's eyes. Yeah, the road was rutted. He should probably get his brother Keen on that. As the youngest, Keen tended to get the crap jobs. The fence was a little run down, wooden posts leaning and in some cases, resting on the ground. And the grass was a little—okay, a lot—high. If they had cows, they could set them free. Let them graze. Unfortunately cows never did do well with bears, so Keen was gonna have to work on that, as well.

His truck creaked and protested as he turned into the driveway. Damn, he needed to get that fixed up, too. At least the final approach to the house was fairly smooth. The gravel was level, and the clan's members had finally learned about organized parking. It'd been a free-for-all when his father was the Itan, but Ty had beaten the clan into organizational submission.

He spared a glance for the still quiet Mia. She grumbled after his pronouncement, but quickly jumped on board with the program. Between the two of them, Parker had been washed and dressed. Not that he'd stayed clothed for long. The minute Mia disappeared to change and freshen up, the boy shifted back into a bear and destroyed the last of his clean clothes.

But at least they got on their way within his thirty minute timeline.

Ty gripped the truck's door handle and gave Mia a long look. Damn, the woman was fine. All curves and sweetness with pale skin. He imagined it tasted like ripe peaches. He'd always liked peaches.

"You two ready?" His bear made the words rough and deep. Hell, he hadn't realized that part of him had pushed so close.

Instead of commenting on it, her attention turned to the cub occupying her lap. It didn't seem to matter to her that she held a fifty pound bear. Nope, to her sweet heart, it was a child.

And didn't that pull at *his* heart and make him wonder. How would she be with cubs of her own? *Could* she have cubs of her own? That was something that had been bounced around more than once, mumblings about whether a human and werebear could produce shifting offspring.

Some old codgers said yes. Other said no. Eli Baker had stood firmly in the "yes" column. His son had been a shifter, even if he was only a half-blood. Eli believed it was the fact that he and his woman had been what he called "fated mates." Out of respect, Ty had bitten his tongue and didn't remind the old man that bears didn't mate for life.

"You ready, Parker?" Her voice was soft and lilting, none of the unease and panic he'd sensed before tingeing her words. At the cub's nod, she turned to him, a blinding yet brittle smile on her lips. "Okay, we're ready."

With that, she swung the truck's door open wide. Parker was fast to tumble from the vehicle, the spray of gravel testifying to the fact that the cub moved faster than his paws could carry him.

Mia was a bit slower, sliding from her seat as Ty rounded the front of the truck. The breeze teased his skin, reminding him of his half-shift and lack of control where she was concerned. Something was wrong—or right—inside him when it came to tempting Mia Baker.

Ty gripped her right arm to steady her, the gravel making her wobble the tiniest bit. The free hand that clutched the handle was a lot less red than hours before, and he inwardly winced at seeing her use it to shove the door closed.

It wasn't until she was fully exposed that he felt her thrumming tension. It pulsed and pounded through her blood like a physical being and his bear reacted to her unease. He immediately pulled her close while his fangs slid out an inch. His human mouth didn't have room for his animal's extended teeth, but the beast wanted to be ready to banish whatever caused her fear.

"You okay, sweetheart?" He leaned down and murmured against her ear, taking pleasure in the tiny shiver that overtook her.

"Fine, there's just so many…"

Ty glanced around and found at least a dozen clan members lingering on the front porch and littering the lawn. "It's the clan den. I live here, but so do a lot of others. A few single bears, and my brothers who are also my inner-circle. Plus anyone in the clan can stop by whenever they want."

"Whenev…" She gulped. "I see. I just never… It's always been me, my father, and Granddad when I visited. They didn't take me around others. Even when I came to Grayslake for a visit, I stayed in the house or the backyard by myself."

"Uh-huh." He eased her forward. "Well, most of us are sweet as pie." She shot him a glare. Yeah, well, he'd said "most" hadn't he? "Come meet my brothers. You'll like them." Only not too much because then he'd have to kill them.

And they couldn't like *her* too much or then he'd have to kill them. Damn, his bear was really freaking possessive of this little woman.

Arm wrapped around her waist and hand resting on her hip, he guided her to the front steps. His bears waved and smiled as he passed, and he returned the greetings, all the while continuing his travels. He wasn't about to get stopped. Not when he was feet away from having Mia in his den. His bear had been demanding this very

39

thing from the moment he'd first seen her, and now his goal was within reach.

Ty grasped the front door's knob, intent on leading his woman—*my woman?*—into his home only to have the opportunity snatched from him. The door swung wide to reveal a smiling Van.

His brother needed a few teeth knocked out.

"Hello, big brother. Did you bring me home a snack?" Van leaned forward and winked. "Let me tell you that this brother," he pointed at himself, "is *just right*."

Ty sensed confusion from Mia and he grinned. "He's making a bad Goldilocks joke. Ignore him."

Not waiting for Van to deliver a comeback, he shifted his hold and snared her hand, twining their fingers together. One tug had her following him deeper into his home.

It was nice. A little sparse, but nice if he did say so himself. Considering it was filled with bachelors, he thought it looked damned good. Yeah, there were a few pizza boxes on the coffee table, but the table itself was sturdy. The couches were high-end leather and comfy.

"Where's Parker?"

Ty glanced back and smiled. "Probably the kitchen. Every cub knows the way to the kitchen." He tugged. "C'mon."

The house was massive, but the common areas were cozy, which meant the walk to the kitchen didn't take long. And that's where they found the cub of the hour.

Gigi, the den house's cook had a now human-shaped Parker plopped onto a stool, paper in front of him and both hands holding crayons. Somehow the resourceful woman had hunted up clothing for the small boy. Well, hunted up someone's tank top more like.

Parker had been easily dressed, but the boy had just as easily shifted as soon as they had turned their back which ripped his clothing to shreds. Considering he'd only grabbed a single change of clothes, he was glad Gigi had found the boy something to wear now that Parker was on two legs. With thin straps and gaping armholes, Ty was able to see the cub clearly. Rage, familiar and hot, burst through him at the sight of the boy's condition.

A threatening growl tore from his chest, pushing through his heart and bursting into the room. Gigi was the first to react, kneeling and focusing on the bit of floor before her. Other nearby bears, his brother Van included, did the same. Each of them fought to soothe his temper through submission. Hell, even little Parker, who didn't understand, whined and laid his head on the table.

The only one still standing by the time he cut off the sound was Mia. No, she wasn't just standing. She was leaning against him, her injured hand flat against his chest and fingers tracing his muscles. It was then he noticed her murmuring.

"Shh… You can gut him later. With a dull knife. Won't that be fun? You can bathe in his blood and drag his body down the street. Entrails everywhere…"

A woman after his own heart.

Ty leaned into her, resting his cheek on the top of her head, and he took solace in her presence. His bear immediately calmed with her touch, receding and silencing the threatening growl that still lurked inside him. He took a deep breath and his bear perked up once again, only this time it was the pleasure of Mia's scent. It was pure, unadulterated sweetness and sex with a hint of home. He didn't want to bathe in blood; he wanted to bathe in *her*.

"Itan?" The trembling voice yanked him from Mia and back to the present.

Ty looked toward Parker and noticed his trembling lower lip. A glance around the room revealed that the other clan members present were still kneeling on the ground though they had raised their heads to look at him. He huffed and ran a hand through his hair.

"Sorry. It's been a rough day." He glanced at his watch. "And it's only ten." He went with levity, grimacing when it fell flat.

Mia tried to pull away, so he tightened his hold and covered her hand gently with his. He didn't want to lose her touch. It was the only thing keeping him grounded and his beast at bay. Every look at Parker yanked at his bear, but each soothing stroke from Mia pushed it back again.

A heavy thump against his back signaled the arrival of one of his brothers. He drew in a deep breath. Youth, knowledge, power, strength.

"Isaac." He eased Mia over, giving his brother room to pass.

"Hey." Isaac grinned at him and then that smile grew sexual as he gazed at Mia. "And *hello*. Who's this?"

"No one." Ty curled his lip and let a little more of his bear out to play as he pushed his brother into the kitchen. *His*, damn it. His. Those thoughts had his heart freezing and then stuttering as it resumed its beat. Bears didn't form attachments. Not really. And a human would want a forever kind of love, like her grandparents and parents. But he wasn't built that way and…

Mia nudged him. "Who's Isaac?"

Now her voice was filled with a threatening grumble and he followed her line of sight. His brother teased and cajoled little Parker through an exam, the gentle, massive werebear treating the cub as they were meant to be treated: with care and love. Based on the look she gave him, she saw too, but obviously didn't trust his brother's actions.

42

He knew as soon as he told her, she'd be half in love with the man in a second; women loved doctors. With a grimace, he answered her. "Our clan healer, and my brother."

Her expression changed, features softening while Isaac did his doctor thing.

No, no, no. He sounded like a child claiming a toy, but Mia was his.

Ty tightened his hold on Mia's waist, intent on dragging her from the kitchen and somewhere brother-less when yet another of his brothers popped in. Why did his mother have to have so many kids? She should have stopped with one: him.

Van bumped his shoulder and tilted his head to the side. "You got a minute?"

"Yeah," he sighed. At least he'd already warned this one off. Couldn't he stand quietly for a moment with a gorgeous woman in his arms without being interrupted?

Keeping his arm around Mia, he tugged her along as they followed Van, his brother glancing back now and again with a frown on his features. They traveled down a side hallway. One mostly unused since it led to his private study and even more private bedroom.

Van paused at the threshold of the room, and his gaze bounced between him and Mia. "This is, uh, police and clan business. Should she…"

Ty curled his lip and released a growl similar to what he'd pulled in the house's common area minutes before. "Yes."

Mia tugged against his grip. "Ty, I can go back to Parker and—"

He turned to her, the woman who'd come to mean more than she should in such a short time. Simply looking at her calmed him. "Mia can hear what you have to say. Especially since it probably has to do with Griss. Am I right?"

43

"Yeah," Van grumbled. Ty sensed the weight of Van's gaze, but he couldn't tear himself from Mia. "Okay then, the human stays."

The bear bristled at his brother's statement. She was only partly human, but she was also so much more.

His brother left them with a shake of his head and Ty grinned. "C'mon. You need to hear this, too."

"But Parker..." She waved behind her.

"Is fine with Isaac and Gigi who will filet anyone who tries to hurt him. She never had cubs so she'll adopt the boy as if he were her own."

He knew he had her when her shoulders slumped. He fought the widening smile. Then his thoughts shifted direction. If it took this much cajoling for her to do something as simple as leaving the cub for five minutes, what would he have to do to keep her at his side?

*

Mia followed Ty into a decidedly masculine room and definitely *did not* stare at his ass. Or the way his hips shifted as he walked. Or the way his exposed muscles flexed when he stalked his way around the desk. Ty's bear coming out to play had scared her, but staring at all that yummy flesh exposed, she had to thank the beast for the lovely view.

Distantly, she noted walls lined with bookshelves; each shelf packed high with books that ranged from new and crisp to faded and old. A massive desk dominated the center, two overstuffed chairs facing it while a single leather chair occupied the seat of honor. The room screamed "male."

She tugged, intent on freeing herself of Ty's hold, but he wasn't having it. He kept his grip firm but gentle as he walked around the end of the desk and settled in the comfortable looking chair. She stood there for a moment, unsure of what to do, but the decision was stolen from her. He easily pulled her closer, and one final heave had her collapsing onto him. Mia released a totally girly *squeak* followed by another when he repositioned her to sit sideways across his lap.

"Ty," she struggled against him, but he merely squeezed her.

"Hush, Van has something to tell us." The man's grin was way too sexy. And cocky. She had to remember the cockiness when she yelled at him later for his high-handed behavior.

Ty's brother merely quirked a brow but didn't comment on their embrace. "Griss is probably getting out around four today."

"Four!" She bolted upright, heedless of Ty's embrace. "Did you see what he did? He—"

Van held up a hand, cutting her off. "I understand. But that's going to be handled in-house."

Mia narrowed her eyes. "How?"

"It's a bear matter." Haughty condescension filled every word.

She struggled against Ty again. "I'll show you a 'bear matter.'"

"Easy." The bear holding her brushed his lips along the shell of her ear, and she immediately stilled. Her body reacted to his closeness and the whisper-like caress. Sharp teeth nipped her earlobe then he lapped at that delicious spot below her ear. "Be easy."

Oh, this man was so much trouble.

"Van?" Ty's voice vibrated against her sensitive skin.

"Yeah?" His brother sounded bored. Good, the man could be bored somewhere else, anywhere else.

"I need you to do some research for me…"

Mia kinda stopped listening. Especially when those fangs scratched along the column of her neck. She was pretty sure she heard something about custody and deaths and… Oh, he sucked on her shoulder. That was very, very nice.

"Does that sound good, Mia?"

She shook her head and fought through her lust-filled fog. "Wait, what?" Except Ty nipped her again. Ooh, evil man. He was distracting her with sexy-times so she couldn't object to anything. "No, nothing sounds good." He slid his hand along her hip and gripped her thigh with his free hand. She slapped at him and pushed away his touch. "No, stop that. Bad furball."

A deep growl, not as foreboding as Ty's but still scary, floated to her from Van. Of course that was countered by another, quieting Van immediately and she turned her head to glare at Ty.

"What?" His expression was all innocence.

"Don't 'what' me. Now, what did you two just decide?" She crossed her arms to emphasize her annoyance but rethought the move when the ache in her hand returned. So, she settled for glaring.

"Based on what Griss did to Parker," Van snared her attention. "As well as some of his ranting in the cruiser on the way to jail, we think it's best to dig into his past a little more. No one in the clan has been particularly comfortable with the way the Holmes' passed and he only came into the area when Parker's parents died, so we don't know much about him."

"You didn't google the man while you had him locked up? Isn't that what investigators do? Investigate?"

Van's mouth tightened, but his tone remained calm. "He was arrested drunk and disorderly, not murder. The clans generally handle their own justice. So, if he caused any shit, it won't be in police records. We have to contact his previous Itans. Which takes time, and I need Ty's permission to reach out to others. To some,

46

asking questions can be seen as a sign of weakness and we don't need someone else coming in and trying to take Grayslake from Ty. An Abrams has led the Grayslake clan for over five hundred years."

Mia rolled her eyes. "Seriously? No questions? That's dumb. It's weak of you *not* to ask questions. There's no telling who you're inviting into your home if you don't at least check a guy's license at the door."

"Mia." Ty's growling of her name had her freezing.

She did a slow pan, gradually shifting her attention from Van and back to the man holding her. "Yes?"

"You'll get used to the way bears do things."

It wasn't a question or suggestion. Nope, it was an outright command.

Oh, heck no.

Just because he was sexy didn't mean he could order her around. She opened her mouth to tell him that when a low, frightened cry rent the air.

Something inside Mia responded, a part of her pushing and fighting to run to the source of that sound. She instinctively knew it was a cub. No, not just a cub, but her cub. Maybe not by birth, but he'd been hers from the moment she'd laid eyes on him.

Before she could move from Ty's lap, Parker burst into the room. The boy's gaze landed on her, and she noted the trembles that wracked his body and the rivulets of tears sliding down his cheeks. In an instant, he was at her side, in the next breath he was on her lap, clinging to her like his life depended on her touch.

"You left."

"Oh, love." Mia stroked his unruly mop of hair. "I'm here, I'm here." She rubbed his back, ignoring the sting the action brought forward. The lingering ache was manageable now, and nothing would keep her from soothing the boy. "You're okay. I'm not going anywhere."

"Ever?" Parker sniffled.

"Never, love." She couldn't deny the driving need inside her to keep the little one safe.

This time the rumbling she felt had a distinctly pleased yet cocky tone. She narrowed her eyes and turned her attention from Parker to Ty. Oh yes, very cocky indeed.

And then she realized what she'd promised. There was no way Griss would ever get his hands on Parker again. So, the boy would — probably end up with Ty, and then Mia had vowed never to leave Parker which meant...

Crap on a cracker.

chapter **five**

Ty stood in the shadows while Mia sat with Parker on the full-size bed and read him a story. The cub was clad in one of Ty's old T-shirts, the neck gaping enough to expose the purple hues of his lingering bruises, but he didn't seem to notice them. The boy had heard the words "nap time" and no amount of cajoling on Ty's part had worked. Then Mia took control. She'd marched into Ty's bedroom, stolen one of his shirts and hadn't even muttered a "thank you" before stomping off once again. She grumbled about Itans and comfort and cocky. "Danged cocky" if he remembered correctly. She'd then swapped out the cub's tank top with Ty's T-shirt and told the cub that it was okay to sleep, his Itan would protect him.

Seeing Parker snuggled in Mia's lap, all smiles and giggles when she purposefully read something wrong… Her smile, her pure joy from spending time with the cub, was a sight to behold. That'd been worth a little disrespect. No one entered his domain without permission or an invitation. Well, except Mia, it seemed.

Damn, she'd make a perfect mama bear some day. Ty's beast rumbled in agreement, the lumbering oaf padding forward and nudging against his mental bonds. He internally shook his head, banishing the idea of Mia pregnant with little werebears. Ty had to father the clan's next round of cubs, groom one of his children to take the reins. Any children from Mia wouldn't be shifters. At least that was the assumption. Maybe. There would definitely be some research done in that area.

Something to think about another day.

Parker's head drooped, slumping sideways until the boy snuffled against Mia's chest. It was wrong that he was jealous of a cub. Really wrong.

His heart clenched when she leaned down and rubbed her cheek on the top of Parker's head. She pressed her nose to his hair and took a deep breath, her breasts straining against her top. Now it was wrong that he got turned on while she tended to a cub. Really wrong. But right or wrong, it didn't change the way the scene touched him and made him yearn for things he couldn't have.

Mia shifted her weight, obviously preparing to leave, and Ty stepped forward. His movement drew her attention, and she gasped, eyes wide in surprise and then she narrowed them in annoyance. Yeah, she had a right to be annoyed and not only because he hadn't announced his presence. He was sure she'd lay into him as soon as Parker was down for the afternoon.

"I've got him," he whispered as he approached. He slid his arms around the boy, and he had to suppress the shudder that threatened to overtake him when his arm brushed her. His beast released that annoying, happy chuff at the contact.

Ty carefully leaned over Mia and eased Parker from her lap to lay the boy in the center of the bed. Their bodies touched, her heat sinking into him while her scent surrounded him in a sweet, seductive cloud. The bear roared, shouting its approval of Mia, choosing her as their own.

Shit.

The moment Parker rested on the soft surface, he eased back until he stood beside the bed, but didn't step away. No, he remained close to Mia, refusing to give an inch. Even when she pushed him with her delicate, slim hand, he didn't budge.

"Ty…" She nudged again and instead of doing as she asked, he snared her hand and brought it to his lips.

Gaze locked on her, he turned his head and pressed a soft, delicate kiss to the center of her palm. The man wanted her, and the bear craved her. It was about time he realized he'd lost the match.

"Hi." He lowered her hand and twined their fingers together, using the gentle hold to help her rise from the bed.

He tugged until they were aligned, her lush curves pressed tightly against his lean body. Her breasts pushed against his chest, the hardened nub of her nipples poking him through the barrier of their shirts. He let his free hand trail down her back and along her spine until he stopped at the top curve of her ass.

"Ty…" Mia's breathing came in shallow pants.

He used his new hold to increase the pressure between their bodies. He wanted her to see, to feel, what she did to him. He wanted her to crave him the way he craved her. Her wide hips would cradle him, welcome him like no other woman before.

"Yes?" Ty grinned. Desire clouded her eyes and—he took a deep breath—the musky scent of her arousal filled the air.

She shook her head, but the need didn't leave her gaze. "I… I'm pretty sure I'm mad at you."

Yeah, he could imagine. He'd sent one of his brothers to her home to gather a few sets of clothing for her. To say she hadn't taken it well was an understatement. Thankfully, Parker had been in the room, and he'd only had to suffer her piercing glare. He was sure there was a shouting match on the horizon. He hoped they'd have worked their way to having sex by then since fights were *always* followed by makeup sex.

"I know. You probably are." He took a step back and forced her to follow him, never losing the connection of their bodies. Every pace, each additional second pressed against one another, increased his arousal. His cock throbbed and pulsed, shoving at his zipper, begging to be released. He wanted to sink deep into Mia and never leave. She'd welcome him with her wet, velvet heat and he'd glory in her acceptance. He just had to get her there. And considering she was *really* pissed, it'd take a while. Ty continued their journey to the door, not letting her pull away for even an instant.

"I am. Really." She nodded, her lower lip pushing out the tiniest bit.

Aw, hell.

That was too tempting. He took a giant step back and hauled her from the room, spinning them so her back pressed against the wall, out of sight of little boy eyes. Ty leaned against her, practically fusing their bodies together, and barely a hairsbreadth separated their lips. She had every reason to be angry. He simply wanted her passionate for a little while.

"I know you are, Itana." The title rolled off his tongue as if it were meant to be. She was the other half of him, the woman to lead at his side. He brushed his mouth across hers, a gentle touch that teased them both. "I know."

He licked the seam of her lips and swallowed her gasp. He delved into her mouth and moaned, her delicate sweet flavors sliding over his tongue. He tasted, groaning when she returned the caress. Then Mia eased away, and he let her. He wanted their passion to be just that: theirs.

"You shouldn't have sent your brother for my clothes." The words were rushed, and then she was back, mouth against mouth and her tongue entering him. He let her take the lead, reveling in her dominance.

This time, it was him who pulled away. He rested his forehead on hers, fighting to catch his breath. "If I had let you leave, you would have dragged Parker out of here the minute I turned my back."

Another passionate meeting of mouths. Shit, his dick had never been so hard, so insistent and demanding. He rocked his hips, growling at the bolts of pleasure the simple action sent through him. When Mia wrapped her arms around his shoulders and clung to him, her short fingernails digging into his flesh, he growled anew.

"He touched my panties." She spoke with a breathy gasp.

Unlike the incident in the kitchen, this time his bear's annoyance was at the mere idea his brother touched her underthings. "Mine."

It was guttural, instinctual, and the truth rang in his soul. He rained gentle kisses along her jaw, tongue tasting every inch of her skin, and he scraped a single fang along the column of her neck. He didn't miss her shiver or the catch in her breath. He definitely didn't miss the way her pulse leapt against his tongue. "Mine."

"Ty," the word held a warning, but he didn't give a damn.

He gripped her hips and rocked against her, enjoying the way she cradled his body while cursing the fabric keeping them apart. He wanted her, wanted to sink into her and roar with the pleasure of possessing and finding his Itana.

"Mine." Her smell, her strength, her fearlessness… "All mine."

When she returned his caress, flexing her hips and rubbing herself along the ridge of his cock, he shifted their position. He eased away, smiling internally at her low whimper, and he returned to slip a leg between her thighs. Mia shuddered, and those tiny nails dug even deeper.

Hands on her hips, he instigated a rhythm that drove them both mad. Her moist heat was snug against his thigh as she straddled him, and he encouraged her to ride him. He rocked and pressed against her, momentarily ignoring the insistent throb of his cock. He couldn't wait until the day she would be astride his hips instead of just his leg. But the whimpers and moans made up for the lack of connection. She trembled in his arms, whining when he took his lips away and sighing when he came back for another kiss. Between the meetings of their lips, she still tried to convince him of her anger.

"I mean it."

"Uh-huh." He sucked on the juncture of her neck and shoulder.

"You can't seduce me out of my mad." When she wiggled her hips he figured he could.

"I know." He encouraged a particularly hard and slow roll of her body.

She whimpered. "Ty…" Her muscles twitched and jerked, their pace stuttering. "I really…"

"Let go." He raised his head from her shoulder, smiling inwardly when he noted the hickey he'd placed there. He couldn't claim her, not until he knew what the hell he was doing—she was almost fully human after all—but he could mark her in that little way. His gaze clashed with hers, those gorgeous eyes boring into him as if she saw his soul. "Let go. I'll catch you, Itana."

Mia initiated the next kiss, plastering her lips against his while she went limp, allowing him to direct her movements. He swallowed her sounds of pleasure, his bear reveling in their ability to arouse her. Her nipples were hard, distended nubs firm against his chest, while the scent of her abundant cream filled his nose. Damn, he wondered how she'd taste, all salty-sweet musk and woman. He salivated at the prospect of dining on her moist heat.

She mumbled words against his lips. Things like "close", "gonna", "need"…

Yes, that's what he wanted. The bear was pissed at him for angering her, and he urged Ty to make amends. When she recovered from her orgasm and remembered why she was angry, he'd do it all over again.

He couldn't wait.

"Itan…" The voice was distant, familiar, and his beast snarled at the interruption. "Itan." This time the snarl built into an audible growl. *"Itan."*

Ty wrenched his lips from Mia's and swung his gaze to the intruder, a roar bursting from his chest. His brother, Van, didn't budge or blink an eye.

Mia sobbed in his arms, draping herself over him with the heartbreaking sound accompanied by a body-enveloping shudder. Those noises quickly turned into a gasp and a tumble of arms and legs as she fought to be free of him. "Oh, my God. Lemme go."

Her obvious embarrassment angered him even more. Damn it, the world was conspiring against him.

"Do you people knock?" Mia clambered away and hid behind him.

"You're in the hallway," Van drawled and Ty felt the rush of heat that encased Mia.

Yup, his brother was going to die—he reached down and adjusted his throbbing cock—painfully. "What do you want, Van?"

He didn't give a damn if his voice was filled with his raging bear. They'd been so close to offering Mia completion, and now she stood stiff at his back.

"Griss's hearing is in half an hour. I need to know what you want to do about it." The man didn't seem the slightest bit repentant at the interruption. Yes, taking care of Griss was important, but so was his Itana.

Ty ran a hand over his head, fingers sliding through his long hair. "Have you found out anything about his history?"

Van frowned and sighed. "Yeah, but you aren't gonna like it. I was going to let you finish with your human first—"

Amazingly, Mia stiffened further and leaned around him. Her next words were filled with rage. "Human? *Finish*? How long were you watching, furboy? And I'll have you know I'm one-quarter bear, thankyouverymuch."

His brother's lips tightened, and Van glared at Mia. Ty noted the tremors slithering through his brother, the slight darkening of his skin that preceded the sprouting of fur.

"Enough," he snapped and Van's shift halted in its tracks. The bear was a good brother—a better enforcer—but he had a bit of a speciest streak when it came to bears mating with humans. Ty calling Mia his Itana went way beyond mating and it had obviously hit Van's "humans suck" button.

"Van, we'll meet in my office. Have Richard keep an eye on Griss for now."

Van quirked a brow. "You know Richard is Sarah's husband, and she's more than a little pissed at you right now."

Ty was getting tired of having his orders questioned. This time, he didn't hold back the bellowing anger that built inside him. It blossomed in his gut, pushed through his chest and vibrated the air surrounding them as it left his mouth. The pictures on the wall rattled and a few crashed to the ground. Hair sprouted from his pores, sliding free with a slight sting, while his nails blackened with the emergence of his beast's claws.

Immediately Van dropped to his knees, chest rising and falling in such a rapid pace that he knew his brother would hyperventilate in no time. He tilted his head to the side, baring his neck fully in submission. "Itan."

Soft gentle hands stroked his back then slithered around his waist and pet his T-shirt clad chest and abdomen. Again her whispered words drew him from the edge even though the bear didn't want to recede. Van was an enforcer first, brother second, and he needed to be reminded of that fact. Actions should always be for the good of the clan, not of the man. Though part of him admitted that taking Mia as his Itana may be seen as something that could weaken them all.

If that was the case, he'd leave and—

"Easy, big guy. Easy." She nuzzled his back and the man and bear sighed as one. The beast was content with her touch, her movements hinting at growing affection. "I've got you."

Yes, she did. She just didn't know it yet.

chapter six

On shaky legs, Mia stumbled down the hallway and toward the guestroom she'd claimed. When she'd chosen the space, Ty had grumbled and growled at her wanting a place to herself, claiming she'd be *more than welcome* in his room. But by then he'd already pissed her off with the whole "my youngest brother is going to dig through your clothes and bring back the most embarrassing bits of lace possible" thing.

Of course, those hadn't been his words to her, but that's what happened. She ended up with a suitcase of dresses that clung to her curves along with the tiniest panties and bras she owned. At least he hadn't hauled the bright red "fuck me" pumps out of her closet. Her best friend had given them to her for her birthday, telling her it was the perfectly discreet advertisement for a man. Mia didn't think six inches was very discreet.

Still trembling from her almost orgasm, she sunk onto the plush bed, flopping onto her back the moment her butt hit the mattress. Her nipples ached and pussy throbbed and dang… she really wanted to come. Like, bad. Just a few seconds more and she would have been one happy chick.

She sighed and shook her head. It would have been a mistake though. Heck, making out with him had been a mistake. The man—

werebear—was all wrong for her. Super, duper wrong. Boinking the clan's head guy would be only that, boinking and boinking alone no matter what he said when passion ruled them. Mia deserved more. She deserved flowers and poems and… Maybe not poems, but at least flowers!

The low ring of her cellphone brought her mind back to the present and snared her from her musings. The familiar, rhythmic beat of the *Cups* song from *Pitch Perfect* filled the air. Well, it was really called *When I'm Gone*, but Mia never could get the image of that actress busting out with a plastic cup and—

The song picked up again, telling her the caller hung up and retried the call. Leaning toward the end table, she snatched the phone and disconnected it from the charger.

"Hello?" She hadn't even bothered to check the caller ID. Great.

"Hey, little cub."

Mia smiled. "Hey, Daddy. What's up?"

"Well, you know I worry and I called your grandfather's house." *My house,* she wanted to growl. It wasn't much, and it was left to her by her grandfather, but she finally had something to call her own. It was *hers.* "And you didn't answer. And then I thought about you surrounded by the clan. Visiting your grandfather in Grayslake is quite different from moving into town permanently." Her father sighed. "I worry."

"The clan here is nice." That was a bit of a stretch considering her altercation with Griss, but stretching the truth was allowed when talking to parents. "I met the Itan and a few other clan members. I'm fine."

A tense silence filled the conversation. "You met the Itan?"

"Well," she cleared her throat and squirmed. There was nothing worse than being on her dad's bad side. Human fathers were protective, but werebear parents were... *whoa.* "Ty needed help with something so I came by and, um, I'm staying for a day or two."

"The rest, Mia."

Silence descended, and she knew he'd wait her out. Dang it. "I, uh," she cleared her throat. "I met the clan's Itan. Ty."

"You're repeating yourself. You're on a first name basis with the Grayslake Itan?" A mixture of skepticism and disbelief tinged his words.

Yeah, she understood his feelings. Humans and non-shifting half-breeds—quarter-breeds—weren't exactly welcome in most clans. It was part of the reason she'd grown up in a human town while her grandfather settled in Grayslake. She'd been tolerated in small doses when she'd visited her grandpa, but moving in was a whole 'nother ball of melon. Van may have smiled at her at when he'd arrested Griss, but his true colors shined through when she'd arrived at the clan's den and gotten hot and heavy with Ty.

"Yeah." She swallowed against the growing lump in her throat. "I'm, uh, staying in the clan's den for, um, a little while." The words were a mixture between a statement and a question.

"I see. Hold on a second, Mia."

Darn it. She'd gone from little cub to Mia. That did not bode well for the rest of the conversation. In a handful of seconds, the thud of a door closing came through the phone, and she figured her father had retreated to his office.

"Mia?"

"Yeah?"

"Why don't you tell me a little more about what's happened. I talked to you after your boxes were unloaded by the movers, and you didn't mention any of this."

She fidgeted. "It's sort of new."

"And what is 'it?'"

More fidgeting. Gah, she felt like she was five years old and about to confess to stealing cookies. "Well…"

She couldn't lie. So, she told him about the cub and Griss and Ty and more of the cub and… She definitely left out the tingly parts. Her father didn't need to know about those. Like, ever.

"I see."

Oh, "I see" was bad. "I see" was what she heard when she got caught by the lake with Bobby Pearson when she was supposed to be at Amanda's studying. And that had been followed by him grumbling about her mother not being alive to handle the girl-boy stuff and a father wasn't meant to talk about *that* and…

Her father sighed. "Ah, little cub. I never shoulda let you go out there. You've gotten mixed up with that clan. Curse the old man to heck and back for giving you that place."

She smiled. Well, if he'd moved on to growling about Grandpa, he couldn't be too pissed about girl-boy stuff. Not that she'd mentioned girl-boy stuff and Ty, but her dad had always had the ability to read between the lines.

She imagined him sitting in his chair, leaning back in the comfortable seat, feet propped on an ottoman and his humidor resting on the small end table at his side. She heard the distinctive clip of him cutting off the end of a cigar and the familiar flick of his lighter flaring to life. In her mind, she scented the sweet smoke and the way it brought comfort to her. If she were five, she'd crawl into his lap. Heck, even at her age now, she'd gladly sit on his lap for comfort.

"Little cub…" His words were filled with hesitation.

"Daddy?" Tendrils of worry snaked through her, pulling and tugging on her nerves.

"I don't," he sighed. "I don't know how to talk about this." The rough scratch of his hand across his cheek reached her. She could practically see him running his palm along his head and then down his face. Something he always did when he was upset.

"Dad... I don't... You're making me worry." Worry was an understatement. Her father said something or he didn't. He wasn't one to waver and waffle. He never had been.

"I should come there. Tell you in person." A sigh came through. "Your mother was young when she turned up pregnant with you."

Mia scrunched her nose at her father's wording, but it was the "old school" that lived in him. "I know."

"What no one has ever told you is... I'm not your biological father."

The words washed through her, sliding into her brain, but she couldn't make sense of them. Of course, he was her father. *Of course!* He'd tucked her in each night, kissed her scrapes, and banished every monster that lived under her bed. He cuddled her and held her close after her mother's death and raised her as a single parent from that second on.

"W-What?" Couldn't breathe, couldn't breathe, couldn't breathe.

"Little cub," the sound of his palm scraping over the scruff on his cheek reached her once again. "Your mother was sixteen. She never talked about it with anyone but me. Told it once, and that was it. Never again."

Mia's eyes burned, the pain stabbing into her. She knew her mom had gotten pregnant young, and her dad stood at her side through it all.

"She went on a date with my best friend, the Itan's son. Her first date, mind you. She wasn't like some girls. And he," her father— whether he liked it or not—coughed and took in a shaky breath. "He raped your mother, little cub. Left her bloody body on her parent's

63

driveway." This time he cleared his throat and sniffled. "Two months later, I found her crying in the park. I was on my way home from a clan gathering, and there she was. Even with tears streaming down her face, she was so beautiful."

"Oh, Daddy." She could sense how difficult it was for him to say the words, but it was just as hard to hear them. No wonder her mother had hated her grandfather, heck, bears all together. "How..."

"She told me the story and I didn't doubt her for a second. That town wasn't like Grayslake, it—"

"Where?" Where did she come from? Where was the man who hurt her mother so she could kill him?

"It doesn't matter. What matters is he's gone for good. I challenged him and took care of him, and I've been taking care of you and your mother ever since. Your biological grandfather didn't want anything to do with you, and you became mine."

A tear streaked down her cheek, immediately followed by another. "I don't look like you. That's why."

"You're the daughter of my heart and that's what counts, Mia. Your mother never wanted you to know all this. She wanted to take it to her grave and made me promise to do the same."

Her grave. Oh, God. Her *grave*. Mia's throat collapsed, but she pushed the mangled words past her lips. "Is that why she..."

Is that why she killed herself?

"She loved you as much as she could, but she finally gave out when you were three. My heart near bursts for you, little cub. Me and you against the world. I watched you take your first breath, I caught you after your first step, and I heard your first word. You're my little girl."

A sob finally escaped. He was right. She knew he was, and she couldn't dismiss the truth in his words, but that didn't make the shock and pain recede. "Why are you telling me this now?"

"I didn't want to ever tell you." He sighed, and she imagined him puffing on his cigar. "But you're in that town and you caught the Itan's eye. Little cub, your biological father was the son of an Itan and even though you can't shift, the blood running in your veins makes you very appealing to other powerful bears. You're not a quarter werebear, but a full half and a very strong half at that. Do you understand what I'm saying?"

"So, this is all biological? With Ty?" She hoped not, but what else was there. She'd gone from practically a virgin to gimme-gimme slut in less than twenty-four hours. "It doesn't mean anything?"

"I'm not saying that. I'm saying take care of your heart."

Mia squeezed her eyes shut and wiped her cheeks with the back of her hand. "He called me his Itana. I should leave, shouldn't I? I don't want some guy because—"

"Itana?"

She nodded and remembered he couldn't see her. "Yeah, a little bit ago."

"Then maybe you don't have to worry about anything. To an Itan, Itana and what the average bear considers a mate are whole different ball games, little cub." He sighed. "I wish your grandfather were still here. He'd explain things better." Another *puff, puff, puff* reached her. "You know you can't shift. It's a result of how you were conceived."

It's a result of my mother being raped.

"When a cub comes from a mixed couple—one being a shifting bear while the other is a half-breed or human like your grandmother— that cub could be able to shift as long as those two were meant to be together. My father called them fated mates. He said that others were ignorant jackasses if they couldn't see past their own assholes."

"Language." Mia let a small smile form on her lips. From the moment she spoke her first word and began picking up others from strangers, her father had been big on the "no cussing" rule.

Her dad harrumphed but stayed on task. "You didn't, because of… Well, just because."

Mia wiped away yet another tear while she tried to absorb her father's words. "So, if it's real, I can have cubs? Everyone says that can't happen. That—"

"Yeah, well, damn near everyone is a speciest pig in bear fur, and they spout what they want you to believe." Oh, her daddy was on a cussing streak. That meant he was really pissed. A low, rumbling growl that she felt in her bones came across the line. "It's the truth. It's not a gamble, little cub; it's love. Plain and simple."

And didn't that leave her a lot to think about. Was this thing with Ty lust? Or the beginnings of love? Was it desire for her or the fact that she had her biological father's blood in her veins? Then again, all questions paled in comparison to the one spinning in her head.

"Is this why she didn't love me?"

"Oh, little cub, you're breaking my heart." He sniffled, and she pretended not to hear. "She loved you the only way she knew how."

* * *

Ty cradled his head in his hands, begging his bear to take a back seat so he could deal with the problems in front of him. There was the normal paperwork related to running the clan's businesses and his job as sheriff, and that was on top of the problem with Griss and Parker. Then there was Mia. Gorgeous, curvaceous Mia.

Who hadn't reached her peak because his brother had been a sarcastic ass.

66

Damn, the bear rushed forward again.

"Ty?" Van eased into his musings, but his beast was still too close to the surface and craved his brother bear's head on a platter.

"Enforcer?"

His brother's gulp was audible. "Yes, Itan?"

Good, at least the man realized his anger still lingered heavily. Normally, Ty wasn't such a hot-head. But the past twenty-four hours had been nowhere near normal. After a few snatched moments with Mia, his life irrevocably changed. Shifting cubs and his clan had taken a back seat to all but Mia and what she cared about. Which meant his world now centered on Mia and Parker. "You have one minute, sixty seconds, to deliver your news." He glanced at his watch. "Go."

"Griss will be tailed the moment he leaves the jail. Calls to neighboring clans revealed that he was born into a clan in Cutler, Alabama. Left when he was eighteen. Bounced around a bit until he showed up here when his brother and sister-in-law died a week ago and he took over looking after Parker. Things are still murky as to whether he even has a right to the cub, so child services has placed him in your care for the time being. Linda over there says it's sketchy, but as long as no one takes a long look at his file, you should be fine. You're not exactly licensed to be a Foster Parent." Van chuckled, but Ty didn't find the pause amusing.

"Why'd he leave Cutler?"

"His parents died unexpectedly." Van's implication was clear. Rumor was Griss killed his parents.

"I see."

"And the facts are that Cutler's Itan, Robert Holmes, is old as hell. He doesn't have any cubs of his own. His only son was challenged by his friend at sixteen and lost. Robert's brother, Griss's father, was in line for the job. Then it was going to go to Griss's brother. Now the only thing standing between Griss and the position of Itan in Cutler is Parker and the old man."

Ty let his eyes drift closed. "So we think Griss is trying to get rid of the cub to give himself a straight shot to the top."

"Yup."

He took a deep breath and let it out nice and slow. "Who else knows he's in our territory?"

Van shifted in his seat. "You, me, and the Cutler Itan. As far as the line of succession, the old man didn't even know Parker's parents had passed."

"Damn it."

"I convinced him to stay put for now. I gave him as few details about Parker as possible and simply told him he's in your household now, but…"

Ty finished his brother's thought. "But Parker is the next in line and Robert will want the boy under his roof so he can be trained." He spat a curse. "Mia's going to be upset."

Van cleared his throat, the squeak of leather against leather as he changed position echoed through the room. "About Mia…"

And the bear charged forward, anxious to hear his brother's words, ready to shove them down Van's throat if he didn't like them. "Yes?"

"I heard what you called her."

His beast huffed. "And?"

"She's human, Ty." Van shook his head. "You can't have a human Itana. Who's gonna lead us when your cubs can't shift? Where will the clan be? You have to think of all of us, not just yourself, man."

Wrong thing to say. Hell, no one should whisper a word about Mia unless it was to praise his choice. The bear was that defensive of what he claimed as his. "Van?"

His brother's gulp was audible. His animal even managed to tune into the rapidly increasing beat of Van's heart. *Thump, thump-thump, thump-thump-thump.*

"Yes, Itan?"

"I grew up thinking of the clan. I live and breathe for the good of the clan. I sweat, bleed, and cry for the clan. From the moment I awaken until the second I go to sleep I do nothing without considering the clan." The crack and snap of the bones in his fingers drew his attention to his hands, the human half of him was quickly giving way to the bear inside. No one questioned his dedication. No one. "And if the clan has anything to say about my Itana, they can leave or meet me in the pit."

"Itan?"

Ty barely heard his brother's gasp over the massive roar his bear shoved through him. The subtle shift of the bones in his hands suddenly transformed to the rapid-fire push of his bear. His skin melted within a breath, slithering back while the beast slammed into him. One moment he was sitting at his desk and the next he stood on back legs, towering over his now kneeling brother.

He bellowed, mouth wide and teeth bared. It'd been less than a day, and already he'd had enough of his clan members talking badly about Mia, giving Mia the cold shoulder, and practically spitting venom at her as she passed. The only welcoming words she'd received had been from him, Parker, Isaac, and Gigi.

Ty climbed over his desk, the wood creaking beneath his weight, but it didn't snap. His forefathers had ordered the table built to withstand the massive heft of their shifted bodies. He lumbered through the center of the room, pausing long enough to snarl at his brother, his enforcer.

He knew the rage was over the top, more than excessive, but it was uncontrollable when it came to Mia. Now that he'd met her, his heart beat for her and her alone. To talk bad about her was to disrespect him, and an Itan *never* tolerated disrespect.

The wide hallway lay before him, the walls built far enough apart to allow full-grown bears to manage the path. He took off down the length, his bear having one destination in mind. Mia could calm him, help him get the bear under control. The beast acted on instinct, it's black-and-white brain not knowing how to combat verbal wounds. And it hated that. It hated that it couldn't protect her from everything. It wanted to claw and destroy every syllable flung against her, but fur could do nothing.

The man could. It knew that, as well. So, the bear would go to the female who could pull the human through him. Then he could soothe her. Promise to care for her and make her their Itana.

He burst from the hallway and into the kitchen, nails scraping over the worn, hardwood floors. The heavy stench of fear permeated the air, and he glanced around the room. His bears, members of his clan, all knelt before him. Good, they should remember he wasn't only their leader by birth, he held it through strength, as well.

No one breathed, each adult still and frozen as he passed. He snuffled and huffed, drawing in their scents, identifying them one by one.

Gigi. Gigi was good. Good to the cubs and liked Mia. His bear half decided she would live.

The human part of his mind shoved, and the bear pushed back. They would go to their Itana, but some of these bears needed a lesson.

Keen. Brother bear. Dug through his Itana's clothes, but was good to Mia. He stayed.

Sarah. Even her name tasted foul on his tongue. The woman had interrupted his breakfast with Mia. Had raged against his Itana's

70

humanity. Had flung a cub across the room. He bared his fangs and enjoyed the increased scent of fear that flowed from her. It would be easy to open his mouth and—

"Ty?" The voice that reached him was like a gentle, soothing breeze. His Mia had come to him.

"No. Just go, Mia. Very slowly, back away." *Isaac.* Brother bear, but he was telling Mia to leave him. Ty roared at the idea, snarling at the speaker.

"Ty." This time she snapped at him, and he swung his head around and glared at her. No one talked to him that way. Usually.

Mia stood, framed in the kitchen's doorway, as sweet and sensual as he'd left her. On her hip, Parker clung to her, his eyes wide and lower lip trembling. Cubs should never fear him. It was the adults he had issues with. The little boy shuddered and stared at the ground, angling his head and mimicking those around him.

Mia returned his glare with one of her own and tapped her foot for good measure. She was gorgeous when angry. In the future, he'd probably annoy her just to see this side of her beauty.

Except the human half of him was pissed and shoved the beast aside while he was distracted. It yanked and pulled the bear back until flushed skin replaced fur. On hands and knees now, he raised his head to look at his Itana, and winced at the annoyance that still lingered in her expression.

"Mia," he rasped her name, the single word soothing him. If only he could touch her…

As if sensing his need, she approached on bare feet, Parker still in her arms. She knelt, easily balancing the cub's weight. Her gaze clashed with his, brown eyes holding a big dose of irritation, attraction and… Sadness?

"Mia?" He pushed to his knees, and his lips twitched when her focus drifted to his cock. Then his *cock* twitched.

A red flush stained her cheeks and her attention immediately returned to his face with that bit of irritation still in place. Before he could say another word she flicked the end of his nose. Hard.

Gasps surrounded them, Parker's included, but he just grinned at her. Which caused another round of gasps.

"What the heck was all this? You're an idiot and a gigantic cornnut."

He shook his head, the grin turning dopey. Damn, she smelled good. "I don't know what that means."

Mia sighed. "I know. Are you done? Because we need to talk."

Aw, shit. Talking was bad.

chapter seven

Mia distinctly remembered telling Ty she was leaving. Yes, that had been a big part of their conversation, but then there had been kisses and suddenly she was back in the guestroom, pajamas in place and toothbrush in hand. Didn't they talk about the fact that their attraction was biological? She was pretty sure that had been one of the topics covered. She stared at herself in the bathroom mirror and frowned. Something had gone very, very wrong.

She was definitely leaving tomorrow. She didn't need to get seduced by a man who only wanted her because of her supposed "strength." Yet her father had said an Itana was different… She scrubbed her teeth harder and faster, forcing herself to focus on hygiene and a little less on the drama in her life.

She spit into the sink and then washed her face. There, she was minty fresh and ready for bed. Not that she'd gotten minty fresh for anyone else. Brushing twice a day was recommended by dentists. Right, she'd keep telling herself she was motivated by her dental health and not by the possibility of exchanging a few more kisses with Ty.

With a sigh, she left the bathroom and padded into the bedroom, exhausted and intent on simply crawling into bed. She glanced at the door, noting it was cracked open the tiniest bit. Convincing Parker to sleep in the room across the hall had taken a few out of this world promises. He'd finally crashed after being assured she'd be a few feet away.

She turned to the bed, shuffled across the wood floor, and flipped off the overhead light. Her feet hit the decorative carpet near her destination and more fatigue swamped her. She knew she'd fall asleep the moment her head rested on the pillow. Just another couple of feet.

Eyes now closed, she fumbled for the blanket and sheet and yanked it aside before crawling onto the soft mattress. She snuggled into the bed, sighing as warmth surrounded her, comforting her, embracing…

"What the frog!" She struggled against the once-welcoming blankets, tugging and yanking at them. A scream built in her throat as the arms wrapped around her tightened and held her fast. A warm, large hand slapped over her mouth, silencing her.

Holy crap, the lumps on the bed hadn't been a pile of decorative pillows like she'd assumed. *Crap on a cheese-covered cracker.*

A soothing scent encircled her, heat and hunger and man. In an instant, she stilled, recognizing the hand keeping her quiet, the arms surrounding her and the warm body at her back.

"Easy." Oh, yes, he was recognizable all right. "I'm gonna move my hand. No screaming. We don't wanna wake Parker."

Right. That was her biggest concern. *Not.* No, her biggest issue was the rock hard cock digging into her pajama clad butt.

In slow increments, his grip eased and then his palm slid from her compressed lips. The moment she was free, she hissed at him. "Are you kidding me?"

"You wouldn't stay in my room." There wasn't a hint of regret in his tone.

"Because we're not doing this." She kept her voice low, barely a whisper. She knew bears had enhanced hearing and she didn't want to wake Parker.

"That's what you said." His hand ghosted her shoulder, slid along the length of her arm and then wrapped around her waist.

"No, Ty. I mean it." It didn't matter if her body craved the big cornnut, she wasn't going to end up some Itan's consolation prize simply because her rapist father was powerful.

"Mia." He pressed his forehead against the back of her neck and his warm breath fanned her skin. "You don't understand."

She struggled against his hold, truly fighting to get away and he finally released her with a growl. She bolted to the other side of the room and took refuge in a welcoming chair near the window. "I understand, Ty. I understand more than you think."

Ty sat up, swung his legs over the edge of the bed and pressed his feet to the floor. The rapid movement exposed more of him, more of his heavy muscles chest, distinctively carved abdomen and way too much of his thick, strong thighs for her liking.

"You're naked!" The words were said with a whispered shout.

The unrepentant man grinned. "I was hoping to get you there, too."

"No, it's not happening. What you feel isn't real and what we did in the hallway…" She shook her head. "Never again."

"What do you mean my feelings aren't real?" A low growl reached her, slithered inside her and she felt something deep within her soul stir. Maybe they hadn't gotten to that part of her complaints earlier?

"I spoke with my father. He explained a few things about me, about my past." Tears stung her eyes and she took a shuddering breath. Her dad's words continued to rattle through her mind and refused to be silenced.

Ty furrowed his brow. "What do you mean?" She opened her mouth to reply and he held up a hand to silence her. "Never mind. It doesn't matter."

He rose from the bed and she got a better look at what lay between his legs. She'd gotten a glimpse in the kitchen, but now she was up close, personal and in high definition with his package. Suddenly she realized she *was* staring at his package and she heated from head to toe. Dang, she had a full-body blush going on.

She snapped her eyes shut and ignored the sound of his feet on first the carpet and then the hard wood floor. She ignored the quiet that descended when he finally stood before her and the heat that came from his nearness.

"Mia, open your eyes."

"Nope." She simply closed them tighter.

She sensed his movement even if she couldn't see it. Large, warm hands came to rest a hint above her knees, palms and fingers easily spanning her thighs. "Mia, open your eyes."

"Are you still nekkid?" Part of her hoped so and that same part was really, really tempted to open her eyes and ogle him. The other part knew it was a mistake. Hormones or instincts or something was driving him to come after her. Nothing more, nothing less.

Ty chuckled. "Yes, but you should get used to it since you'll be nekkid soon, too."

"Nope. You're not listening to what I'm saying, Ty." She sighed.

"I'm listening, I just don't like what I'm hearing so I'm gonna ignore it. It's a benefit of being Itan."

She opened her eyes and glared at him. "You're not *my* Itan," she snapped.

Aw, crap on a cracker, looking had been a mistake. Especially since now she could stare into his chocolate-brown eyes that were quickly darkening to black. Dang he was temptation on two legs and four. His eyes drew her in, but his lips… Maybe she could have one last kiss.

No, bad horny girl, bad.

He released one leg and brought his hand up and cupped her cheek, running his thumb over her lower lip. Tempted beyond control, she flicked her tongue out and tasted his skin. Yet another mistake. His flavors burst over her tongue, spicy and sweet and she ached for another sample. She repeated the move, this time taking the tip into her mouth and suckling the digit.

"Mia, you can't do things like that and expect me not to touch you."

Amazingly, her skin heated further and she released him with a soft pop. "Sorry," she whispered. "Couldn't help it."

"Uh-huh." His gaze bore into her, searching and hunting. For what, she didn't know. "You don't think my feelings for you are real? That's the problem?" She nodded. "How about trusting your own?"

"But I…" She what? She craved him like a drug? Wanted nothing more than to jump into bed with him? Feared him wanting her simply because of her father?

All of the above and then some.

"You're my Itana, Mia. You're not some game to me, or a way to waste time. I won't pick you up today and throw you away tomorrow."

Tears pricked her eyes and clogged her throat, cutting off any words, and she shook her head.

"Yes." He brushed stray strands of her hair aside and tucked them behind her ear. "But I'll prove it to you. We'll take things slow. I want you more than air, ache to claim you as mine, but I won't. Not until you tell me you're ready."

"What if I'm not ever…" Saying the words hurt her heart.

"You will be. And then the clan will celebrate."

"Ty, they're not going to celebrate a human Itana. Most bears are disgusted by humans. And," and if his feelings were nothing more than lust and anything less than love, "and they'll expect cubs. They'll be livid that—"

"You said the word cubs while referring to the two of us joining. That's enough for me. It's one step in the right direction and I refuse to let you talk yourself backwards." He removed his hands and rose to his full height, putting his flaccid cock at eye-level.

Oh, that was never, ever going to fit. It twitched and she slammed her eyes shut once again, much to Ty's amusement if his manly chuckle was any indication. He grabbed her wrist, encircling it with his fingers, and tugged her standing. His heat scorched her and his scent invaded her senses.

"Come to bed, Mia." He pulled her and she pulled back, opening her eyes to stare at him.

"We're not sleeping together." She'd never be able to resist him.

He looked at her over his shoulder. "You won't sleep in my bed because Parker needs you near, so I'm sleeping in yours."

She shook her head. She seemed to be telling him "no" all the time, but it hadn't made a difference yet.

In a single step, he was against her, cupping her cheek with his free hand. "Just to sleep, Itana. I promise, no matter how much you beg, I won't fuck you."

* * *

78

Ty's balls were gonna fall off. They'd been blue for hours and he knew that the moment he tried to move, they'd turn to dust and crumble. But he wouldn't change a thing about how he'd spent the night.

Tucked against him, Mia wiggled her ass and snuggled closer, pressing her rear against his still-hard cock. Damn. It hurt, but oh so good. The feel of her skin against his had his bear purring like a cat. It was annoyed at the delay in claiming her, but satisfied that the human half was doing all he could to hurry the process along.

He tightened his hold on her waist, smiling at the soft sigh that escaped her. Conscious, she wouldn't admit to their connection, but asleep…

Ty couldn't resist nuzzling her, pressing his face against the length of her neck and breathing deep. His beast truly did purr and the sound was followed by a rumbling chuff. He wasn't sure what her father said to her, but it seemed to have pushed them back a few steps. It wouldn't matter in the end. He was sure he could shuffle her alongside him once again. By the time he was done, she would be begging him for his mark. He took another, deep, lung-filling breath and released it on a long, slow sigh. Hopefully it would happen sooner rather than later.

Mia snuffled and nuzzled the pillow, mumbling low. "Ty…"

And there went his cock hardening further. She couldn't do things like that. His Itana wanted him, he simply needed to get her to admit it.

The low squeak of a dry hinge had him tensing, his bear rushing forward and ready to protect their mate. He focused on the bedroom door, watching as it opened further to reveal a bleary Parker. The cub's eyes widened and he gasped, backing up a step.

"Parker?" He kept his voice low, but knew the boy's enhanced hearing would allow the cub to hear him.

"Itan?"

"Come in, sweet cub." He was a sweet cub and he internally grimaced as he thought of the boy's future. Hell, the kid's present life was bad enough. He had a homicidal uncle and would soon be handed off to an elderly great uncle.

Parker shuffled into the room, bare feet sliding over the carpet. He tugged on his borrowed shirt, pulling it back onto his shoulder, and then rubbed his nose. Wiping it, of course, on his shirt.

The boy stopped at the edge of the bed. "What do you need, sweet cub?"

"I want Mia." The whisper was loud and he flicked his attention to Mia, but she didn't stir.

"Mia's sleeping. How about breakfast? I'm sure Gigi has something for you."

Parker shook his head. "No, want Mia, Itan."

He closed his eyes and sighed. He knew that tone, he'd heard it from other cubs often enough. "What about if I take you to the kitchen? Mia didn't get much sleep last night."

"B'cause you're in her bed. Mom says grownups only sleep together when they love each other and are mated and you're not mated."

Mom says…

Present, not past tense. Parker must have realized his words as well since large, rounded tears appeared in his eyes.

"But she's the Itana. We should let the Itana sleep, right?" At Ty's question, Parker rubbed his balled, chubby fist across his eyes and nodded. "You and I will go see what Gigi has for us."

Ty slowly extricated himself from Mia, easing his hand from around her waist. He dropped a soft kiss to her temple before swinging his

80

legs off the bed. He snared his discarded boxers from the floor and slid them on as he stood. Turning around, he found a wide eyed Parker staring at him.

"You were *naked*." Another boy-volume whisper.

"That's how your Itan sleeps with his Itana, sweet cub." He rounded the bed and held out his hand for Parker. "Let's go see what Gigi has."

The child grabbed his hand, so much smaller in his. The differences between them astounded him. So tiny, so helpless, so very alone. No, the cub would always have the Grayslake bear clan. Always.

"Come, Parker." He led the boy from the room and into the hall, their dim path lit by the glow filtering through the windows.

As they passed one of the larger panes of glass along their path, he noted the sun peeking over the horizon. The varying shades of pink, purple, and orange filled the sky and appeared to dance over the mountains.

The small hand in his squeezed, the cub weaving the tiniest bit. It wasn't quite a stumble, but Ty didn't want Parker getting hurt on his watch. He scooped the child into his arms amidst his tiny, tinkling giggles.

Parker laughed, high-pitched and pure, and bracketed Ty's face with his hands. "Itan!" He laughed along with the cub and play-snarled then pretended to snack on Parker's arms. "Ty!"

He tickled Parker's stomach. Had anything ever been more fun? Just toying with a cub and making him smile, laugh, with pure joy. He couldn't wait to do the same to his and Mia's cubs.

They slid into the kitchen and he found his brothers seated at the island while Gigi bustled around the stove.

He wasn't quite ready to end his game with the cub. "I'm a big, scary bear and I'm gonna have *you* for breakfast." Parker froze in his arms, tiny body stiff and his heart rate increased. "Parker?"

"He scared me, Itan. He was gonna eat me." His voice was whisper soft.

Ty hugged the cub close, knowing that a physical connection helped soothe little ones when they were upset, and Parker was definitely upset. "Who, Parker?"

Mentally, he ticked through the list of clan members staying in the house and tried to imagine them through a child's eyes. Truly, he was the only one he'd ever consider "scary." The rest of them were nothing compared to him.

"At my window." The cub whispered, but Ty knew everyone could hear.

He eased them toward the island and slowly edged Parker from his body until the boy sat on the smooth granite. Ty met his brother's gazes and then refocused on Parker.

"Who was at your window, sweet cub?"

"He was a scary bear and he," a shudder overtook the boy. "He scratched my window, Itan. Don't let him get me."

The boy launched himself at Ty and he easily caught the slight weight. Rubbing Parker's back and soothing the cub, he focused on Van and knew he and his brother shared the same thoughts.

Patrols had increased, but no one and nothing should have come within a hundred feet of the house. Not even the guards. They sure as hell shouldn't have been hanging around Parker's window. There was only one man who would risk getting close to the Itan's den and he was supposed to be under surveillance.

"Van, give Richard a call." The man nodded, gulped his coffee and took off.

The click-clack of high-heeled shoes pacing across the wood signaled someone entered as Van departed. Normally, Ty couldn't have cared less about who came in for breakfast, he liked being available to his clan, but the owner of those shoes had him gritting his teeth. It also had him tightening his hold on Parker. Even more so when a high-pitched growl vibrated from the cub and the pink skin beneath his hands slowly turned furry.

"What about Richard? What do you need with my mate?" Sarah's familiar, grating voice rose above the *clang* and *clink* of Gigi's cooking.

"Where is he right now?" Ty kept his gaze on Parker. Fur slowly coated the boy's face. Something wasn't right. He knew of cubs who didn't care for strangers until they'd grown into their fur a little more. Parker's current behavior coupled with the incident in Mia's kitchen told Ty this went beyond a little unease or lack of control.

Sarah chuckled. "Sleeping, I'm sure." She leaned against the counter within eyesight yet the majority of the kitchen remained between them. He kept his body turned so the cub hadn't seen her yet. "Last night was tiring for him."

Even with the distance that separated Sarah and Parker, the cub vibrated with suppressed anger. Parker was nearing feral in nature, the bear in the small child pushing through. Tiny fangs dropped and his little mouth was rapidly becoming a snout.

Ty narrowed his eyes. "Tailing someone was tiring and leaves that kind of smile on your face?" Parker's nails lengthened and pricked Ty's arms. Sarah merely sipped her coffee instead of answering. His bear was *not* amused. "*Sarah?*"

"Apologies, Itan." The bitch wasn't apologetic in the least and Parker sensed something from the woman because suddenly the boy wasn't there. No, a small, agile cub replaced the human child and that cub launched itself from the counter.

Parker flew through the air and landed on the tile with a grunt and scramble of limbs, his claws not finding purchase at first. The moment he righted himself, he barreled toward Sarah. Every inch of his fur stood on end, his little teeth bared, and saliva dripped from his mouth.

Ty was on Parker in an instant, snaring the boy around the middle and hauling him from the ground. Distantly he heard shouts, Sarah's screams and yells for someone to muzzle the feral kid along with his brother's growls. But he only had eyes for the cub. He scruffed Parker, gripping the skin behind his neck and pulling. Not tight enough to hurt him, but enough to remind the cub who was boss.

"Parker." The boy continued to struggle and snarl so he shook him slightly. "*Parker.*" Louder, larger growls filled the space, joining those of the cub's. Unable to control the child's aggression, he called for his youngest brother. "Keen, take him." With more than a little bloodshed, he managed to transfer his snarling bundle to Keen's control and then he took hold of Parker's muzzle. Staring into the child's eyes, he let his bear push forward and borrowed a little of the beast's power. "Parker, you will shift. *Now.*"

It didn't take much compulsion for the boy to change, fur receding and suddenly Keen held a small, sobbing child instead of an aggressive cub. Parker reached for him and he gladly took the slight weight, nuzzling his small head when Parker buried his face against Ty's neck.

He looked around the kitchen, noting the disaster before him. Sarah was gone, but coffee puddled on the ground surrounded by shards of the woman's mug. A huffing, puffing Isaac stared at the kitchen door, more than a little hint of the man's fur coating his arms.

The way the small child shivered in his arms, he wondered if he needed to give something to the cub to soothe and calm him as well. It was what they did for distraught bears and those nearing the feral edge after spending too much time in bear form. He was sure they could do the same for Parker.

Then again, he was awfully small…

"Isaac?"

His brother shook his head as if clearing it. "I ran her off. She was near her shift and there was no doubt…"

The man's words trailed off, but his expression told him more. For some reason, Parker hated Sarah and it seemed the feeling was mutual and very deadly on Sarah's part.

"Okay, I need you to check outside Parker's window. See if there's evidence of a bear and if they left anything behind to identify them."

Isaac nodded and left.

If any biological evidence remained, Isaac would run it through their updated DNA catalog. More than once they'd used the equipment he'd purchased for the clan to catalog the DNA of their members. There had been many times when other clans had stumbled upon dead bears and been unable to identify them if they didn't belong to their clan. That led to post-mortem photos emailed to the various Itans. He encouraged others to adopt the same procedures as Grayslake within their own clans and slowly but surely others followed him.

"Keen?" His brother's attention quickly centered on him. He was young, barely twenty-one, but the eagerness on the man's features reminded Ty that he rarely gave the youngest Abrams much responsibility. "You're good with computers."

Keen snorted and rolled his eyes. "Something like that."

"I need you to find everything you can about Sarah and Richard."

"Richard?" Keen furrowed his brow.

"I know he's been in the clan since birth, but I want you to dig around. I want to know everything." He kept his gaze level, serious. "I also want you to do the same for Cutler's Itan, but quietly."

85

"Define 'everything.' We talking simple like bank accounts or you gonna make me work a little and hit the FBI and Department of Homeland Security?" Excitement lit Keen's eyes.

"You can do that?" Ty only received another snort. "Listen wise as—," Parker stirred and sniffled, reminding him he had a cub with little ears like sponges in his arms. "Wise-rear... I need whatever you can get me."

"Sweet." Keen twined his fingers together and cracked his knuckles. "Gimme an hour or two."

His brother bounced on his toes, filled with excitement and Ty realized something saddening and heartbreaking at the same time. Keen had been last born and over ten years separated them. Growing up, that distance had been like a million years and he'd spent more and more time pushing Keen away rather than pull him closer like a brother should.

Shaking his head, he huffed and looked to the boy that wasn't a boy any longer. "I don't know you at all, do I?"

That excited expression slid away. "It's fine."

"It's not. Meet me in my study. Not because of this, but just..." It was a request, a true request, not an order. The Grayslake Itan didn't ask anyone to do anything, he commanded.

"Yeah." Keen nodded and then pointed toward the door. When his brother spoke, Ty pretended not to hear the way his voice broke. "I'm gonna get to work."

He nodded and Keen strode from the room, his back a little straighter and shoulders a little higher.

"You know," Gigi, amazingly enough, still clanging away with her pots and pans, spoke behind him. Piles of food sat on the counter and it looked like she hadn't even paused when all of the drama transpired. "I think that was the sweetest thing you've ever done."

Great, suddenly he was sweet.

Parker sighed against his neck and a piece of his heart fell in love with the little boy right then.

Damn, Gigi was right.

chapter **eight**

Mia followed Ty under protest and glanced back at the house every so often. It'd been three days since Parker's outburst in the kitchen—which no one had woken her for—and Ty assured her Sarah wouldn't be coming by the house in the near future. At least, not while the cub was in residence. The "in residence" portion of his statement still worried her. When wouldn't Parker be "in residence?" He was staying with her, well them, so he'd be "in residence" forever. He would never go back to Griss.

Ty said Van and Keen were working on gathering evidence against Griss before they took him down. But once the werebear was out of the picture, where else would Parker go? She could tell him where he *wouldn't* go and that was away from her. No ifs, ands, or bears about it. He'd turned up in *her* pantry, dang it.

"Ty, I don't think this is a good idea. Parker might…" Eyes trained on the clan's den, she didn't realize he'd stopped until she was plastered against his very solid, very delicious front. "Oomph."

She frowned and looked up into his smiling eyes. Wow. The man really shouldn't smile. Ever. It melted her insides and made her want to agree to anything he said.

"He'll be fine." Ty brushed his lips over hers and she shivered. "Van will take good care of the cub."

"But what if he needs me or—"

He silenced her with a kiss, this one much deeper and it held a passion that made her knees weak. He traced the seam of her lips with his tongue, lapping, and licking until she opened. Only, once she opened, he eased the kiss and drifted away.

"He knows Van will take care of him and that you're coming back. If we're needed, Van knows where we're going. We also pulled in a few more guards to patrol the grounds." Yeah, he'd said that before, but she still wasn't happy about leaving Parker.

"I know…" She nibbled her lower lip.

A soft *thump* caused by Ty dropping their picnic basket sounded a moment before he gripped her chin and tugged her lip from between her teeth. "He'll be fine and we're not going far."

"You're sure?" She glanced back at the massive house.

"I'm sure. We're only going to the lake. It's a ten minute walk." He tilted his head toward the path. "Come on."

The grin, it was the grin that did it. That little boy, you can trust me, of course I didn't break grandma's china serving bowl, smile.

His thumb still rested on her lower lip and she couldn't help flicking her tongue out for a tiny taste. She let the tip slide over the end of his finger and his spicy flavors danced over her taste buds, drawing a delicious moan from her chest.

Ty echoed her sound and his bear slid forward, stealing the milk chocolate from his eyes and darkening to black. "Mia."

"Sorry." She pressed one last, chaste kiss to the end and eased back. "I'm ready." He narrowed his eyes, as if he didn't believe her, and she nodded to reassure him. "I am. Promise."

90

He still seemed skeptical, but with his fingers still wrapped around her wrist, he spun, grabbed the picnic basket from the ground, and returned to leading her through the forest.

Trees surrounded them, bracketing the path and casting dancing shadows on the well-trodden trail. Dead leaves and pine needles cracked and crunched beneath their feet and the whistles of the birds added to the chorus. Each step took them deeper, each foot led them farther from Parker. Before long, she couldn't see the house at all and was left with the surrounding woodland and... Ty's ass.

And what an ass it was.

Nice and firm, rounded just enough for her to ache to bite and nibble. The man had been parading around her for *days*. All those manly muscles on display with an occasional appearance by aforementioned ass and his cock. Ty had a thing for being naked around her and she was quickly developing the same sort of craving. And he still refused to sleep in his own bed.

Mia was his Itana and he wasn't sleeping anywhere but beside her. How could he protect her from down the hall? Nope, his werebear buttocks were staying put.

The first night when she'd unsuspectedly crawled into bed with him it had annoyed her.

The second had frustrated her.

The third was a whole 'nother kind of frustration: sexual.

She'd known the man for five days and all she wanted to do was crawl into him. Pieces of her soul were already chipping away and forming a nice little pile, stacked together just waiting to be handed into his keeping. The more time she spent with him, the more she realized that maybe what they had went beyond biological urge. Just maybe...

"Here we are." His words tore her from her musings and back to the present.

"Oh, Ty."

The forest gave way to one of the most beautiful sights she'd ever witnessed. The placid, blue lake spread for what seemed like miles. The water gently lapped at the shore, the soft rush simply adding to the music from the birds. The scents of trees and water surrounded her and a calm she hadn't felt since she'd found Parker enveloped her.

"Let me show you one of my favorite places."

Eyes trained on her surroundings, she allowed Ty to draw her forward, trusting him to not lead her astray. Her sandals crunched over damp sand and before long, they stopped once again.

Ty released Mia and she split her attention between the majestic view of the water and that of his rear end.

He'd brought her to a secluded space. A massive cottonwood, its leafy canopy casting a wide circle of shadows, dominated the area. He spread a blanket near the base and rested the basket on one corner. On another, he dropped his shoes.

He caught her watching him and smiled wide. Oh, that smile did funny things to Mia's insides. She pressed a hand to her stomach, begging the butterflies to ease. Yet another sliver of her soul joined the growing pile.

"Just weighing it down so the wind doesn't snatch it from us." That was followed by a wink. She was in so much trouble. Ty held out his hand. "Come sit. Lemme feed you."

Mia blushed, but managed to force herself into motion and closed the distance between them. When she reached the edge, she slipped her sandals from her feet. She gingerly stepped onto the spread sheet and stood, awkward and unsure yet again. She still hadn't figured out what Ty wanted from her, heck, why he *wanted* her.

"C'mere." He wiggled her fingers and she went to him, shoving aside her worries for now.

It was an afternoon picnic, not a lifetime commitment. Hadn't he told her he'd convince her of his sincerity? Hadn't he said over and over that she was his Itana?

After another, tear-filled conversation with her father, he stressed the difference between a mate in today's werebear society and an Itana. Bears in the wild weren't inclined to bind themselves to a forever mate and werebears were somewhat similar.

Except there were times—when a bear wasn't a pigheaded speciest cornnut and had an open mind—that werebears could find their fated mate and happily commit to them for life. Otherwise, they found love and devoted themselves to a single person when they were ready for cubs. The soul-deep connection she would share with Ty was so very, very different. It was stronger, unbreakable, and forever. An Itan only ever joined with his fated mate, his Itana, period. An Itan and Itana would never part.

The whole idea of fated mates and finding a bear's other half outside their species went against the very vocal majority, but he urged her to look at what her grandfather had with her grandmother. Her dad guessed that bears weren't necessarily meant to stick with bears, that humans and halfers were needed to breathe life into the clans.

Because Ty was calling her his Itana and taking his time with her, her father said it was highly likely she *was* meant to be with him. A man obsessed with simply claiming her and tying them together due to the strength of her blood wouldn't be so patient.

Mia eased to her knees beside him as he pulled container after container from the basket. He laid out the feast he'd brought along and she salivated at what was spread before them. Man, she loved Gigi. She was really going to miss the woman once Griss had been dealt with and she returned home with Parker. Except Ty didn't know that tidbit quite yet. She internally winced, imagining the confrontation to come. Ty would demand custody of the cub while Mia would be just as adamant. She'd adopt Parker, even move home with her father to ensure the cub had a warm, werebear upbringing, but she wasn't leaving him in Grayslake. She wasn't sure of her success, but a young cub needed a woman's influence and the clan's den was filled with men. No telling what kind of bad habits Parker would pick up from the Abrams brothers.

"What has you thinking so hard?" Ty's words interrupted her thoughts and she plastered a smile on her face. Today was about spending time together and enjoying their surroundings as they got to know one another. It wasn't about her jumbled thoughts that raced from "give me forever" to "I need to run far and fast."

Mia shook her head. "Nothing." Her stomach grumbled and she scrunched her nose while heat suffused her cheeks. "What else do you have in there?" She scanned what had emerged from the seemingly bottomless basket and realized there was something missing. "Like, another set of silverware?"

His answering grin was wicked. "Nope, just one set." He held out his hand. "Come closer. I'm gonna feed you and my bear is dying to give you what you need."

It was one of the few times he'd mentioned his inner bear. Sure, she'd seen him close to losing control of the animal as well as one spectacular, fur-filled display in the kitchen, but otherwise he didn't acknowledge its existence.

"Feed me?" She raised an eyebrow and he gave her a jerky nod.

"Feed you." Ty waggled his fingers. "C'mere. Or are you scared? I told you, I wasn't going to fuck you until you were ready. Not even if you begged."

"Crude much?" She sniffed. She enjoyed giving him a hard time, even if she secretly reveled in his sexual teasing.

"Honest. Now, get that pretty little ass over here."

She sighed and rolled her eyes, but crawled to him just the same. "Nothing about me is little."

The second she got within reach, Ty went into action. He snared her hand, tugged her forward and she went from kneeling to snuggled comfortably between his legs, her back pressed to his front. Of course she let out a high-pitched squeak that had him chuckling.

He leaned down and rubbed his cheek along her neck and nuzzled her below her ear. "Right where I want you."

She moved to pull away, put some space between them. She couldn't resist him when he got close and all sweet and affectionate. Ty was so gentle with his touches, smooth and soft when he caressed her. Whether it was the simple act of brushing his hand over hers or a passionate kiss, she melted.

Instead of getting free, she ended up closer to him. His arms wrapped around her waist, his palms coming to rest on her rib cage and his thumbs teased the underside of her breasts.

"What would you like, Itana?"

His lips? His tongue? His shaft sliding into her over and over again?

Ty nipped her earlobe. "Gigi packed strawberries for us. Just a hint of sweet. How about we start there?"

Oh. Food. At least one of them was staying on target. She nodded, not trusting her voice.

Ty leaned forward, jostling her, and chuckled when his reach came up short. He tried again, pushing her down a bit with the stretch. When it was evident their positioning wasn't going to work, he slumped back. "All right, this went differently in my head." He placed his hands on her waist. "Up you go. We're swapping places."

Before she could object, or even agree, Ty manhandled her into position. Now she was the one with her back against the tree while he knelt on the blanket facing her.

"Ah, that's better. Now I can see your face as I feed you." The grin was very, very wicked and very, very tempting.

Yet another blush stole over her cheeks and she wondered if she'd spend the rest of her life perpetually red when in his presence. Of course, that thought had all color fleeing her face. There wasn't going to be a "rest of her life" with Ty. Because… Well, just because. He was going on instinct, his bear guiding him and shoving the human half of him toward her because of her supposed strength. There wasn't love there. And maybe she was his Itana. Maybe. But that didn't negate the fact that a certain set of emotions were missing.

Ty turned and perused the various containers. He snatched one and turned back to her, naughty smile back in place. "Open those legs for me."

"What?" She widened her eyes. She wasn't opening anything. She'd done that in the hallway days ago and came very close to begging him to take her.

Instead of answering, he moved forward, inching along and nudging her thighs apart with his presence. Wider and wider her legs went, her skirt rising higher with every centimeter. And still he came nearer. She snared the hem of her flimsy dress and pushed it down. She didn't manage to keep it lowered to her liking, but she did draw Ty's attention to her predicament.

"Shy, sweet Itana?"

"Ty," she shoved the word past gritted teeth.

"No reason to be. One day soon we'll get intimately acquainted." He gave her a wink and she glared back at him. "You're beautiful, Mia.

Lush and curved in all the right places. You shouldn't be shy, not with me."

Mia rolled her eyes. She wasn't a downer, but she *was* realistic. "Lush? You mean fat."

Ty curled his lip and released a low growl. "Gorgeous. The bear and I agree you were made for us. You are perfect."

She snorted.

"I mean it." He glared.

Her stomach grumbled again, breaking into their stare off, and the sound pushed him into action. "We're gonna finish this, don't think we're not." He popped the top on the container he held and the sweet, delicious scent of strawberries drifted to her. He snared one and brought it to her mouth, tracing her lower lip with the plump fruit. "Take a bite, Itana."

"No forks?"

Ty shook his head. "The bear wants to provide for you. Open up."

Mia kept her gaze on Ty, relishing the subtle shift of the colors of his eyes, brown darkened to black and then back to brown. His skin rippled and she imagined his beast lurked beneath the surface.

He rubbed the tip of the berry along her lower lip, teasing and tempting her until she finally relented and opened her mouth. Ever so gently, he slipped the end past her lips and she bit into the juicy fruit. The delicious sweetness of the strawberry danced over her taste buds, but it was the scent of his skin that called to her most.

She chewed and swallowed the bit she'd taken, licking her lips the moment the bite was gone. This time his eyes didn't return to a chocolate brown, but remained black. He held the strawberry to her lips and she repeated the process: nip, chew, swallow, lick. Now dark brown fur peppered his arms.

The last bite was barely worth mentioning, the tiny sliver remaining held between two fingers. Each nibble had given her more of the berry, but it'd also given her more of his seductive scent.

With the next bite, Mia didn't second guess her desires, didn't shove back the need to taste not only the berry, but him as well. She accepted the fruit and so much more. She opened her mouth slightly wider than necessary and slid her tongue over his thumb then index finger. The strawberry slid into her mouth, but she sucked his pointer finger in as well. She swallowed the sliver of strawberry with ease and focused on Ty, on the digit in her mouth, and how her teasing affected him.

She treated him much like she'd treat his shaft, suckling and caressing with her tongue. She flicked the tip and then stroked him, sliding along the length in gentle glides. The rate of Ty's breathing increased, the rapid expansion and contraction of his chest accompanying the huffs and puffs leaving his mouth. More of his brown fur covered him, traveling down his arms and rising along his neck.

"Mia." The word was more growl than human speech.

Ty eased his finger free and returned to her with another strawberry so they could repeat the process once again, teasing them both. Bite, chew, swallow, lick. Bite, chew, swallow, lick. They were back to a tiny sliver, a small piece she swallowed without hesitation. Which left her mouth free to taste and savor Ty's finger.

Mia let her gaze wander to the juncture of his thighs, to the bulge that lurked beneath his jeans. Her body responded to his condition, reacted to the arousing teasing she'd initiated. She heated with every suckle of his finger, panties dampening and an unfulfilled ache spread through her. She needed him. Those pieces of her heart she'd already given him urged her to succumb to his desires.

When he attempted to retreat, she increased her suction and swirled her tongue around the tip. "Mia, you need to stop."

She shook her head, still unwilling to release him.

"Mia, you're two seconds away from *being* lunch." His nostrils flared and she realized he scented her need for him which stoked her cravings.

Slowly, she slid her mouth along his finger, exposing more and more of the digit to the warm air. Instead of letting him slip free without any further teasing, she nipped the very tip, nibbling the pad of his forefinger. A shudder overtook him, his entire body shaking with the uncontrollable move, and then her world tilted.

Ty gripped her thighs and in one lightning fast jerk, she was spread before him on the suddenly near-barren blanket. A quick glance at her surroundings revealed the containers were scattered on the fringes of the blanket and the two of them occupied the center of the smooth cloth.

As before, he knelt between her spread thighs only this time he eased much, *much* closer to her heat. So much so that her skirt was now bunched around her hips and her panties were exposed to his gaze. She knew what he saw. His brother had only brought the tiniest and frilliest panties he could find and today's were the worst of the bunch.

Had she subconsciously picked them, knowing she'd come to him like this?

Probably.

The panties were made of black lace and midnight satin. The thin weavings hid her skin from view while the tightly woven fabric obscured her center. Under the heat of his gaze, her blood warmed further, sending floods of sensation to her pussy and clit. She throbbed and tightened, body silently begging for him. Her nipples pebbled and pressed against her bra and even her breasts pleaded for his touch.

Rough hands traced her legs, sliding along her calves, past her knees and on to her outer thighs.

"Mia?" His questioning gaze met hers and the warmth of his hands halted where her legs met her hips. His thumbs teased the crease, easing toward the elastic hem of her panties, but going no farther. "What do you want?"

He wanted words? Actual words?

Mia whimpered and wiggled a little, drawing his attention back to the apex of her legs. A growl escaped his lips. He tightened his hold, and slid closer to her center. The very tips of his thumbs delved beneath the edges, ends stroking the perimeter of her lower lips, and a shiver raced down her spine.

"Ty," she whispered his name, the sound seeming so loud against the quiet forest.

"Tell me." The two digits delved deeper, stroking more of where she desired him most.

"Touch me."

"Here?" He stroked what little bit of flesh he'd reached.

"Yes."

"With my hands?"

"Oh, God yes." She arched and rocked her hips, hoping to force him to give her more.

"With my tongue?"

She trembled from head to toe, arousal and pleasure washing over her with those three words. "Yes."

His hands moved away, the sexy roughness no longer caressing her inner thighs, and the retreat was immediately followed by the renting of cloth. The day's warm air bathed her wet pussy, grazing her in a gentle caress. Now she was exposed to him, fully, completely exposed.

Those delicious hands returned, palms scraping over her flesh and fingers coming to meet at her center. He stroked her, digits sliding along the seam of her lower lips, petting her with a barely-there pressure.

"Ty," she whispered.

"Right here."

A finger slipped deeper, gliding over her sensitized tissues and causing a full-body shudder to overtake her. Smiling, he repeated the caress, her cream easing his way as he tormented her. Up, then down, and up again. The pad of his finger grazed her throbbing clit and her pleasure spiked, yanking a gasp from her chest. A purely satisfied masculine chuckle followed her sound and he gave her another barely-there stroke. Again a bolt of bliss hit her.

Then it got worse—better? His touch returned south and delved deeper, sliding farther until his finger circled her very center. He teased the edges of her heat, going round and round the rim of her soaked pussy. She rocked against his caress, aching to have any part of him inside her.

"Please, Ty?" She shifted her hips once again. She was on fire, burning for him, her entire body aching for his possession and demanding she submit to his every whim. "*Please.*"

Ty eased his finger into her, sliding effortlessly into her moist entrance. His digit teased her inner-walls, stroking them, and the touch aroused her even further. Her body burned for him, ached and begged and throbbed with desire for the man between her spread thighs. He retreated and then pushed into her, establishing a slow, gentle rhythm that drove her mad.

"Not enough," she whimpered.

He withdrew completely, and she whined, wiggling her hips in an effort to entice him to return. And he did return, giving her more than he had before. Two fingers slid into her, stretching her pussy.

"Better?"

She nodded, unable to do much more. Especially when he began that slow, steady pace once again. The calluses on his fingers teased her while the tips of his digits slid over her G-spot with every gentle thrust and withdrawal.

"So much better," she moaned.

Through it all, she kept her gaze centered on him, absorbing every emotion that flitted across his face. Lust, desire, animalistic need. It was all there plus a hint of something else, something she wasn't quite ready to identify.

Ty continued to torment and tease her, drawing her pleasure higher and higher with each beat of her heart. His free hand rested atop her mound, thumb so close to her pulsing clit yet so very, very far away. She wanted him to flick and circle the nub and the caress would send her soaring over the edge.

Then he sent that hope crashing down around her. He withdrew from her pussy.

"No," she wailed and sobbed.

"Shh… I just want a taste."

Then he did the most erotic, delicious thing she'd ever seen. He brought his fingers to his mouth and lapped at them, sucking them deep, and he moaned. His eyes rolled into the back of his head and he sucked harder, hollowing his cheeks.

Mia glanced down, noting the even larger bulge hidden from view by his jeans. She wondered how *he'd* taste.

He released his fingers and stared down at her, his eyes fully black. Brown fur dusted his cheeks and neck, the light sprinkling continuing on to his biceps and forearms.

"More." He lowered fully to the ground, resting on his stomach between her spread legs and he brought his face level with her weeping pussy. "Need."

Mia pushed up to her elbows and stared down at him past the swell of her stomach. The move made her aware of her body, of the curves that covered her and how they compared to the perfectly trim Sarah. But then it didn't matter because Ty's heated gaze met hers, his expression telling her that he wanted her, craved her, and needed her more than anything else in the world.

Still focused on her, he lowered and eased forward to hover over her desperate pussy. Talented fingers teased her opening once again and slid deep into her as before. At the same moment, he fused his mouth to her pulsating clit and flicked the bundle of nerves with his tongue.

"Oh, *fuck*." Oh, holy fuck. If ever there was a curse-worthy time, it was that second. And the next moment when he sucked. And then when he rubbed her G-spot with the pad of his fingers. And then when he…

Mia rocked against his hand, meeting his every thrust and fighting to have more of him inside her. She wanted to be stretched completely, filled entirely by him. Soon the pleasure became too intense, overwhelming her with the sensations of his hand, his mouth, and that wicked tongue.

Ty settled into a steady, lightning inducing rhythm that drove her wild. Flick, suck, thrust, rub, repeat. Mouth and fingers tormented her, sending sparks of pleasure and shards of rising desire through her veins. More and more he gave and more and more she took.

"Ty," she whimpered and his gaze bore into her, seeming to look into her soul and whatever he saw pleased the bear. A vibrating rumble traveled from his mouth to her clit and she screamed at the pleasure his action caused.

Unable to stop herself, she reached down and sifted her fingers through his hair, fisting his strands. She tightened her hold, fighting to direct his actions, and the move had him growling against her clit. Fuck, the vibrations added to her pleasure. Feelings of bliss and ecstasy rocketed through her from head to toes and back.

Her cunt clenched and tightened around his fingers, milking him, and she readily admitted that she wished she were being penetrated by his cock. He'd slide deep into her, plunging in and out in rapid succession.

Holding his hair tight, she rocked against his mouth, shifting and flexing in time with every thrust and retreat. Mia cupped her breast with her free hand, kneading the mound and rubbing her nipple through the fabric of her top and bra. She needed a little more…

"Ty," she sobbed his name. "Close…"

His rhythm changed, his tempo increasing and she gladly matched him, reveling in his attentions. Their gazes were no longer intent on each other, but she sensed his feelings through every flick of his tongue and slip of his fingers into her sheath. His actions demanded she come and snatch that final completion.

She raced to the edge, to the very precipice, and hovered along the brink of release. A little more and she'd…

Another rumbling growl and then a hint of pain stole through her. Oh shit, he'd scraped her clit with his fang. And then again. And once again. With that small hurt, she flew. The ache threw her to the brink and right into the abyss of her orgasm. Her body tightened, muscles spasming and clenching as the pleasure overtook her.

No, overtake was too bland a word.

It conquered and claimed her, stole every hint of control and she could only succumb to the pleasure of his mouth and hand. Heedless of her screaming, he continued, his actions sending crackling spears of ecstasy through her veins. Her toes curled, muscles tensed, and the bliss of her release crawled into every corner of her body. Trembles robbed all voluntary action from her and the only thing she could do was go along for the ride that never seemed to end.

"Ty!" She jerked and twitched, the bliss shorting out her nerves. A sob tore from her throat and she fought against his hold. To get closer? Or father away? "Please." He scraped her clit once again and this time it was to get away. She jerked, pushing on his head instead of fighting to bring him nearer. "Too much..."

Ty hummed against her sensitive flesh, and his torment eased. The suction on her clit ceased and the rapid plunge of his fingers in and out of her soaked pussy slowed. But the pleasure... Her cunt spasmed and a small tremor slithered up her spine causing Mia to whimper.

Ty released her clit and placed a soft kiss to the blissfully abused nub. Those talented fingers slipped free of her and she finally stirred enough to release her hold on his hair. Pushing to her elbows once again she found him licking his lips, the bear's eyes practically glowing in pleasure.

"Delicious."

chapter nine

Ty lapped at her slit once more, enjoying the musky flavors of her cream as they danced across his tongue. His cock ached and throbbed within the confines of his jeans, but he held himself in check. Barely. Mia still had too many doubts, too many questions, and he wouldn't push her until she was truly ready to be his. No matter how much his dick complained. Come to think of it, his bear complained a hell of a lot, too.

He placed one, last lingering kiss to her flushed pussy and then rolled back to his knees. He'd never seen anything more beautiful than a debauched and thoroughly satisfied Mia. Her dark hair formed a midnight halo around her head, her face glowed with satisfaction and her clothes barely clung to her.

He held out a hand to her. "Come on, Itana. Let's eat."

Mia giggled. "You did already."

He rolled his eyes and wiggled his fingers. "Uh-huh. Time for you to eat. Gigi will kick my ass if I bring all of this food back. Plus there are a few more things I want to show you."

"Naked things?" She waggled her eyebrows.

"Wench." When she finally placed her palm on his, he grasped her and tugged, pulling her upright. "No more today."

She harrumphed and he found that gorgeous as well.

In two seconds they resumed their positions only this time, Ty remembered the forks. He gathered a bite of potato salad and held it out for her. His bear continued its growling commentary, but was slightly appeased by the idea of feeding her.

She opened her mouth to accept the morsel, but the echoing roar that rolled over them had him halting immediately. The second, more urgent than the last, had him tossing the food to the ground.

"Shit." Ty rolled to his feet and snatched up Mia's shoes. "Put those on. We need to go."

"Ty?"

"Now, Itana," he snapped out the words and cursed himself for his tone, but Van wouldn't have called for him if it hadn't been urgent. He'd threatened to kill anyone who interrupted his picnic with Mia.

With his brusque order, she scrambled into action, as if sensing his need to leave quickly. The moment her sandals were in place, he hauled her to her feet and took off toward the path.

"What about the food?"

He shook his head. "We need to get back."

Another round of roars came.

"Oh, God, is it Parker?" Her footsteps faltered.

He turned back to her and noted that every feeling inside him was visible on her features. "I don't know. Can you run?"

Her nod was all the agreement he needed. He released her and broke into a jog, glancing over his shoulder to make sure his Itana kept pace. Gradually, he increased his speed. Later, he'd be smug about the fact that his human mate kept up with him. They burst past the tree line and raced toward the house, the rapid pounding of their feet against the hardened earth never lessening.

Van spotted them first, his brother lowered his head from its raised position while the last roar he released still lingered on his lips. "Itan."

Ty slowed when he got to the small gathering of his brothers, all three of them standing together and at least fifty feet from the clan den. He opened his mouth to question the men, but Mia got to them first.

"What's wrong? What happened? Is it Parker?" She fired the questions at Van, Keen and Isaac, one after another, and turned toward the house.

"Itana, wait." Isaac, held out a hand to stop her.

Ty's beast reacted instantly, snarling at the idea of any other touching her. He was still surrounded by her scent, the musk of her cream sticking to his skin, and that drove his possessive and protective instincts even higher. He grabbed his brother's wrist and tightened the hold until Isaac winced.

"Damn it, Ty," Isaac muttered the words.

"Ty? Seriously? You're playing with your brothers when there's something wrong with Parker?" She scolded him and Ty noticed that his brother's eyes widened.

"It's not Parker, Itana." Van, her harshest opponent, had finally adopted the title. It seemed that after three days, his brother had gotten the hint. "It's… something else."

"Oh."

Ty still hadn't released his grip on Isaac. His bear was having too much fun watching the different shades of red fill his brother's face.

A small, delicate hand punched him in the shoulder followed by a whining "ow."

From the corner of his eye, he saw Mia shake her hand. "Your body is like concrete. Now, stop hurting Isaac so they can tell us what happened and then we can hurt all three of them." Mia's glare encompassed is brothers. "Do you have any idea what you interrupted?"

Based on the flaring of their nostrils and the grins that suddenly decorated each of their faces, he figured they did.

"Focus," Ty snapped. He wanted this done and then he'd sneak Mia away...

Keen gulped, and stepped forward. "Richard was running late this morning and someone finally found him."

Ty sighed and released Isaac. He pinched the bridge of his nose and waited for Mia's rapid-fire questions to pick up again. He'd wanted to save her the stress, wanted to keep her happy and free of worry while they got to know each other over the past few days. Telling her that Richard—one of the men responsible for trailing Griss—had been missing for a day wasn't exactly something that gave off a worry-free vibe.

That decision was about to bite him in the ass.

"Found Richard? He was missing? I thought he was watching Griss." A single, slim finger poked his arm. "You said he was watching Griss while Van did bear research."

He couldn't cater to her right that second. He needed to be the clan's Itan. Straightening his spine, he turned to Van. "What happened?"

"Ty?" She gripped his bicep, tugging on him.

"Just listen, Itana. I'll explain later." The furious expression on her face assured him he'd probably have a quite a few things to explain later. Probably something about keeping secrets. And, based on the murder in her eyes, he wasn't going to enjoy the discussion.

Not much could be done about it now.

Van ran a hand down his face and this was the first time Ty noticed the fatigue dragging at his brothers. All three of them wore haggard expressions, dark circles lingered under their eyes, and their clothes were wrinkled.

"What happened?"

Keen spoke up first. "You know I didn't discover anything crime related about Richard and Sarah in the government database, but I went ahead and tagged their financials." His brother stared at the ground a moment and then refocused on Ty. "There was a twenty grand withdrawal from Sarah's account this morning."

"And an officer found Richard in a dumpster behind the diner this afternoon. He was last seen having breakfast there yesterday and then never showed up for his shift. So between then and two this afternoon, he was beat to hell and left for dead." Van's voice was quiet, solemn.

"It was Martin's turn to watch Griss. What did he have to say about the asshole's whereabouts?" This shouldn't have happened, they already knew the man had probably killed Parker's parents, his brother and sister-in-law. Hell, maybe even his own parents in an effort to get a shot at the position of Itan. The Sheriff's office in Cutler had forwarded a box of evidence to see if they could discover anything new, but that wasn't arriving until later in the day.

Damn it, his people were supposed to keep an eye on the male.

"Martin's missing." Van's lips formed a solid, white slash across his features. "Griss is out there on his own."

"*Fuck.*" There was no better word in the English language. Mia's shaking hand embraced his, squeezed until a throbbing ache assaulted him. Scenarios pinged through his mind but there was only a single conclusion that could be reached. "Find Sarah." Keen whipped out his cell phone and punched the screen. His brother felt it was okay to play damned games? "Keen?"

"Two seconds." Another few pokes and prods.

"Keen…" he growled. He *would* have his brother's full attention.

Keen finally looked at him. "Her phone is at the corner of Main and Seventh. Car is on Sycamore near Pine."

"What?"

His youngest brother shrugged. "You wanted everything on them, I gave you everything. The cell was easy to hack and her car is hooked up to one of those services where if you're in an accident, they call you. I got into both systems."

Yet another surprise from Keen.

He'd missed way too much. As soon as this crisis was over, he'd remedy that. For now, he needed his inner-circle, not a band of brothers wandering around.

"Good. Van, you're acting as enforcer. Go find her and bring her to me. Battered is fine, dead is not. Put her in the cell in the basement. I have no doubt she's helping Griss somehow. Keen, keep him up to date on her location."

Van's eyes darkened to black as his brother accepted the responsibility of his position.

Keen held his hand out to the clan's enforcer. "Give me your phone. I have an app that'll track her."

He dismissed his two brothers and focused on Isaac. "I need you to go through everything inside that box coming from Cutler and find me a reason to end Griss. Undisputable proof would be best, but I'll take something I can use to reason with the Southeast Itan if it comes to that."

Ty knew the man had been behind the deaths of his own parents and his brother and the male's wife. He needed proof before he could finish it all.

"Yes, Itan."

By the time he was done, Van and Keen had refocused on him. "I want more men near the den and in the forest. He's not coming near the Itana nor Parker."

They spoke as one. "Yes, Itan."

With that, they strode away, three werebears intent on their orders. Which left him with a wide-eyed, shaking Mia. She still clutched him, fingers digging into his skin, but he barely noticed the sting. He was more worried about the wildness in her eyes.

"Mia?"

"What else haven't you told me? Why is he doing this?" Her eyes cleared for a moment. "You can't keep secrets from me. Not if…"

Ty clenched his jaw, fighting against the lie that ached to spring to his lips. He wanted to tell her there was nothing left to reveal. There was nothing more going on other than a missing Griss and Sarah the heartless bitch. It was obvious the two of them somehow found one another and were working together.

"Mia," he forced himself to be calm and collected while he shoved his bear back into its cage. The animal raged at him—*raged*—for upsetting their Itana.

She released him and stepped back, holding up her hand to forestall him when he would have followed. "No. That *man*," she spat the word as if it were poison, "nearly killed Parker. The male who was supposed to be watching him *did* die, another is missing, and Sarah is involved in it all. Parker hates that woman and has tried to take a

113

chunk out of her twice. Have you looked into that? Because something about her stinks." She took a deep breath and another step back. "You need to clean up your clan, Itan."

With that order—and it was an order—she spun on her heel and stomped toward the house. At her approach, the back door burst open and a smiling, tumbling Parker stumbled down the steps. Mia didn't halt, merely scooped up with cub with a laugh, raised him above her head and blew a raspberry on the boy's stomach.

You need to clean up your clan, Itan.

Wasn't that the truth.

*

With every step, a little more pain crept into Mia's veins. He'd kept secrets. Not about tiny, insignificant things, but ones that affected her and Parker's safety. She knew about Richard's initial screw up. The man hadn't been appraised of Griss's crimes and had been lured by his mate into shirking his duties. A brief dose of clan discipline had corrected the man's behavior. Locating Griss again had taken a little time, but from that moment, he and the other guards had been intent on keeping the evil male under constant watch. Mia realized Sarah's distraction had probably been intentional. The woman was definitely working hand-in-hand with that piece of cow poop.

Parker giggled and tried to tickle her and she laughed as he expected, even if bits and pieces of her were dying.

"You little tease." She laughed and tickled him in return while stomping up the stairs into the home. The moment they crossed the threshold, she placed him on his feet. The scent of warm cookies stroked her and she smiled down at the cub. "Why don't you go see Gigi and beg for a cookie? Tell her I said you could have one."

"Two?" Parker held up two fingers.

"Okay, two." She was such a pushover for a smiling face.

"Three?" Another finger joined the first two.

Mia rolled her eyes and laughed. "Be happy with two, mister." She nudged him toward the kitchen. "Off you go. I need to find Keen."

The boy giggled and raced off, feet sliding over the polished wood and he nearly wiped out as he raced around a corner. Shaking her head, she did as she'd told Parker, she hunted Keen Abrams.

Ever since Ty discovered his youngest brother's magic with computers and anything tech related, Keen could always be found in his new office. Mia slipped off her muddied sandals and then padded through the den, navigating the halls with ease now that she'd been in residence a few days. She rounded the next corner and smiled in relief to see the door open. More than one clan member had earned Keen's echoing roar by going in when it was firmly shut. Some hacking attempts needed quite a bit of concentration.

Mia poked her head in. "Keen? Got a minute?"

"Always for you, Itana."

She internally winced at the title. The Abrams brother's acceptance had been a sort of domino effect. First Isaac, then Keen and finally Van. From there it was slowly filtering down through the clan.

Mia moved deeper into the room and slid onto a heavily cushioned chair. "I want to know everything."

"Everything, Itana?" His eyebrows rose to his hairline and a sweet look of innocence graced his features. If it wasn't for her experiences with Parker, she would have believed him.

"Everything, Keen. I know there's more than what you four discussed in the yard. There has to be. So, I want to hear it."

"Itana…" He squirmed in obvious discomfort.

"Glad you agree."

"Oh, but I didn't—"

"Well, you called me your Itana and the clan's Itana rules beside the Itan. She shares his knowledge and his burdens. I believe I've been neglecting my duties in that area, so let's fix that, shall we?" Mia gave him her best *aren't I sweetness and light* smile.

When he frowned and squirmed, then sighed, she knew she'd won.

"It all goes back to Cutler, Itana…"

Fifteen minutes later, Mia had the short version of Griss's history and a timeline of events. Starting with the Cutler Itan, Robert, and his dead son. Then on to the Itan's dead brother and family which left only Parker between Griss and control of the Cutler clan. Added with what happened in Grayslake, and she was sick.

"You need to go into Sarah's past, Keen." She pressed a hand to her roiling stomach.

"I've already—"

Mia glared at him, he didn't deserve the brunt of her anger, but she didn't exactly have Ty hanging around. "You missed something. Did Parker's parents hang around Richard and Sarah much?"

Keen shook his head. "No, they stuck with other families with cubs. Clans aren't about being buddy-buddy. We get together once a month for a run, but most of the time, there are smaller individual groups—cliques—that socialize more than we do as a larger group."

"So Parker—who has probably seen Sarah from afar, but didn't know her—suddenly decides to take a chunk out of her leg? His behavior is probably new for him. He wants to harm a near stranger while he's been sweeter than anything to everyone else, including me." She kept her gaze steady. "How is it I'm the only one seeing something there?"

"His parents just died—"

116

Mia raised a single brow and waited.

Keen's shoulders slumped. "Yes, Itana."

She gave the man a jerky nod, and rose from the chair. In a handful of steps, she was in the hallway and hadn't even bothered to say goodbye to Keen. She had too many thoughts writhing in her mind. She bounced between decisions, shifting from confronting Ty or simply stealing Parker away while no one was looking.

One thought clung to her, one part of Keen's explanation that refused to be ignored.

The Cutler Itan, at one time, had a son.

A son that was killed at sixteen by his best friend.

chapter ten

Ty entered Mia's room, their room, with trepidation dogging his every step. He waited for her to yell and scream at him, to demand that he leave her space and never return, but the order didn't come. Instead, she ignored him, ignored him standing just inside the doorway as she padded past him and into the bathroom.

He quietly eased the door closed, wincing when the click of the latch sliced through the silence. He stepped deeper into the room, moving toward the bed, and he paused just beside the piece of furniture. The quiet stretched, occasionally interrupted by the splash of water and low thump of the various bottles of creams and treatments she slathered on each night. Usually, he joked and poked fun at her routine, assuring her that nothing in a bottle could make her more beautiful to him. Tonight, however...

Ty cleared his throat. "Mia?"

"Just a minute."

She disappeared from view for a moment, the half-closed door blocking his line of sight, but then it swung wide. She was revealed to him in all of her shorts and T-shirt clad glory. He glanced at his watch and noted it was nearing nine. Technically, it was early for a lot of the bears in the clan, but with tucking Parker in, they usually headed to bed before everyone else.

"Did you want to go out?"

Mia shook her head, then paused and nodded. "In a way."

She went to the bed and it was then he noticed the duffel bag resting there. The duffel that had originally been brought over by his brother when it'd been decided she'd stay for a while.

"Mia?"

She tossed in a few bottles and then tugged the zipper closed. She grabbed the handles and lifted the bag from the bed before turning to face him fully. "Parker and I are leaving."

"You can't. Griss—" He snapped his mouth shut when she raised a hand.

"I'm not an idiot. I understand everything now. Do you get it? *Everything.* I spoke with Keen this afternoon, and he laid it out for me. I know Parker needs to stay under the clan's protection until Griss is dealt with. I also know you intend to hand him over to the Cutler Itan."

"He's the boy's great uncle, Mia." He ran a hand through his hair, frustration battering him while the bear seethed at the idea of Mia being away from them.

"He's a beast you know nothing about beyond his familial ties to the cub. You don't know the kind of boy he will raise, the kind of man he'll mold." Tears glistened in her eyes, and she shook her head. "I'm not leaving Parker or the grounds, I'm not that stupid. I wouldn't risk Parker's life by leaving entirely. We're going to Van's."

Ty couldn't have withheld his growl if his Itana's life had depended on it. The mere idea she'd be anywhere but at his side… "No."

"You don't have a choice. Two thirds of the security have been pulled from the house and transferred to Van's home. We'll be at the bottom of the hill and we'll be protected. Keen has added additional safety measures to Van's house. It'll be safer than here."

"Safer? There's nothing more safe than being with—" Another rolling growl slid from him.

"Safer. I know Griss hasn't been spotted around here recently, but he got through that one time, didn't he? That first night? He lurked outside Parker's window and scared him, didn't he?" She glared at him. "Yet another secret. They're piling up, Ty. You better start shoveling your shit before you drown in it."

With that, she strode past him, snapping and breaking off pieces of his heart with every step. When she passed through the doorway, he followed, unable to stand the growing distance between them.

They emerged into the kitchen to find several guards along with his brothers gathered near the back door. A bouncing Parker came to him, and Ty automatically scooped the boy into his arms.

"Ty, we're gonna spend the night at Van's house and watch movies and play video games and eat popcorn and…"

He only half-listened, his focus remaining on his Itana. "Mia?"

Her gaze strayed to him but quickly centered on Parker. "Come on, little cub. Let's go have our adventure."

A pair of wet lips pressed against Ty's cheeks, and he forced his attention to the boy in his arms. "Have fun, okay?"

A huge smile was the only answer he received, and then he lowered the cub to the ground, forcing a farewell grin as Parker scrambled away.

Mia grasped Parker's small hand in hers and followed the boy toward the back door. An unfamiliar burn overtook his eyes, the slight,

121

stinging pain annoying yet unknown. Wetness slid over his cheek, and he dashed it away, refusing to acknowledge the tears.

"Mia?" He didn't recognize the croaking voice that came from his throat.

"I'll see you around, Ty."

"We should talk." He took a step forward.

She shook her head sadly. "I know you were trying to protect me. I understand that." She shrugged. "But I'm not a little cub. I was your Itana, and I rate better than secrets and lies. It's not real. I tried to tell you that. Biology, it's a sick duck."

Her words cut through him like a burning knife, slicing his flesh away from bone. *I was your Itana.* No, he couldn't have lost her. It was a bump in the road, a stumble. Nothing more, nothing less. It wasn't about biology, their attraction and feelings weren't created out of anything as simple as blood. She was just overreacting a little. They'd talk, she'd understand and...

The thump of the back door closing drew his attention, and he noticed the kitchen was empty, every guard and all of his brothers were gone. He moved to the kitchen window and tracked the progress of the group, keeping an eye on them as they traveled to Van's. It truly wasn't a long walk, just to the bottom of the hill, but the distance seemed like hundreds of miles.

Lights flicked on inside Van's home signaling their arrival, and it was easy to see several large, lumbering forms move around the outside of the house. The guards obviously slipping into position. She'd be safe; his brothers would make sure of it. Of course, the knowledge did nothing to mend the pain in his chest.

"Whiskey or coffee?" Gigi's voice cut into his worries and agony.

Without tearing his eyes from Van's home, he whispered his answer. "Whiskey. Definitely whiskey."

The thump of Gigi's retreating steps were immediately followed by the clank of glasses. The alcohol swished in the bottle as she returned, and the two glasses and bottle clinked when she placed them on the granite countertop.

Still his gaze remained on Van's home.

The sweet scent of whiskey hit his nose, and he finally tore his attention from the bottom of the hill, turning it toward the woman who'd been in his life since he was born.

"C'mon and drink so I can tell you what you did wrong." She slid a half-full glass toward him.

"I didn't—"

"Oh, I'm sure you think you didn't, but I know better. Have a seat and drink up." She nodded to his tumbler of whiskey.

His bear told him no, that he needed to get the hell out of their den and down that damned hill to get their Itana back. But Ty's human half knew better. Instead of demanding Mia return, he padded to the kitchen bar and slid onto a stool. He tugged the glass closer, cradled it in his hands for a moment and then simply tossed the burning liquid back. It seared his throat, clearing his sinuses on the way down, and he coughed the moment he swallowed the last drop.

"Shit." He sucked in a breath. "Damn." He nudged the glass toward Gigi. "Another."

"One more and then we'll talk about you mucking things up." Gigi was good to her word and poured more of the amber liquid into his glass.

When she stopped at halfway, he gestured for more. "If you're gonna rake me over the coals, give me something to dull the pain a little."

"I shouldn't give it to you. You need to feel it to learn from it."

Ty rubbed his chest, remembering the pain etched in Mia's features. Remembered the way tears lurked in her eyes and how her hand shook when she'd reached for Parker. Then there was the tremble in her voice as she'd spoken to him, berated him over his secrets.

"Tell me where you went wrong." Gigi's tone told him that no matter what he said, it wouldn't be the answer she was looking for.

"I lied to her."

The woman raised an eyebrow and gave him a look that said he had to do better.

"I should have told her everything from the start. She's my Itana," he coughed to cover up the crack in his voice. "She needs to walk beside me, not behind me."

Damn hadn't he heard his mother yell that at his father just before she dumped his dinner on the front porch. *If you want to act like an animal, you can eat with them.*

"You're getting closer, but you need to back up a little to get to your biggest mistake." Gigi sipped her whiskey.

He pressed his lips together and clenched his jaw. "I lied to her—withheld the truth, whatever you want to call it—in order to protect her instead of having her help me make decisions. I don't see what else I've done wrong."

Well, there were probably other annoying things he'd done to piss her off, but the little stuff didn't seem bad enough to walk out over.

"Have you sat and talked to her?"

Ty rolled his eyes, earning him a slap to the head. He glared, but answered her question instead of getting snarly. "Of course, I have."

"Uh-huh."

"I have."

"*Right*."

"Damn it, Gigi." His teeth were gonna shatter the way this was going.

"Fine. Did you ask her to come here? Or tell her?"

"I…" Well, he hadn't given her much of a choice, really. He'd played off her affection for the cub to trick her into coming to the den. Then he'd tricked her further to get her to stay.

"And when you decided she was your Itana, that was it, wasn't it? You just said it aloud, and everything was supposed to be happy."

"Well…" Ty winced. "Yeah, sorta."

"You haven't done a bit of wooing, Ty Abrams. You've made decisions and brow-beaten her into going along. Said things over and over, sure, but between running the clan, trying to be sheriff and worrying about Griss, you two haven't spent any time getting to know one another. Not really."

"I took her on a picnic." He didn't care if he sounded like a two year old.

"Uh-huh. And came back smelling like sex. I don't think much talking happened out there." Gigi gave him a deadpan look.

Yeah, he hated when she was right.

"You want her to trust you and love you, Ty, but you need to give her a reason to. 'Because I said so' isn't going to cut it. It won't work with her, and it sure as hell ain't gonna work with her daddy when he gets here."

That statement had him sitting up straight, eyes wide as he stared at Gigi. "What? Her father?"

The woman nodded and swirled her glass, watching the dark brown fluid spin round and round. "Tomorrow afternoon. He submitted a request to the Southeast Itan on his daughter's behalf, and he wants to be here for her in case the man calls with questions."

It couldn't have hurt more if she'd ripped out his heart and punched him in the gut. "Does she think I won't let her go? Is that why he contacted the Itan and is coming here? I keep telling her she's mine, but I'd never keep her against her will. I love her, damn it."

The air left his lungs and his heart stopped. Dear God, even if he'd come at things in a totally fucked up way, he loved that woman.

"It's good for you to admit your feelings, but I doubt she's worried about you forcing her to stay. You need to ask her why she called in the big guns." Gigi filled his glass once again.

"But you know the reason."

She nodded. "But I know the reason. Eavesdropping is wrong, but it's one of the ways I come to know everything here. You boys have tighter lips than a virgin sacrifice's vagina."

Ty smirked.

"Now, as for the rest, you need to do some shopping." She pulled a sheet of paper out of her pocket and slid it across the counter. "You can start there."

"Shouldn't I get to know her? To find out what she likes so I can—"

Gigi smacked him. "Boy, her daddy is coming tomorrow. You need to get her happy before that big old man turns up here and rips you in half." She nudged the page toward him again. "Wooing any woman begins with something like flowers and sweet notes, but there are some ideas just for her, too." She sipped her whiskey. "The superstore in town is open twenty-four hours."

The hinges on the back door's screen squeaked and then the wood panel swung wide to grant Keen entrance. "Itan?"

Ty jumped from his seat. "Mia? Is she okay?"

126

"She's fine." Ty worked to ignore the pity in his brother's gaze. "A program I was running just spit out some information you need to know."

He looked down at the list, scanning Gigi's neat scrawl, and weighed his responsibilities as Itan against his love for Mia. He sighed and stood, digging into his pocket. He tossed his keys to his brother. "C'mon, you drive and tell me at the same time."

Keen furrowed his brow but caught the keys with ease. "Where are we going?"

"Shopping."

chapter **eleven**

A tiny poking finger woke Mia. The small, chubby digit tapped her shoulder, drawing her from sleep. Which was something she hadn't had much of after leaving Ty last night. The Abrams brothers supported her as their Itana, choosing to serve and protect her instead of stepping into the middle of things and making the disagreement between her and Ty worse. They chose a side. Done.

Unfortunately, even if she believed she was in the right, she wasn't able to sleep without Ty beside her. In a few short days, she'd become accustomed to his presence, to his scent and the way he wrapped around her as they slept. He protected her even when they crawled into bed, making sure he lay between her and the door.

There was only one body in the bed now. Well, one body and one little boy who apparently wanted her out of bed.

"Mia." *Poke poke.* "Are you awake?" *Poke.* "Mia, you hafta see."

On the next prod from Parker, she snatched at the little boy and pulled him atop her, tickling and growling at the small cub. Giggles and laughs filled the room with a few high-pitched squeals for good measure. Heavy, thumping stomps announced a near stampede and then the tiny bedroom was filled with Isaac, Van, and two other clan members.

"What's going on?" Isaac's voice boomed in the small room, and she noticed their eyes were black as night.

"Sorry," she gulped. "Parker and I were kidding around and got a little out of hand. We're sorry, right Parker?"

Wide-eyed, he nodded. "Sorry."

As one, their shoulders slumped and they exhaled, those black eyes fading back to their natural colors.

Van came forward and ruffled Parker's hair. "It's okay, little cub. We just want to make sure you and the Itana are safe." He turned his attention to Mia. "Gigi's here and said breakfast is ready."

They filed out, leaving her and one grinning little boy behind. "Come on, you little rat, let's go eat."

Parker scrambled from her, kneeing her in the process, and then raced from the room. She knew the moment he hit Van's kitchen because his high-pitched, joyful voice filled the house.

With a sigh, Mia rolled from the bed and snatched a hair tie from the dresser. In less than a second her hair was secure in a lopsided pony tail. She glanced down at her body and shrugged. She was scraggly looking but covered. She'd borrowed a set of brand-new pajamas from Van, teasing him about why they weren't worn when he handed them over. He'd blushed, mumbled something about "nekkid" and then rushed off. It pleased her to no end that she was able to make the big bear squirm.

Chuckling, she shuffled from the small guestroom and headed toward the rising voices in the center of the house. She easily recognized Isaac, Van, and a few guards' tenors tumbling over Parker's. Keen's was noticeably missing, but last night the man said he was chasing a lead.

Before long, she emerged into controlled chaos, Gigi barked orders while the massive men rushed to do as she asked. Even Gigi had abandoned Ty, and Mia wondered who was making the Itan's breakfast this morning. Gigi pointed at her and crooked her finger and Mia instantly headed toward the woman. *She who controls the kitchen must be obeyed.* Hadn't she heard that from her father often enough?

Her dad. He was coming to see her today, hitting the ground at noon and then driving over from the airport. He'd arrive around three or four. She glanced at the analog clock on the wall, five or six hours and then she could slump into his arms and let him bear a little of the weight she carried.

"Morning, Gigi."

She tugged Mia close and gave her a one armed hug while planting a kiss on her forehead. "Sleep well?"

Mia frowned and shook her head. "Not so much."

"Uh-huh." The heavy thud of a car door slamming reached them. "'Bout time he showed up." Gigi nudged her. "You've got a visitor. Go on out."

"But my dad's not supposed to be here until—"

"It's not your daddy."

Mia shot her a questioning look, and Gigi rolled her eyes. "Little boys aren't the only ones who know how to eavesdrop. How am I supposed to know everything if I don't do a little spying?"

"So you know who's out there? And I want to go outside?"

"'Want to' is a stretch. 'Need to' though… You definitely need to go out there."

Frowning at Gigi's cryptic statement, Mia strolled from the kitchen toward the front of the house. The men who had been talking and laughing in the living room were now suspiciously absent, as was Parker.

The rapid knock of the visitor broke into the silence, and Mia peeked through the peep hole. It took one quick glance to identify the person on the other side of the door. The moment she saw him, she stumbled back. Her heart beat rapidly, pounding out an ever increasing, unsteady rhythm.

Ty. Dang it. Why had he come to Van's? She'd said what she'd wanted to say, and that was it. Done.

Another handful of knocks. "Mia? I can scent you. I know you're there. I just need a few minutes."

She didn't move, not an inch.

"Please?"

It was the "please" that broke her. The single word held heartbreak and hope, pain and longing and something a lot deeper. A feeling that neared her own.

Padding to the door, she reached for the deadbolt, only to find it already unlocked. A quick twist of the knob and a tug had the wood panel swinging wide to reveal Ty.

Ty who looked a lot like she felt. Bags lingered beneath his bloodshot eyes; his clothes were wrinkled, and his hair stuck up on its ends. He looked exhausted and delicious at the same time.

He cleared his throat and shifted from foot to foot. "Hi."

"Hi."

His gaze stroked her, slid over her from head to toe and back again, and the nervousness vanished. His eyes darkened to the bear's black, and she idly wondered if any of the werebears in the clan knew how to control their beasts. "You're wearing Van's clothes."

Mia nodded. "Yes, I didn't think a slinky nightie was appropriate here. Van has never worn these, and he offered them to me."

He stepped closer, and his nostrils flared while he breathed deep. "You don't smell like him."

She barely restrained the urge to roll her eyes. Dark brown fur now coated his biceps. "No, because they're new *and* I slept alone until Parker got me out of bed this morning."

He compressed his lips and his attention strayed from her, his gaze settling on the landscape in the distance. Seconds of silence ticked past, neither of them speaking. Part of her felt like giving in, jumping into his arms and saying to heck with the rest. But she knew she'd never forgive herself if she relented so easily.

Dang, she loved the man, but she wasn't about to subject herself to a lifetime of lies and secrets.

"I'm sorry." The words were low but clear. He turned back to her, his stare intent. "I'm sorry for so, so many things."

She nodded, acknowledging his words, but she wasn't quite sure what her response should be.

"If you'll let me, I'd like to take you out today." She opened her mouth to reply, but he spoke again before she could get the words out. "No funny business and our clothes stay on. Someone," he cleared his throat. "Someone reminded me that you and I—that *I*—didn't take the time to get to know you. So, I'd like to do that if you're willing."

"I—"

"She says yes." Gigi's shout came from deep within the house, and Ty's chuckle came immediately on its heels.

Mia wanted to say yes, wanted to commit and leap into his arms, but doubt still lingered. "Ty, I don't know."

He closed the distance between them, stopping just short of touching her, and stared intently at her. "I messed up. I know it. But I've never done this before. I've never cared about anyone but myself and my clan. You'll always be my Itana, Mia, but give me another chance to prove I can be the Itan you deserve." He took a deep breath and she pretended there weren't tears swimming in the big, bad Itan's eyes. "Please."

When he looked at her like that, when he whispered those soul-wrenching words for her ears only, she had one answer: "Yes."

A wave of relief rippled over him, and it looked as if a massive weight left his shoulders. A blinding smile spread his lips, and he leaned the tiniest bit closer. He pulled one hand from behind his back and presented her with a single yellow tulip. He brushed the soft petals against her cheek and the delicate, clean scent of the flower filled her.

"For you." His voice was rough and deep. Mia slid the tulip from his grasp and clutched the delicate stem. "A red rose seemed too ordinary for you, but the meaning remains the same."

She stared at the thin, yellow petals while his words tumbled through her mind. Red roses meant love… She'd heard him, but she wasn't sure she wanted to accept the message.

"Ty," she sighed.

"Go change, Itana. Wear something comfortable because we'll be gone for a while."

Mia nibbled her lower lip. "I have to be back—"

"By two-thirty because your father will be here between three and four." He placed a fingertip on her chin and pulled down, forcing her to release the bit of flesh. "I'm not the only one in this relationship with secrets being revealed." Ty removed his touch, cleared his throat, and stepped back. "Go change. I'll wait here."

Mia swallowed, panic overtaking her. How much had he discovered? What did he know?

134

"Go ahead. We'll have time to talk once we get where we're going."
His words didn't hold the gruff, emotional tone any longer.

She moved back and let the door swing closed, cutting off her view
of Ty. She stared at the solid piece of wood while thoughts tripped
over each other in her mind. Which secrets had come into the light
overnight?

"Well?" Gigi's question cut into her racing thoughts.

"He wants to get to know me." She twirled the yellow tulip in her
fingers. *A red rose seemed too ordinary for you, but the meaning remains the
same.* She turned back to the sweet, yet annoying, woman. "He gave
me a flower. Can we put it in water?"

She padded toward the other woman, intent on getting to the
kitchen. She'd get dressed, just as soon as she ensured Ty's token
would last more than a few hours.

"At least he listens every now and then."

"Huh?"

Gigi waved her away. "Nothing." She plucked the tulip from Mia's
grasp. "He did good, though. Hopelessly in love. That's what a
yellow tulip means."

Hopelessly in love.

Mia shook her head, unwilling to let her heart head in that direction.
At least, not yet. Or rather, again.

*

Ty tried sitting on the porch swing, but the way his knee bounced
when he sat jangled the chain and annoyed the hell out of him. Then
he paced, the thump of his boots on the worn wood annoying him
even more. He finally decided pacing on hard land would work
better, so he kept walking over the same fifteen feet of ground while
Mia changed. Out of his brother's clothes. His bear was still angry

about that. Even if Van had never worn them, they belonged to the other bear.

"She called out for you last night, you know." Isaac's words had him halting in his tracks.

"And you know that how?" The bear inside him rose to its hind legs, flexing its muscles and preparing to shove the human half of him aside.

"She's not exactly quiet and I was stationed outside her bedroom window. Hell, I'm surprised half the clan didn't hear her." Isaac took another pull on his cigarette and then lifted his foot, snubbing it out on the bottom of his shoe. "Damn things are gonna kill me," he mumbled. "That woman is so hung up on you, you'd have to be blind not to see it."

"And she left me. Yes, I can see what you mean." He snapped his mouth shut, swallowing his bitterness.

"Uh-huh. I'd feel sorry for you if you didn't deserve it."

"You know what—" A snarl replaced the rest of his sentence. He had a shit-ton of pent up energy and he knew just how to get rid of it. Ty took a step toward Isaac, ready to beat the man bloody.

Except then the front door swung open, and there was Mia looking gorgeous and fresh and his. The bear rumbled in appreciation and dropped back, happy to bask in her presence. They could always kill Isaac later. Wasn't like the man was going anywhere.

Ty strode up the steps, fingers tingling with the need to touch her. Just a small connection, nothing sexual. He held out his hand and waited, hoping that the two of them hadn't destroyed things beyond repair. Because it was true, he wasn't the only one holding secrets. It seemed she had a few herself.

"Ready?" The word was deep and rough, but his bear refused to take a back seat.

She nodded and placed her hand in his. For the first time since she'd walked out of the door, he was calm. Just her touch soothed him like nothing else.

"Where are we going?"

"One of my favorite spots." He smiled wide when a bright red blush suffused her cheeks. "Not that one. I've got a few others." He winked and smiled even wider when the red turned near burgundy. "C'mon." Ty tugged her toward his beat up truck. They'd be roughing it a little, but the battered thing was the only vehicle he risked going over the bumpy roads.

In a handful of moments he had her in his truck and then they were on their way, heading deeper into the forests that surrounded the clan den. The vehicle bounced over the deep ruts and dragged through big patches of mud. The angle of their ascent had the tires slipping every now and again. The man-made road they traveled had been created by the clan and couldn't be found on any map. It was hidden, it was sacred, and it was theirs.

The silence that blanketed the cab was both comfortable and tense. Ty's human half was on edge, hunting for something to say, some way to smooth the strain that surrounded them. While conversely, the bear was finally at ease, content with its other half nearby.

The few miles to their destination passed and they finally emerged into the massive clearing. Trees had been uprooted and transported elsewhere in the forest to make the space flat and open. He kept driving until he reached the leveled top of the hill, and he maneuvered the truck until the bed faced the valley.

"Where are we?" They were the first words from Mia since they'd entered the vehicle.

He kept his gaze trained on the tree line, unwilling to see her reaction to the place he held so dear. "The clan gathering spot. I thought it'd be nice and peaceful. A place for us to talk and get to know each other uninterrupted."

"Oh."

That was all he got from her—a low, murmured "oh."

"Oh good, or oh bad?" He hated the uneasiness in his voice. He needed to find his footing again, needed to hunt up level ground so he wasn't stumbling around in the dark.

Ty sensed the weight of her gaze, was able to see her look to him in his periphery. "Good."

One word and then the clunk of the door handle being tugged was followed by the grating squeak of the hunk of metal being swung wide. He stared at her then. Stared at the back of her head, the soft curls, and the curves of her body exposed by the snug fit of her sun dress. She hopped to the ground and was hidden from sight when the door slammed closed once again.

Well, he was doing okay so far. She had at least gotten out of the truck voluntarily.

Ty was quick to follow, quick to head to the back of the vehicle and meet her by the tailgate. He found her staring down into the valley below and he focused on it, as well.

The green, rolling hills appealed to his bear. The forests were home, but it was nice to be able to wander safely and without worry of someone sneaking up on him. Homes dotted the landscape, the dens of his clan members spread across the grassy valley. He spotted Van's place, the house surrounded by shifted bears and assorted cars.

"It's beautiful." Her whispered words were carried to him by the breeze.

"It is. It's home." He reached over and tugged on the handle to the tail gate, releasing the latch and then slowly lowering it. In one quick move, he vaulted into the back and grabbed the things he'd brought along.

Blankets and pillows overflowed his arms, and he dropped them on the end.

"What are you doing?" Trepidation edge her words, and he glanced at her, wincing at the uneasiness coating her face.

"We're just talking, eating a little something. Nothing more, Mia. I promise." He waited for her, waited for her acquiescence.

When she nodded, he went back to work, laying things out over the clean truck bed. He'd washed the thing once he and Keen had returned from their shopping trip. He didn't want his Itana anywhere near the dirt and grime that had been caked on the metal. Next he snared the massive outdoor umbrella he'd found and rigged it into place.

A chuckle had him looking to Mia, and he grinned at her. "What?"

"You thought of everything."

He shrugged, a little heat rushing to his cheeks, and turned back to his task. "You're pale. The last thing I want is for you to burn and be in pain." Umbrella in place, he took a step back and surveyed his work. Satisfied everything was as he planned, he moved to the tailgate and held his hands out. "C'mon up."

He wiggled his fingers, and she shook her head. "No, I'm too—"

Unwilling to hear the end of her sentence, he snared her anyway and easily lifted her onto the truck bed, smiling at the squeak that escaped her lips.

"Dang it, Ty."

He couldn't help but chuckle in response. That turned into a loud laugh when he caught sight of her outraged expression. "We would have been arguing forever, Itana. You think you're too big to carry, and I think you're absolutely perfect. You're made for me. I just need you to see it."

*

Oh, Mia saw it, more than she cared to admit out loud since there was still a crap-ton to work through. Sure, they'd shared a home for nearly a week, but his days were consumed by clan business plus the house was constantly filled with other bears. With Parker added into the mix, the only time they'd spent alone was when they slept. And even that was occasionally interrupted by the small cub. All in all, six days later, she still stared at a near stranger who she was half in love with and angry with at the same time.

Deciding not to argue, she settled on one of the piles of blankets and pillows he'd created. "So, what did Gigi make for us today?"

Ty shook his head. "Gigi is firmly in the 'Ty is an idiot' camp. I made this myself." He delved into the basket and returned with a wrapped bundle. "I can take care of you even if I am feeding you lunch for breakfast."

"I know." She nodded. She knew he could.

The first packet was unwound to reveal a large sub. That one was immediately followed by another. Then chips and cookies and... more food than she could ever eat. Ty set everything out between them, each tidbit within easy reach. It also kept them apart.

Mia quirked a brow. "You're not feeding me by hand this time?"

The annoying man smirked. "If I got that close to you, you'd end up naked and screaming my name. Again." He winked at her and then gestured to the array of food. "This keeps us both a little safer."

"Uh-huh." Not commenting further, she dug into the food, savoring the flavors and smiling when she realized he'd taken the time to put it all together, to provide for her. The flower had been from the human half of him, but the feast was all bear. A bit early in the day for lunch fare, but then again, eating on a hilltop wasn't conducive to bacon and eggs.

His gaze remained intent, and she fought to hide how he affected her. Of course, there was no concealing the way her nipples hardened or her pussy dampened due to being in his presence. Every once and again, he'd flare his nostrils and breathe deep. She couldn't help but blush then, knowing he could scent her desire for him. It was difficult to rationalize telling him no when her body screamed yes.

Their meal passed in relative silence, the quiet only broken by the chittering of animals and the songs of the birds that filled the forest. When she finally popped the last, remaining berry into her mouth and finished the sweet morsel, she let her gaze linger on him.

"So…"

Ty squirmed and then he slumped his shoulders. "So, I don't know how to do this. It's caveman as hell, but my bear and I crave you. We want you in our den, and we have no problem throwing you over our shoulder and locking you in." He took a deep breath. "But you deserve better. Just tell me what I need to do to make you happy, Mia, and I'll do it."

He looked so heartbroken that she nearly caved right there, but crumpling and giving in wouldn't solve anything.

"Tell me about yourself, Ty." She snuggled deeper into the pillows and enjoyed the shade from the umbrella and the soft breeze that ruffled her hair. "Just tell me about yourself and I'll tell you about me."

And so they talked.

His parents retired six years ago, leaving him in charge while they lived in Florida. The heat was tough on bears, but it made his mother happy so his father had gone along. Their electric bills were huge.

And oh, by the way, they would probably be in residence by the end of the week, two days from now at the earliest. He'd sorta told them he'd found his Itana.

Ty had the grace to blush and wince as the confession rolled off his tongue which went a long way toward her deciding not to kill him.

Then she'd sorta told him about her father's impending arrival (which wasn't news to him), the fact that he wasn't her biological father (which was), and her relationship to Parker (which threw him for a loop).

"He's your cousin." Ty drew the words out, as if saying them slowly would help him understand them better.

"Yes," she nodded.

"And the Cutler Itan, who will be here soon, is your grandfather."

"Yup."

"So Griss is…"

"A cousin." And it boiled her blood to think of the man that way, but facts were facts.

Ty blew out a slow breath and leaned back. "What about the papers your father filed with the Southeast Itan? Is he," Ty gulped. "Is he taking you back with him?"

Her heart broke for him then. The defeat in his gaze went bone deep, and snippets of their conversation came back to her.

"More than anything, I don't want the ugliness of the werebear world to touch you, Mia. This thing with Griss… It's ugly. I want you wrapped in a bubble, protected from anything that could upset you."

"No," she shook her head and his eyes brightened a bit. "I asked for custody of Parker in light of my grandfather's child rearing practices and the way he failed to act when my biological father ra—" She swallowed the bile rising in her throat. "When my biological father raped my mother. Plus, Griss attempted to beat Parker to death. With Sarah's help, I think."

142

"You want to keep Parker." It wasn't a question, just a statement, but she nodded nonetheless. "He's going to be the Cutler Itan, Mia. I don't want you to get your hopes up. The clans take the line of succession very seriously and believe future Itans are better left with the previous Itan for training."

She had thought of this; she and her father had thought of this. "If he's with me, he's with a family member and you can train him. I don't think there's anyone better to train Parker than you."

A hint of joy lit his eyes and then they deepened to black. "The only way I could do that is if you stayed."

Mia's heart thundered, pounding against her rib cage and fought to burst through her chest. Excitement and nervousness warred within her, and she knew there was only one answer she could give him. While today had been enjoyable and reinforced her decision, she'd already made her choice the moment he brushed a yellow tulip across her cheek.

Hopelessly in love.

"Which I am." She held her breath, waiting for his response.

Deep brown fur rippled and slipped through his skin, sliding over him to coat his arms and neck. Hints of the hair decorated his cheeks and it looked like the midnight black of his eyes was there to stay.

*

"Mine."

Nothing could ruin this moment, the culmination of a lifetime of waiting. He had always figured he'd find a suitable female bear and have a few cubs, but this happiness… It had seemed unattainable. Despite his parent's mating as an example, he hadn't believed what he would soon hold in his arms was possible.

He'd take her and love her and tie them together forev—

Ty's thought was cut off by a pouncing Mia. His formerly timid Itana practically mauling him.

Okay that was in his imagination. In reality, she leaned toward him, easing closer until she was within his reach, and *he* pounced.

Damn it, that didn't happen either because the shrill ringing of his cell phone sliced through their peace. Ty growled. They weren't supposed to be interrupted for anything short of the world coming to an end. Since things were still bright and shiny outside, he didn't think that was about to happen.

His Itana whined and slumped into the pillows. Yeah, Ty wanted to whine a little too. His mouth watered at the thought of getting another taste of her... and more.

The ringing continued while he dug through the scattered blankets and pillows. He'd tossed the thing aside when making their mounds of pillows and never hunted it down. The annoying sound repeated over and over until he answered the call.

"Hello?" He hadn't even bothered checking caller ID.

"I'm sorry, Itan, but you need to come back." Van's words held more than a hint of stress, hell, it held a boatload.

Reacting first, Ty rolled to his feet and headed toward the tailgate. "What happened?"

"The perfect God damned storm." An echoing roar came through the phone, and he heard his brother respond with one of his own before the phone went dead.

"*Fuck.*"

"Ty?" Mia's creamy skin beckoned him, and he couldn't do a damn thing about it. Any other time, he'd dive between her thighs, claim her, and then happily die there. Any. Other. Fucking. Time.

"Something is happening at the den. I don't know what, but we need to go." His words were clipped. He figured he'd owe her an apology later, but his worry had to be for his bears.

Without another word, Mia scrambled toward him. She grabbed her shoes before jumping down from the bed. She didn't even pause to put on her sandals and simply ran to the passenger door barefoot. Ty was quick to follow her actions, sliding behind the wheel in less than a second.

"We'll come back for the rest of this shit later." Ty turned the key, and the engine roared to life. He pressed the pedal down hard and fast, and the truck instantly obeyed. It didn't look like much, but the old bucket of bolts moved when she needed to. The evidence of their visit flew from the bed, blankets, pillows and trash flying from the open back. Eventually, the umbrella lost its battle with the wind.

Yeah, they'd come back for everything later. Assuming there was a later.

chapter **twelve**

The drive back to the den sent Mia's heart racing, each bump and jarring thump forcing her heart rate even higher.

Ty gripped the steering wheel tighter and tighter with each passing mile, his knuckles glowing white. More of his fur came out to play with every second until his arms were entirely brown. His mouth had already lengthened and thickened to his bear's snout while his forehead flattened and widened.

Oh yes, the bear was coming out.

Mia scooted closer to him, wiggling across the bench seat until they sat thigh-to-thigh. She let his touch soothe her nerves while she hoped hers did the same to him. When his shoulders slumped and grip on the wheel eased slightly, she figured it had.

"I don't know what we're going into. The last I heard was another bear and my brother going after him."

"Okay," she gulped.

"I need you to stay in the truck." He reached down and squeezed her knee. "I need you safe."

Mia nodded. "All right."

Silence remained their only company as they bounced down the hill. The truck tires squealed the moment the rubber hit the asphalt. The back end swung out, vehicle fish-tailing for a moment before Ty wrenched it under control.

They sped past the trees that lined the road, her vision was filled with blurs of green and brown, but her gaze remained firmly on the blacktop before them. She watched the clock, her heart racing faster and faster with each passing minute. Soon they'd be back at the den and could figure out what sort of madness they'd stumbled into.

Eventually she recognized her surroundings, noting the massive boulder where they'd turn right onto a dirt road. It wouldn't be much longer...

The land lay flat before them and slowly the small specks representing their visitors' cars grew larger as they approached. Mia didn't recognize any of them other than those that belonged to Ty's brothers. A Cadillac was off to one side while a large SUV was on the other.

But it was the two bears between the vehicles that worried her most.

"Holy shit," she whispered the words. "That's my father." She glanced at the dashboard clock and noted the time. "And he's really, really early."

"Shit." Ty slammed on the brakes and brought the truck to a sliding stop that sent gravel spraying. "Who the hell is the other one?"

The strange bear's fur was light brown with hints of grey and white showing through the coat. It was obvious the animal was older than her dad. It took slow, heavy lumbering steps while her dad's were more quick and agile. The other's eyes were dull and cloudy while her father's were bright and filled with an anger that was foreign to her.

Daddy was *pissed*.

With a shouted "stay put," Ty jumped from the truck, slamming the heavy door so hard the entire vehicle shook. The man raced for the two battling bears, tearing off layers of clothing with every step. First the shirt, then the shoes and then his jeans. By the time the last article slipped from his skin, he was already halfway through his shift. Bones and muscles reshaped lightning fast. Fur seemed to burst forth, and his nails transformed into deadly claws between one blink and the next.

She went from watching Ty get naked to staring at an enraged werebear intent on breaking up the fight between the two males.

Stay put? Like heck.

Mia yanked on the door handle and shoved the heavy metal panel wide, hopping from the truck the moment she had enough space. She raced from the vehicle, intent on getting to the two men who held her heart. She made it ten feet, ten feet of worry and running, before another body barreled into her, slamming her to the ground.

"Don't you even think about it." The snarled words were deep and filled with deadly intent.

Self-preservation kicked in, demanding she freeze and listen to the massive male atop her. The gravel beneath her palms scraped and scratched her skin, but it was the man crushing her that worried her most.

"Nod if you understand."

Of course, Mia nodded. The large mass of man holding her down eased some of his weight from her, and she took a chance to glance over her shoulder. It was Keen, but a Keen she'd never seen before. Muscles bulged and flexed all over his body, the harsh, carved lines digging into her. His mouth was a snout, long and thick and covered in near-midnight fur while wicked fangs stretched past his lips. His forehead was flattened, eyes now farther apart. She looked to the hands on either side of her body and shuddered. Fingers were claws, deadly nails now inches long.

Gradually his weight eased, lessening until he rolled to his feet and towered over her. He reached down and hauled her upright while his gaze remained firmly on the ongoing carnage before them.

The older bear continued snarling and clawing at her father, hunting for blood, while her father did the same. The burgundy fluid coated each of their coats, blackening the fur and matting the strands to their massive bodies.

Ty raced into the fray, shoving aside her father and then roughly doing the same to the other bear. Her dad didn't seem to take too kindly to being denied his kill and attacked Ty, turning his enraged attention to the man she'd decided to spend her life with. A ginormous claw scraped down Ty's side, opening him from shoulder to hindquarter, and Mia couldn't withhold her scream.

"Ty!" Anguish filled her voice and pain for him raced through her body. She took one step and then another toward the tangle of bears, but it was Keen's unrelenting grip that stayed her.

"Damn it, Keen." She yanked against his hold, never tearing her gaze from the battling bears.

The older bear pushed back into the fight, and Ty shoved him, sending him tumbling and stumbling back a half dozen steps and then he turned his attention to her father once again. Blood continued to flow from the gaping wound, and the bears' focus remained intent on one another. Her dad raised his claw, ready to strike, and she realized Ty wasn't going to defend himself. He wasn't going to fight the man who'd raised her.

This time, when she heaved against Keen's hold, she broke free. One minute she was a captive and then next she was racing across the gravel driveway, screaming as loud as she could.

"Daddy, no!" Sobs choked her voice, so she tried again. She dug deep, hunting within herself for every ounce of energy she possessed and let loose another shout. "No!"

Her father's downward strike stuttered in mid-air, claw freezing in place, and Mia didn't slow a bit. No, she moved faster, sandal-clad feet pounding over the loose gravel. She slid across the uneven surface, stumbling until she stood between her father and the man she loved.

"No," she gasped and fought for breath. Wetness coated her cheeks, tears streaming from her eyes. "No."

A growl came from behind her, the sound so familiar, and it was answered by the massive bear in front of her. Her father bared his teeth, curling his lip and snarling at Ty.

"No more!" She screamed as loud as she could, fighting to be heard over the growing growls.

Another bear's sounds joined in, coming from her left. She quickly stooped, grabbed a rock from the ground and threw it at the offending animal. She may not be a skinny model-like woman, but she'd played hard with the boys growing up. One of her favorite games had been baseball. Mia put all of her strength behind the throw, flinging it across the expanse and nailing the bear right between the eyes. Blood immediately welled from the wound she'd inflicted. She glared at the fang-bearing bear and mimicked his snarl.

"I fucking said enough."

A rolling whine came from her father and she turned back to him, intent on his slow and steady shift. Her dad was getting older which made his shifts a little painful. Arthritis was a witch, he said, and being a bear didn't make it any different.

Before long, he was on his hands and knees, panting. Some of the scrapes he'd received were now healed, a few deeper ones still bright pink against his pale skin.

His first words to her was actually a single word. One she should have expected. "Language."

Mia rolled her eyes and turned away from him and back to Ty. He narrowed his eyes, his bear glaring at her, but she didn't care. He was hurt and in pain, his expression telling her without words how much agony he was in. She cradled his snout, running her fingers along its length.

"Are you going to shift back for me, Itan?" She ran her fingers along the top of his nose.

A snarl came from somewhere, and she glanced around to find the source. So help her, she would fling rocks all dang day if that's what it took. Her gaze landed on the bear she'd injured earlier, but he was handling the graying werebear currently shifting back to his human form.

Satisfied the bear she'd hurt was on her side and the greying bear was being watched, she focused on Ty once again. She leaned down and pressed a kiss to his bloodied nose. "You're injured. Shift so I can take care of my Itan."

A bright ray of hope entered his eyes and she nodded, answering his unasked question. Did he think she'd take the words back after witnessing him fight her dad? Hardly. Bears were bloody creatures. She didn't like it, but it was true. A bone-shaking tremble overtook him, the movements transferring to her, and then she was faced with a bloodied and naked Ty.

The crunch and shift of gravel reminded her that she stood between two men she loved the most. And they'd been trying to kill each other moments before. Great.

"Keen." She raised her voice slightly, and the still half-shifted bear was at her side in an instant.

"Itana?"

"Can you help my father into the house?"

"I don't need no help," her dad grumbled, but she knew he'd take the assistance anyway.

Besides, she was going to help one of the two men and she sure as heck didn't want to be cuddled up to her naked father. Slipping beneath Ty's arm, she turned him and urged him toward the house.

"You shouldn't have done that." His voice was low and strained. The wound had begun the healing process but it was far from over.

"Uh-huh. And have the two men I love more than life kill each other?" She snorted and then coughed when she realized what she'd said.

"You love me." The man sounded so darned smug about it, too.

"I have no idea what you're talking about," she sniffed.

A bellow followed them into the house. "Who is the other man you were fighting and who the heck did I bean with that rock?"

"I have no idea who you're talking about and Isaac." He groaned when she lowered him into one of the kitchen chairs. A grunt came from her father seated nearby. She glanced over to find Gigi poking and prodding him but not rushing around so she figured he couldn't be too hurt. Which meant she could focus on Ty.

"Ty?"

"I'm fine." He sighed. "You love me." His grin was goofy, but his face still bore the evidence of his pain.

"I'll never say it again if you don't tell me what I wanna know and let me patch you up." She snared a wet washrag from the pile Gigi had plopped in the middle of the table.

"Aw, Mia," Ty whined.

"You might as well give in. She's damn stubborn."

Mia dropped the cloth in Ty's lap and straightened to glare at her father. "*I'm* damn stubborn?"

"Language." Her father grunted, and she glared.

"I'll give you some language, you old coot. You damn near gutted Ty!"

"Language."

"I will put you in an old folks home so fast it'll burn your fur off." She ground her teeth and glared at him.

Mia's dad glared back at her. "He got between me and my kill. I called it damn it. Challenged the man. Was gonna win, too, until that male of yours got in the middle. The world would be a better place without that piece of shit."

She growled and flicked her attention between her father and Ty. "Will someone tell me who the frick that was and why the driveway seemed like a good place to do battle?"

Isaac shuffled into the kitchen, rubbing his forehead and wincing as he made his way into the room. He turned to her with a half-smile. "Nice aim. Hurts like a bitch though."

"Language," her dad grumbled once again and Mia sighed.

"Thank you." She kinda felt bad for beaning him, but not really. "Well, is *anyone* gonna answer my question?"

Isaac spoke up first. "Parker's great uncle."

Mia froze, heart no longer beating and the air in her lungs turned to ice. She turned toward Ty, searching for his support, and he granted it without question. Suddenly his arms were around her, his hand urging her to lay her head against his chest.

"And Mia's grandfather. That's why I was doing my best to kill him."
A growl followed her dad's words.

"We had days. You said we had days. I heard you. You said *later.*"
Her body had gone back into motion and then some. Now her heart
raced, and adrenaline flooded her veins. An uncomfortable silence
surrounded her, but she couldn't stop the babbling. The words
poured from her, filling the quiet in the kitchen. "He's ours. He
won't take him. Tell him, Ty. Parker's ours now. We're keeping
him."

"Shh… Your father and I will figure it out. Trust me." Any other
time, and with any other man, she would have laughed at the
absurdity of the order. Instead, with Ty, she immediately calmed. He
said he'd figure it out and he would. "Here, take a sip of this, you're
shaking."

Mia gladly took the juice, the orange liquid fresh and sweet against
her tongue. It slid down her throat easily, and she savored every
drop, including the bits that were a little bitter. Bits? "Ty, I think…
this… is…"

*

Mia slumped into his arms, her body going from tense to dead
weight in half a second. "How much did you give her, Gigi?"

The older woman looked at him with a single eyebrow raised.
"Enough." She waved him away. "Go put her in bed, shower, and
put some clothes on."

Half-ignoring her, he turned to Isaac. "Where are Van and Keen?"

"Van is keeping an eye on Robert, the Cutler Itan, while Keen is on a
teleconference with the Southeast Itan and his second-in-command."

That had him stiffening in his seat. "What?"

His brother placed a hand on his shoulder. "It's fine. We keep
treating him like he's five, but Keen knows more about clan law and

155

the dozen ways Robert has shot it all to hell. I really think you need to make him the clan's keeper when this is done."

"Keeper?" The Grayslake clan hadn't had a keeper of the knowledge in decades. His father had always told him that Grandpa never had one, he hadn't had one, and there was no reason for Ty to have one.

Maybe it was time to stop living beneath his father's edicts.

"We can talk about it."

"Good. Keen is more than capable of presenting evidence and explaining what happened. That'll give you all time to clean up."

"Listen to him, boy." The gruff voice belonged to Mia's father, Thomas.

Ty's bear bristled at being called "boy," but the man was older than him by quite a few years, and he'd taken care of Mia and her mother after what Robert's son had done. Thomas deserved his respect.

"Fine." He stood, not caring about his nudity, only worrying about the drugged woman in his arms.

His wounds stung and pulled, but the pain was nothing compared to taking care of Mia. That started with putting her to bed to sleep off the drugs she'd been slipped and ended with possibly executing the Cutler Itan. The bear was excited by the prospect of getting rid of the man.

Ty turned toward the hallway that would take him to his room. Now that he had Mia back under his roof she'd be in *his* room in *his* bed.

"Isaac," he called over his shoulder. "Tell Keen to come see me when he's done and have Van throw Robert's ass in the basement cell and post a guard. If we find Sarah, they can share." He strode farther down the hallway with each word, steps eating up the ground. "I want all three of you in my room as soon as possible."

156

Foot after foot disappeared in a blur, but it wasn't until he neared a particular door that he slowed. He glanced into the room, noting the messy sheets and scattered belongings.

Ty turned back toward the kitchen and found that Isaac, Gigi, and Thomas stared after him. "Gigi, where's Parker?"

By the stricken expression that overshadowed her face along with the surprise coating Isaac's, he knew the answer.

Damn it.

"Have Keen inform the Southeast Itan that we're moving on Griss and Sarah."

"Wait. Sarah?" Thomas raised his eyebrows. "Tall, brunette, stacked?" At Ty's nod, the old man grunted. "Huh. If it's who I think it is, I thought she died when Griss's parents were killed. It was never talked about publicly, she was a bastard, but gossip is she's Griss's half-sister."

"How did we not know about this?"

Thomas shrugged. "I don't live in Cutler, but I still have a few friends there. It's not written anywhere. Just one of those things everyone knows."

Well, fuck. That explained a hell of a lot. "No, Sarah is alive and well and we think she had Griss kill her mate. I also think she was involved in Parker's beating, but I have no doubt she worked with the man to steal Parker." He scented the woman all over the cub's room, the aroma reaching out to him in the hallway. Ty looked to Isaac. "They won't make it to sunset, Isaac. You make sure the Southeast Itan knows that."

"Ty, you can't take out another Itan's heir. Legally…"

"Legally Parker is the heir, not Griss, and we don't know who the boy belongs to. I never saw a will. All we do know is that he turned up in Mia's pantry. The cub belongs to Mia, and Mia belongs to me.

No one *ever* takes anything that's mine." Ty's bear rushed forward in agreement. Even though the cub wasn't of their blood, the animal had decided to keep the child as his own. His muscles bunched and grew, thickening and stretching. Fur sprouted, and he felt his nails sharpen and lengthen. "If one hair on his head is harmed, they're dead. If they don't turn him over without a fight, they're dead. No matter what, those two aren't seeing tomorrow. You tell the Southeast Itan that, Isaac."

chapter **thirteen**

Mia woke slowly, head feeling as if it were filled with cotton and mouth dry as the desert. She rolled her head to the side and forced her eyes open. Dang, she was tired. Her body felt heavy, weighted down by hundreds of pounds of mush. Her arms and legs refused to respond, remaining still no matter how much she fought her unmoving form.

She looked around the space, noting the foreign, manly décor, and realized she wasn't in her room. No, she would bet her last dollar she was in Ty's. A clock with glowing red numbers displaying the time caught her attention and she frowned.

Eight o'clock? When they'd been hauling butt back to the den, it'd been just past one. What the heck happened to the time?

Groaning, she jerked and forced her body to roll over, putting her on her side. Another lurch and she'd managed to flop onto her stomach. Well, at least she was a foot closer to the edge of the bed. That last foot—man—that one took a lot of wiggling, grunting and moaning, but finally she was right on the rim.

Panting, she fought against the mud holding her captive, and demanded her body respond to her commands. Before long, she was vertical, sitting upright and only slightly swaying.

She looked to the clock once more. Dang, ten minutes had passed.

With a deep grunt, she shoved herself to her feet, and gripped the bedside table when her balance threatened to falter. She rocked, a wave of dizziness overtaking her, but something inside her nudged her to keep going. She didn't have time to stop. She definitely didn't have time to whine about seeing double and feeling like she'd puke at any moment.

Mia shuffled, forcing one foot in front of the other. It took her forever, but she finally managed to traverse the room. She was thankful Ty wasn't a man who had a ton of belongings.

By the time she reached the room's door, she was panting and out of breath. The darkened hallway stretched before her, and she groaned, imagining the way she'd feel once she got to the kitchen.

The kitchen.

Just thinking of that one room had memories creeping forth.

Thoughts of her father fighting her grandfather... Ty jumping between the two bears... Oh, God, the massive wound that went from her Itan's shoulder to hip.

So, why the heck was she half asleep and feeling like an elephant stomped all over her when she needed to be at his side?

With every flex of muscle and inch she scooted forward, more of her strength returned. The unsteady stumbles turned into a wavering gate, but she managed to stay vertical by using the wall for support. She eased along the hallway, pausing now and again. She came to an open door and slowed—if that were possible—and peeked inside.

Ah, Parker's room. That meant she was halfway to her destination. She observed his room in one sweep, noticing the rumpled bed sheets and strewn toys. She'd have to teach the cub to clean up after himself.

She stumbled past the boy's room, but a small spot of deep burgundy caught her eye. The dark color contrasted against the lighter wood flooring, and it was definitely a stain she'd never seen before.

Mia pushed away from the wall holding her up and lurched deeper into the room, tripping over discarded toys and little boy shoes. Uncaring of the scrapes and cuts she'd suffered earlier in the day, she dropped to her knees and reached out for the near-black spot. No, *spots*.

Sticky. They were sticky… She brought her stained fingers to her nose. The color should have told her, the deep hue cluing her in on what she was seeing, but the scent left no doubt. Blood. In Parker's room. And there was no Parker to be seen.

A wailing scream surrounded her, consumed her, the sound filling her mind until she could think of nothing but the blood coating her fingertip and the knowledge Parker was gone.

Then rough hands were there, large and callused and oh, so familiar. The low voice that accompanied the touch soothed her, gentled her as he had so often over the years.

"Daddy. Parker's missing isn't he? It's his blood, isn't it? Why didn't anyone wake me? Why—"

He pulled her close and forced her head to his shoulder. "Hush now. Getting upset won't fix things."

She swallowed past the growing lump in her throat. "What happened? I remember sitting on Ty's lap in the kitchen and then nothing."

"Gigi drugged you."

"What—"

"She had a good reason. Your Itan doesn't think anything bad about her actions, so you're not allowed to get angry." He harrumphed, and she knew that tone, knew he believed every word he'd said and that last bit had been an order.

Mia pushed away from her father, scooted back until she could stare the man in the eye. "What's going on? If she had a good reason, what is it?" Her father squirmed. "Daddy?"

"Your grandfather—"

"I had one grandfather and he's buried in Grayslake's cemetery." She snapped off the words. The man who'd shown up here sure as hell wasn't her grandfather.

"Language," he grunted. Darn him. He always knew when she cursed, even in her head. "The *Cutler Itan* is in the basement cell while Ty, Van, Isaac, and a few others search for Griss and Sarah."

"They have my Parker." She whispered the words, but her dad heard and nodded. "I want them. I want my cub and then I want those two gone, Daddy."

He grunted. "Always said you were a bloodthirsty little thing." He nudged her aside. "Come on then, let's go see what the old man has to say."

Mia stumbled to her feet, leaning heavily on her father when she finally stood. "You think he has something to do with this?"

He led her toward the door and into the hallway. "I'd be surprised if he didn't."

And that just pissed her off. No, it made her angry. Fucking. Angry.

"Language."

"I didn't even say that out loud! Damn it, Dad."

"Language."

162

Mia huffed. "One of these days, I'm going to yell every bad word I know and then hide behind Ty."

He patted her hand, leading her farther down the hallway, and the light of the kitchen slowly crept over them. "You do that, little cub, you do that. Then you can patch your man up when I'm done with him."

"Daddy, you know it's not fair. He's not going to hurt you."

"That's what makes it fun."

Shaking her head, Mia followed her dad, shuffling along until they entered the kitchen. Keen sat at the counter atop a barstool and immediately popped to his feet when she entered.

"Itana! Should you be awake yet?" Then the man at least had the grace to wince. "I mean, uh, I…"

She shook her head and waved him away. "I'm not happy about being drugged but it wasn't like you were the one who did it."

"Nope, that was me and I'd do it again, missy." Gigi popped right into the conversation. Her voice held just enough conviction that Mia knew she was bluffing her way through what was coming. Normally, doing anything against the Itana meant expulsion at best and death at worst.

Taking a deep breath, she turned toward the older woman. Yes, thinking back on the panic she'd felt at hearing the Cutler Itan had arrived was overwhelming. The only choice available at that point was physically knocking her out or drugging her. She'd been too scared to think clearly.

"Good." She nodded to make sure the woman knew she was serious.

Gigi narrowed her eyes. "That's what I thought." She tossed the rag she held onto the dark granite counter top. "Now, sit down and have something to eat. The boys," Mia assumed she meant Ty, Van and

Isaac, "will be calling in again soon. Griss and Sarah have been wily, but they're both idiots. They'll mess up before long."

Her stomach told her to slide onto a stool beside Keen and take Gigi up on her offer. But her heart screamed at her to go down and beat the hell out of the Cutler Itan. For some reason, this whole catastrophe began and ended with that aged bear.

With a shake of her head, she nudged her father toward the door that led to the basement and the man who'd raised her piece of crap sperm donor.

Mia trudged down the steps, gripping the banister and praying she stayed upright. Robert's weak roars and snarls greeted her as she entered the dimly lit basement. The air in the room was stale, the heavy scent of the Itan's blood soaking the air and the coppery tang invaded her senses.

A guard met her at the base of the steps, his face a study of grim lines and banked anger as he moved to block her. "Itana."

She didn't remember his name, but then again, she hadn't been introduced to the entire clan, either. "I'd like to see Robert."

The guard huffed. "Itana, the Itan was clear—"

"He's not here. If you won't let me see the Cutler Itan, you can surely let me see…" she swallowed against the bile rising into her throat, "my grandfather."

The words tasted vile on her tongue, but they'd been necessary. She was the clan's Itana, yet not. Once she and Ty solidified their bond, it'd be different. For now, it was a matter of finesse.

"Itana, I'm sorry—"

A deep, rolling snarl cut off the guard's words. The sound vibrated through her, pulsing and pounding along her veins and then into the poor male that stood before her.

Dang, she loved her father.

"Move." A single word from her dad combined with those threatening noises had the guard jumping aside in an instant. The guard's Adam's apple bobbed along his neck when he swallowed hard, and Mia fought against the smug smile that wanted to jump to her lips.

She strode past the male and deeper into the large basement, heading toward the single light that illuminated a cell against the far wall. Well, the entire wall *was* a cell. At least thirty feet in length and fifteen feet deep, it held a single, graying, and pissed off bear. It would have been more frightening had he not been covered in blood, limping, and missing patches of fur.

Her bare feet slapped against the naked, concrete floor, drawing the animal's attention. Upon her approach, he pulled back his lips, baring yellowed teeth. One fang was broken in half, the bright red root showing against the pale nub. She wondered who ended up with the missing piece embed in their flesh. Ty or her father? Either option merely increased her anger, her rage, at the male coming into her territory and interfering with her clan.

She rounded the lone chair in front of the cell and easily lowered herself onto the seat. The last remnants of the drug she'd been given drifted away as adrenaline took its place. Her heart thumped and raced. She'd get answers, damn it. She wanted to know why and who and where and…

"Shift." The bear bared his broken fang, and she internally rolled her eyes. Right. Very scary. Mia leaned forward and glared at the bear. "Shift, you no good, piece of shit."

She didn't miss her father's murmured "language," and she would have apologized had the shuddering animal before her not kept her attention.

The familiar crack and snap of bones drifted to her, and she focused on Robert. Not her grandfather… *Robert*. Fur receded to reveal pale,

165

wrinkled skin. Age spots covered every inch and his veins were easily seen beneath the near translucent surface. Before long, his face was completely transformed, the bear's snout now replaced by a human's visage.

Her first thought was that he looked old. Not just old, but ancient. The bags beneath his eyes had bags of their own and his face drooped, the right side pulling down so much he wore a half-frown. When he glared at her, his right eye didn't follow the movement, and she realized that somewhere along the way, Robert had endured a stroke.

Good.

He swayed on his feet, finally stumbling toward the bed and collapsing onto the thin, padded surface. He grabbed the folded blanket and wrapped it around himself, covering his aged and withering body with the thick covering.

"What d'ya want?" His words were thin and reedy, voice cracking at the end of his sentence.

She wanted a lot of things, really. She wanted a mother who loved her and hadn't taken her own life. She wanted to bring her biological father back from the dead just so she could stomp on him. But most of all...

"Parker."

He pinched his lips together but didn't say a word.

"I want Parker, Robert."

"I'm the Cutler Itan, you stupid whor—"

"And I'm Grayslake's Itana and you're in a damned cage." Her father didn't bother chiding her. Good. Because she was just getting started. "I know *you* know where Parker is. You show up, and he goes missing? Too convenient. I want him back. He's mine."

Every cell in her body screamed in agreement. That little cub belonged to her and her alone. She might share him with Ty... someday.

"He isn't anything to you. You're just a piece of trash."

"I'm your granddaughter, you stupid ass." Mia pushed to her feet and fisted her hands at her sides. "And Parker is my cousin."

"You're nothing but a bastard whelp your mother tried to shove off on our family." Robert harrumphed, and her father's growl filled the space. "Somehow the slut managed to get that one to take you." The caged male waved at her dad, and she was waiting for her father to rip the bars apart and gut the Itan. She was actually surprised when he didn't. "Griss is that boy's uncle."

"Who tried to kill him," the words burst from her lips with a whip of rage.

"No," the old man shook his head. "He wouldn't. I sent him here to bring me the boy. Got to raise him right. Can't let him die like my pussy nephew."

Mia took a step toward the cage, glaring at him, hoping he suffered under the weight of her anger. "What you did was send a monster to pick up a boy that stood between him and being Itan." She kept walking until she clutched the metal bars. "And your nephew didn't die. He was murdered right along with his wife. You need to think long and hard about who would do such a thing."

She stared at the tired, decrepit man and waited for the truth to dawn.

"No."

"Yes," she snapped.

Mia tightened her hold, fighting back the emotions threatening to swamp her. She ached to scream for the guard and demand his gun, ached to kill the man before her. He was the reason her mother was

167

no longer at her side. Him. The Itan's son wasn't around any longer, but her grandfather was.

Taking a deep breath, she continued. "Yes. Parker's parents are dead, and it wasn't an accident. I found Parker hiding in my home in bear form. After Ty arrested Griss, Parker shifted. The boy was covered—*covered*—in bruises. If he hadn't been a werebear, he would have been dead." She kept her gaze intent on him, watching for any evidence of caring… and found none. "Now one of my people—" God she felt the truth of those words down to her bones. The Grayslake bears *were* her people. "One of my people is dead. Griss, and now Sarah, have Parker."

"Sarah?" Her grandfather grunted. "Always liked that girl. Too bad women can't lead. She would have been one tough bitch. Aw well, I'll have to toughen up the boy."

Shock pummeled her, and she turned toward her father. "He's delusional. Bat-shit crazy." Surprisingly that didn't earn a "language" from her dad. She looked to Robert. "You actually think you'll get Parker back? Griss and Sarah will kill him if we don't find him soon."

He shrugged. "Then I'll take Griss."

"I don't…" Mia shook her head. "You don't give a damn about anyone, do you?"

"I care about my clan." Robert growled, and she couldn't find it in herself to fear him. Not when she looked hard and saw the way age had ravaged his body.

Fine. If that was how she could get to him, then that's the angle she'd take. "If you care about your clan, who will lead them after Ty guts you for simply *existing*, you need to know a couple of things. Griss and Sarah *will* kill Parker if Ty doesn't get to them in time. And no matter what, Griss won't see morning. A Holmes will no longer lead in Cutler. So, is there anything you have to say about where we can find your nephew? Or are you happy with your clan going to the strongest bear in your territory?"

Cold, dead eyes met her gaze, but she didn't flinch or look away. Right then, right there, Mia wasn't a half-breed, bastard mongrel. She was the fucking Itana of the God damned Grayslake clan.

"Language."

chapter **fourteen**

Ty glared at the map spread across the hood of Van's cruiser. Hour after hour had passed and still there was no hint about where to find Griss and Sarah. The trace on Sarah's car and phone led to nothing, both being ditched at opposite ends of town. The clan interviewed the businesses along the main street and even ventured to some of the outlying homes, but no one had seen a thing.

It was as if the three of them had disappeared, and that was unacceptable.

"Van!"

His brother materialized at his side, a grim yet determined expression on his face. "Itan?"

"Have we checked near the border of our territory? By Redby?" It was a long shot. Hell, Ty knew better than to screw with the wolf pack, but he couldn't return to Mia without Parker.

Van raised an eyebrow. "You think he'd be dumb enough to fuck with the wolves? Two against a pack are shitty odds."

"Van, I want Parker. Make a call."

His brother pressed his lips together, obviously not liking his order, but nodded and moved away. Van yanked his phone out of his pocket and dialed, and Ty turned his attention back to the map. He noted the markings, the areas they'd searched and others they had yet to explore. Fuck, their territory was big, and Griss and Sarah could be anywhere.

The ringing of his cell drew his attention, and he answered the call without glancing at the caller I.D. "Abrams."

"Ty?"

He swallowed back a groan. He should have looked first. "Mia. I'm sorry about—"

"It doesn't matter. I spoke with Robert."

Shit. "Mia, you shouldn't have gone down there. The guard had orders to—"

"Keep the Itana from visiting her dear, dear grandfather."

He imagined her quirking a brow, her expression daring him to explain that yes, the guard *had* been ordered to keep her the hell out of the basement.

"Mia…" He didn't know what else there was to say.

"Robert understands things now and knows if you don't get to Parker before," she sobbed, and he ached to pull her into his arms. "If you don't get to Parker, he won't have anyone to inherit his title. He thinks you should look to your enemies. Griss will go to whoever will help him work against you. Robert believes Griss has convinced another group to hide him for a while and then make his getaway." She cleared her throat. "That's what Robert would do in this situation."

"Fuck." The word burst from his lips. "All right." He took a deep calming breath. "Just fuck. I'm going to make a few calls, including

172

one to Keen with orders to keep your ass in the house and away from the basement."

"Ty…"

"No, Mia. I need you to stay away from him. He's evil and vile and—"

"He can't hurt me. I get it. He's not my family, Ty. You are; my father is. That man is nothing to me." Conviction filled her words.

"Okay, but he's still dangerous. Promise me you'll stay away from him and stick to Keen like glue. I'm sending a few more guards your way and—"

"No. I want them all fighting to get Parker back. Period. I'll be fine."

"Mia…" He huffed and looked around the gathered bears. If what she said was true, if they were going to have to go against his enemies, then he really did need every male he had. "Fine. But what Keen says goes. Do you hear me? Nothing can happen to you."

"I'll be fine. I promise." He heard the wavering of her voice and knew if he were there, he'd see tears in her eyes. "I need to be in perfect condition so my Itan can claim me after he brings our cub home."

Ty shouldn't be joyous at her words, not with his world crashing around him, but he couldn't help the emotions rising in him. "Good. I'll call you as soon as I know something."

"Okay."

"Mia, I…" He swallowed hard. He shouldn't be saying the words over the phone in the middle of a crisis.

"Me too, Ty. Me too," Mia whispered.

A low click told him she'd cut the call, and he gripped his phone. His beast roared with joy, interpreting the words as a return of his feelings. They'd joked before, but this agreement had been intentional and filled with pure emotion. Except he didn't have time to be too happy. Not when so much could still go wrong in the coming hours.

Shoving his phone in his pocket, he sought out his enforcer. "Van!" His brother turned toward him, eyebrows raised. "Ask the wolves how they feel about taking on the hyenas."

A half hour later it seemed the wolves were more than happy to kick some hyena ass. Four black SUVs with limo tinted windows rolled to a stop beside Ty's clan, five males alighting from each, giving him twenty wolves in all.

The largest, meanest looking wolf approached, his steps predatory and sure. There was no doubt Ty was facing the pack's Alpha. His bear ceased its pacing inside his mind and turned its attention from grumbling about Parker to snarling about the Alpha's presence. Not much he could do about it now, the man had come to help. In a way. Ty didn't kid himself. The Alpha hated the devious hyenas just as much as he did though he sensed the wolf Alpha's hatred went much deeper than Ty's.

"Itan," the man's voice was smooth, and he tilted his head ever so slightly. Not in submission, but at least with respect.

"Alpha," Ty repeated the man's gesture. "The Grayslake clan thanks you for your assistance." It grated on him to ask, but hyenas bred like rabbits and Ty wouldn't risk his males. There was always the chance the bastards would swarm. Bears were tough, but no one could survive a half dozen of those fucks attacking each of them.

"Your enforcer indicated your son has been taken."

The words stabbed him in the heart. Yes, Parker was his son. "Yes. He's the son of my heart. He won't be the next Itan." He glared at the Alpha. "So if you think this will create a blood bond..."

174

The man's smile was wicked, his inner-wolf peeking through his eyes. "Any bond will do, Itan. My father began the war between us, and I'd like to end it."

Ty thought their animal nature had been the true catalyst. Like hyenas, wolves birthed litters and their packs tended to reproduce at twice the rate of bears. If the pack wanted to, they could amass and run the bears out. Of course, they'd be down three-quarters of their members when all was said and done since Ty would be damned if he disappeared without a fight.

Ty grunted at the man's words. He wasn't sure what to make of the male just yet. "Let's get Parker back and then we can share a meal." He thrust out his hand. "Ty Abrams. You spoke with my brother Van. I've got another brother, Isaac, here, as well. He's our healer and will deal with the wounded when we're done."

The Alpha grunted. "Reid Bennett. Van wasn't clear on why you believe the hyenas have your pup."

"Cub." Another grunt from the Alpha. "And it's the boy's biological uncle who has him. He's a coward, and second in line to take over as Cutler Itan. He wants Parker out of the way. I thought maybe he'd head to your pack."

Reid released a low growl and the wolves scattered throughout the area froze. As one, their gazes centered on them. Ty pretended not to hear the warning. "Then I realized you'd probably kill him for wandering into your territory without permission." The growl cut off, and that grunt returned. "The current Cutler Itan is locked in a cell in my basement—"

"You locked up one of your own?"

Ty nodded. "And he'll probably be dead by morning by my hand or the Southeast Itan's when he arrives." Not that the notion worried him much. "He passed along the idea that he'd hide with my greatest enemy." Ty smirked. "You're dangerous, but those pieces of shit

175

can't care about anyone but themselves. They're bottom feeders. I
know they'd let Parker and his uncle onto their land."

"What if you're wrong?" Yellow eyes met his and Ty shrugged.

"You go home with a few cuts and bruises and there are a few less
hyenas hanging around. We'll keep searching." Pain at Parker's loss,
rage at Griss and Sarah for taking the boy, ate at him. "I'm not
returning to my Itana without my cub."

Reid grunted and reached out, thumping his hand onto Ty's shoulder
and giving it a squeeze. Ty's bears froze and the tension surrounding
them intensified, growing and thickening with every passing second.
Ty's bear snarled at the touch, urging him to rip out the Alpha's
throat while they had the chance.

"We'll find your pup." Another squeeze.

The bear wasn't satisfied. It wanted to eliminate the threat standing
before them, and Ty shoved the animal back. They needed peace
with the wolves, at least long enough to find Parker. It could go back
to hating the wolves once he had the boy in his arms.

Ty nodded. "Van!" His brother appeared in an instant, halting when
a couple of feet separated them. "Speak with Reid's enforcer…" He
raised his eyebrows in question.

"Beta. Morgan."

"With Morgan, make sure we're all on the same page. I want to be
out of here in fifteen minutes."

"Yes, Itan." Van immediately strode away and toward a large wolf.

"What's the plan?" Reid's words drew his attention back to the male
before him.

"We go after their Alpha."

Another grunt.

* * *

The stench of urine and grime grew as they rolled through the decrepit town. It didn't matter that the A/C was set to recycle the interior air, the stink managed to creep into the SUV. Ty parted his lips to breathe through his mouth, and now he tasted the rank aromas of the hyenas. They truly were like dogs, pissing on everything to mark their territory.

They rolled to a stop before a seedy, run down home. The fence was half-fallen, pieces of board littering the scraggly, brown grass. Shutters clung to the walls of the house by a handful of screws, and the wind battered the panels, sending them banging against the brick.

Ty gazed at their surroundings, noting the absence of people, human or hyena, along the street. Not a soul strode down the sidewalk. No children playing in yards.

Quiet.

"Itan, I don't like this." Van's tone held more than a hint of worry.

Yeah, he didn't like it either.

"Hate to admit it, but I agree with the bear." Morgan's voice immediately followed Van's and a new tension filled is brother.

"The men are in position surrounding the house." Reid cut in, slicing the rigid hostility in two. "We're going in. But if you're too much of a pussy, Morgan, you can keep your ass here."

With Reid's pronouncement, Ty climbed from the SUV, not bothering to close the door quietly. The hyenas knew they were there. They were destructive assholes, not stupid.

Ty and Reid, flanked by Van and Morgan, approached the seedy, run down home. The wind shifted, blowing from the south instead of north, and familiar scents drifted to him. Griss. Sarah. Parker.

Increasing his pace, Ty went from a determined walk to a flat out run toward the door. His booted feet pounded on the pavement, and he distantly recognized the other men trailing in his wake. Fur sprouted from his pores, coating his arms, chest and neck before sliding higher to his face. His jaw cracked and the bones around his mouth snapped, reshaping into his bear's muzzle. His snarls were joined by the rip of cloth as his chest expanded, muscles enlarging with his impending shift. Seams burst and fabric tore into small pieces with every inhale. It'd been a stretched assumption that the hyenas aided Griss and Sarah, but now it was a certainty.

Pausing for the briefest of seconds, Ty kicked in the flimsy wooden door and strode into the dim interior. Aided by his bear's senses, he swept the room with his gaze. He noted the occupants that rushed to their feet, bodies morphing into their beasts before his eyes. But it was the single man in the back of the room that drew his attention.

The male was bigger than the other hyenas and a shroud of menace clung to him like a cape. He easily neared six feet in height and his chest was broad and heavily muscled, but he had nothing on Ty. Nothing.

Ty strode toward him, intent on his target. This was the Alpha, the leader of the hyenas, and the man he needed to tear apart with his paws. Splatters of dried blood coated the other man's clothing, droplets clinging to the fabric and dyeing them a morbid burgundy. Even more decorated his exposed arms. Ty had no doubt it wasn't the Alpha's. The man was a sadistic fuck and probably wore the blood of one of his pack members, or worse, Parker.

"Van, keep these bastards back," he called over his shoulder.

He didn't wait for a response. He knew his brother, his enforcer, would do as ordered. He also had no doubt that Reid and Morgan would stick to the plan. The Alpha was his and he didn't give a fuck about what happened to everyone else.

He weaved around one shifting body and then another, discarding the idea that the writhing hyenas were a threat. Whines and groans

178

came from the shifting hyenas. Weaklings. Shifting didn't hurt unless the human was disconnected from his animal and refused to respect the beast. They thrashed on the floor, their clothes sagging as their animals took shape.

Pathetic.

So intent on the hyena Alpha, Ty didn't notice the only other threat in the room until it was too late. A clawed hand swiped across his abdomen. The owner of said hand quickly followed and stepped into his path. Fuck, the man was huge. Bigger than the alpha by six inches and fifty pounds. But he was still a hyena, a fucking *dog*, and alone he was no match for a grizzly.

Pain radiated from the wound, the ache slithering through him and burning him from inside out. Fuck, it hurt a hell of a lot more than it should. He'd endured a shit-ton of pain over the years, but this ate at him.

He glanced at the Alpha, noting the smirk the man wore and the cocky attitude that surrounded him. All that stood between Ty and the hyena leader was the massive stack of dumbass in front of him.

The battle raged behind him and Van's roar was quickly joined by Reid and Morgan's howl. The call had been sent and was immediately returned by the males outside. Their men would join the battle, more blood would flow and seep into the ground and Ty was ready to add this hyena's to the river of red.

The man snarled and brought his claw-tipped hand back, shifting his weight as he prepared to strike once again. Hell no. Pain in his side or not, he wasn't about to fall to this piece of crap. As that deadly hand descended, Ty ducked and countered with a swipe of his own, digging his nails into the hyena's flesh. He tore at the skin, sinking his claws into the male's hip and then dragging them across his body. Deep furrows were left in his wake, the marks stretching from hip to ribcage.

An anguished snarl followed the attack and then the male was on him again, swinging at Ty with no rhyme or reason. He wasn't a fighter, wasn't trained to protect his pack and Alpha. He was a bully who'd obviously gotten by on his size alone.

Ty had grown up with three brothers and none of them had a problem with bloodying the other when their bears got the best of them.

The only difference was the burning wound that ate at him and enraged his bear. It wasn't normal, wasn't the type of pain he was accustomed to. Blood still flowed freely with no hint at when the wound would begin healing.

He ducked the male's next strike, dipping low to avoid his claws and popping back up on his other side. Without hesitation, he returned the attack. He drew his claws across the man's body, forming a bloody, macabre "x" that allowed even more blood to escape. His opponent's incensed bellow overrode the sounds of the fight that surrounded them, but Ty only had eyes for the man with murder in his gaze.

With rage overriding sense, the male sloppily attacked. Claw-tipped hands struck out at him. The movements were random, unplanned and fueled by fury.

Ty returned each one, connecting when the male didn't and wincing when he did. His arms and chest were covered in scratches and scrapes. Each one burned and sent fire through his veins. Fuck, something was wrong.

His opponent circled right and Ty mirrored him, unwilling to allow the man behind him. Each shift of muscle sent a renewed ache through him, the agony pulsing and throbbing in time with his heartbeat. But he fought through it, fought through the aches and pain. He remained intent on putting the male down so he could get on to more important things.

Like killing the hyena Alpha.

Movement drew his attention and he watched his brother Isaac take on a partially shifted hyena. They grappled and swung at one another, colliding and then shoving apart only to attack once again. Blood decorated Isaac's shirt, turning the white fabric to a deep red. Every drop flowed from a deep gash that dissected his brother's face and Ty decided that particular hyena would die slowly… Except his brother chose that moment to snap the male's neck and stole his fun.

Damn it.

Nails digging into his shoulder wrenched Ty's attention back to his own battle. The claws dug deep into flesh and muscle until they collided with bone. Another explosion of agony rocked him and he decided he'd had enough.

Ty threw off the hold, and plowed his deadly nails into the male's shoulders. He let his bear out to play, allowed the beast to transform his mouth into a snout and release his fangs out in full force. Saliva pooled in his animalistic maw, the bear inside him excited at the prospect of drinking the other man's blood.

The moment his opponent was close enough, Ty hit. He opened his jaws wide and struck, sinking his fangs through soft flesh. The coppery liquid flowed over his tongue, danced across his taste buds, and sated the bear's hunger. The massive body against him struggled. Claws scratched and dug into him, but Ty wouldn't be denied his victory. He tightened his jaws until his teeth scraped against each other, and then he jerked his head, bringing the male's throat along with him.

The bear wanted to savor the feel of his opponent's flesh sliding down his throat while the man was disgusted with the idea. Instead of enjoying his meal, Ty spat the lump of muscle and skin on the ground so that it lay beside his opponent. The man wrapped his hands around his throat, but Ty knew it was hopeless. The guy would be dead in moments.

It was then he noted the silence, the quiet that invaded the space. He let his gaze wander over the room. He took in the cowering males, the gore that coated the walls… The blood that crept out of the bodies of the males he'd brought with him.

A new rage filled him, an anger that overrode the pain of his wounds and pushed his bear forward even more.

And it had one source.

Ty spun toward the hyena Alpha. A little of that smarmy smile had fallen from his expression, but the belligerence and arrogance remained.

"Where is he?" The words were garbled by the beast's snout, but he got them out nonetheless.

"Who?"

"You have something that belongs to me. And I want it back. Where is he?"

"Do I?"

The bear roared inside him, it demanded that he slice hunks of flesh from the hyena Alpha. Slowly.

Ty strode toward the male, not caring about anything or anyone but the piece of shit before him. A wave of Sarah's scent washed over him with just the slightest hint of Parker's added. "You have mine."

He should have stopped five feet away—or even four—but he strode right up to the hyena Alpha and went for the male's neck. Hand outstretched, he realized his mistake the moment he was within grabbing distance. The Alpha shifted his weight and ducked then dug a clawed hand into the steadily bleeding wound on his abdomen.

The pain… No, not pain. Pure, unadulterated agony assaulted him. It beat at his insides, tearing into him and wrenching muscle from bone. The bear within him wailed at the hurt that assaulted them.

182

The male made a fist, burrowing deeper into Ty's flesh. "Hurts, doesn't it? All that poison running through your blood."

Fuck, he should have realized… Poisoned claws. Fucking pussy-assed hyena pieces of shit.

Ty brought his hand to the male's throat and sunk his nails into his flesh. "Where the fuck is he?"

"Kill me and you'll never know." The Alpha squeezed harder.

Ty countered the other man's tightening. "Or I can just fucking kill you. They have my fucking son. Where are they?" He shook the Alpha, smiling through the pain when a crack of bone followed the move.

"Release me." The words were garbled and accompanied by a dribble of blood escaping the Alpha's mouth.

Ty bared his fangs. The bear was quickly growing accustomed to the throbbing hurt that attacked them. "Give them to me and I might let you live."

Claw-tipped fingers scraped his forearm, but the new physical pain was nothing compared to the loss of Parker. He shook the hyena Alpha again.

"Where are they?" Ty squeezed harder, and his animal rejoiced in the Alpha's whine. The male would be dead soon, he'd make sure of it. Ty may bleed to death, but the Alpha would be gone.

In one swift movement, the Alpha released Ty and shoved him. The move surprised Ty and his grip involuntarily eased enough for the Alpha to break free. Ty stumbled back until he was no longer within striking distance. Blood coated him from head to toe, each and every scratch reminding Ty that his wounds bled liberally and were numerous.

He didn't care. He couldn't care. Not when he had a son to find and an Itana to claim. The male before him stood between Ty and happiness and he'd be damned if a fucking hyena was going to end him.

Ty strode forward and the Alpha did the same until they rushed one another, arms locking, claws piercing skin and digging into the other's body. He lived and breathed the coppery fluid now. Nothing existed beyond bone, flesh and blood. His world centered on destroying the male before him and nothing else mattered. Nothing.

He snapped his jaws, reaching for his opponent's vulnerable throat, but was merely met with the other man's teeth. More of the shift rushed through him. Legs bulging and pressing against his jeans. His feet stretched in his boots, the space within them lessening with every heartbeat.

"*Itan!*" Isaac called to him, but the bear wanted this male's blood covering his claws and sliding over his tongue. He'd been injured by the now dead hyena, but he still had more than enough rage to fuel him. The hyena Alpha would die. Quickly or slowly, he would be dead. Soon. "I have Sarah, Itan!"

The single name broke through the haze of bloodlust that had captured him. He paused in his attack, but didn't let his guard down, keeping his muscles tense while he held the Alpha. "Isaac?"

The heavy thump of booted feet crunching bodies and bone announced someone's approach and the scent of the forest reached him. A wolf. *Reid.*

"I've got this one, Itan."

"Don't—"

"I won't kill him. At least, not yet. He and I have unfinished business, also."

Ty let some of the tension flow from him and eased back, shoving the injured hyena away. "His claws are—"

"Poisoned. Fuckers can't win a fight without it."

184

Ty spared a glance at the wolf Alpha and noted the steadily flowing wounds that decorated his body. His animal's healing should have sealed the wounds by now, but hadn't. He took a look around the room, noted the broken bodies that littered the ground and the pieces that splattered and clung to the walls.

"They died too quickly." His gaze landed on one of his own bears with his lifeless eyes staring directly at him. "Way too quickly."

A low whimper drew his attention, the sound soft and distinctly feminine.

He met his brother's gaze and Isaac threw a beaten body toward him. The woman's scent identified her, but visually, the person looked nothing like the female he remembered. Blood coated every inch of her skin, her clothes clung to her in tatters and more than one cut decorated her flesh. She was a broken, battered woman.

And his bear didn't give a fuck; not when pain and rage pumped through his blood. She'd more than likely been involved in the death of Parker's parents and had probably participated in the initial attempt at killing the cub. She had definitely paid to have her husband murdered, and she'd succeeded in kidnapping Parker.

No, he didn't have an ounce of pity for Sarah.

Only her whimpers and his heavy panting broke the silence, as if everyone held their breath in anticipation of his next actions.

They'd all seen so much death and they may see one more.

Ty crouched beside the whimpering female. He buried his fingers in her blood-matted hair, fisted the strands, and yanked her head back until she was forced to look at him. Her lip was split, both of them swollen, and her left eye wasn't much better. The right was able to focus, and it was zeroed in on him.

"Where's Parker?"

"I'm sorry, Itan." She spoke with a raspy breath, her lungs rattling with her exhalation.

"Where is he?"

"I'm sorry…"

Ty yanked on her hair and eased closer to her, baring his impressive fangs. He had no doubt about what she saw. Blood filled his every breath and the liquid coated his furred muzzle. It clung to his lips and painted his teeth and he wouldn't hesitate to add hers to the mix. "Where. Is. He?"

More of Sarah's scent invaded him, a combination of blood and cum wrapping around him. She hadn't just been beaten but raped, as well. Where had Griss been through all of this? Were they treating the male the same? Inwardly, he hoped so. But that left him with the question of Parker's location, and whether they were…

The hyena Alpha's snarl followed by the smack of skin against skin reached him. Good, let the wolf get in a few strikes.

Ty looked over his shoulder at the hyena Alpha. The male was bent over, one hand clutching his throat while the other held his stomach. "Tell me."

"Did you really think I'd let them stay permanently? That old man needed you distracted, and this lovely was payment." The hyena Alpha rasped out the words.

Fucking Robert. He'd kill him the moment he found Parker. More pieces fell into place. The bastard was old and would probably die soon. He would want someone as strong and twisted as him to take over Cutler. Apparently he'd found it in Griss. Except Parker's parents and then Parker himself stood in the way.

A trembling hand gripped his steadily bleeding forearm and he looked to Sarah. Tears filled her eyes and a tiny piece of him ached for the pain she'd suffered. But then he remembered Parker, Mia,

186

and one of his bears lying dead ten feet away. That emotion vanished.

"Have you checked in at home lately, Itan?" The hyena's words grated over his skin.

The blood in Ty's veins stilled and froze, his heart ceasing to beat for one second and then two. The truth was etched into Sarah's features. Griss had gone to his home.

"Will I find Parker there, Sarah?"

She gulped and nodded. "Forgive me."

Ty let her head thump to the ground and shifted his weight, muscles bunching as he prepared to rise and face the hyena Alpha. He'd kill the male and then tear Griss apart.

"No. Please, Itan. *Mercy.*"

The true plea was in her eyes. She didn't want forgiveness—wasn't begging for leniency—she begged for death.

Making a choice he hated, Ty let his claws lengthen fully, sharpening and growing until his hands were beyond deadly. Despite his need for vengeance and his dreams of killing Sarah slowly, the reality of his position hit home. By her actions she was a traitor to the clan and yet she was still a woman. A woman he'd sworn to protect and care for as her Itan.

"Please."

He tilted her head back, exposing the blood-caked line of her neck. "May your soul be welcomed with loving arms."

It was the standard prayer, one recited by rote even if he didn't believe her soul would be embraced. With one, lightning fast strike, he slit her throat, pushing deep with his claw and ensuring her death came quickly.

He rose to his full height then, watching her life fade until her heart no longer beat. His beast was satisfied with her death. It wanted to fight and destroy Griss, but it detested the idea of challenging a female. Her request for mercy appeased the animal's need for retribution.

Letting his gaze sweep the room, he found everyone's attention on him; bear, wolf, and hyena alike. A glance through the dirt-caked window revealed the home was surrounded by his and Reid's men. Good. He focused on the hyena Alpha then. Defiance still lingered in his gaze but that cocky attitude was no longer present. His beast yearned to tear the man limb from limb, but if the Alpha and Sarah were to be trusted, he needed to get to Mia.

"I'm ordering a purge. Twenty-four hours for singles. Forty-eight for family units. This is my town now. I don't want a fucking hyena here in two days."

A glowing rage entered the hyena Alpha's gaze. "You can't—"

Ty snarled and flexed his claws. "I can't what?"

The Alpha's intent focus burned him, the look promising retribution, but Ty's rage burned hotter. When the man said nothing more, he returned his attention to the wolf Alpha. "The Alpha and inner-circle die regardless."

Reid raised an eyebrow.

"What?" Ty didn't have time for games. He felt more of his life sliding away with each breath. His wounds still bled liberally with no hint of stopping any time soon and fatigue clawed him. Griss was on his way to Mia and if he hurt her...

Reid shrugged. "We'll do more wet work and get rid of these pieces of shit and even help in Grayslake if we're needed, but this will become *our* town. Not just the bears' or the wolves', but *ours*."

"You think we can work together?"

"Yes," Reid jerked his head in a quick nod.

"Done." Ty forced himself to stand tall as he reached for Reid—his wounds making themselves known. They each gripped the other's forearm, digging in their claws to seal the alliance between their peoples. Ty didn't have much blood to spare—the poison in his veins was seeing to that—but they needed the connection. More would have to be settled before a true bond could form, but for Mia and Parker's sake, he would work with the wolves.

A growl drew Ty's attention back to the hyena Alpha. "He dies. Slowly."

chapter **fifteen**

Dinner had been a quiet affair, the posted guards cycling through to grab a bite to eat while Mia put plates together. She'd shooed Gigi out of the kitchen once the cooking was done. There was no reason for them to both fret and pace the area. Hour after hour passed and still… nothing.

Keen occasionally got a call and his expression grew graver with each, darkening further until it seemed a storm of rage swirled inside him.

Yet another guard slid onto a stool, and Mia nudged a full plate in front of him with a smile. "Here you go."

He shook his head. "You shouldn't be serving us, Itana. You should—"

"Sit on my happy ass while you work to keep me safe? Not happening, eat your salmon." She smiled to lessen the rebuke and smiled even wider when he did as she asked.

The trill of Keen's cell phone had her looking toward the living room once again, and tension filled her veins. Every time it made a sound, her worry ratcheted higher. Had Ty found Parker? Were they okay? Was Griss dead?

Keen's face flushed, red rising to cover his neck and face, and then the hue was immediately followed by the rush of brown fur covering his skin. Muscles bulged beneath his shirt, shoulders growing in breadth. The hand holding his cell phone grew larger and she had no doubt his nails were now thick and blackened.

In an instant, she was off her stool and racing across the kitchen, intent on getting to Keen and discovering what had him shifting in the middle of the living room.

"You're sure." Keen inhaled slowly. "How many?" He paused. "How far?" Another lull. "Yes, Itan."

Then the phone crumpled beneath the pressure of Keen's grip, plastic cracking and splintering in his fist. The obviously furious and rage-filled Keen turned black eyes on her.

"We need to get you to—"

The sound of glass shattering cut Keen off, the tinkling still filling the air as a bright red spot formed on his chest. It grew and grew, spreading and soaking the fabric. Another noise, an echoing *crack*, came next and yet more red bloomed, covering his side.

Keen roared, more of his bear taking over, and barreled toward her amidst the destruction of the living room. Objects exploded in his wake, and it finally clicked in her mind. He was being shot at. Someone *shot* him.

And still he raced to her.

The moment they hit the kitchen, the male nearby launched across the counter separating them and tackled her to the ground, covering her with his massive body. A huffing Keen soon joined them, the front and side of his shirt now painted in red.

"Keen!"

He grunted, but otherwise ignored her. "What have you got, Ash?"

192

"Teeth and claws, man." The male atop her spoke but didn't release her.

"Fuck." Keen wrenched a cabinet door open and reached inside, yanking off a piece of wood to reveal a hidden panel. A press of several buttons on the concealed keypad had shelves retreating, and a cushioned tray of handguns came into view.

"How?" Ash gasped in surprise and Mia did the same.

"I'm responsible for security, aren't I? Training was gonna start today, but with Parker…" Keen reached for a gun and hissed. "Fucking bastards had to hit me twice."

"Keen?"

"I'm fine, Mia. Ash, look under the sink. There's a panel on the left, rip it off."

The man atop her moved away, doing as Keen ordered. "Got it."

"Good. Punch this in…" Keen rattled off a string of numbers that never seemed to end, but finally there was a hiss followed by a click.

"Holy shit, man." Ash's voice was filled with awe. "Talk about a fucking equalizer." The male emerged from beneath the sink, two large guns in hand. "What the hell are these?"

"HK416s. Point and shoot."

Mia watched with wide eyes while Keen shoved pieces of the hand guns together, pushing and pulling on different parts before moving on to the next.

"Keen, what the hell is going on?" Her voice wavered.

"Griss is outside. Probably with friends." A rapid fire of bullets tore through the large kitchen windows and door while another handful hit the front of the house. "Definitely friends." Keen eased from the cabinet and shoved a gun toward her. "Mia, point, pull the trigger. Keep your arms straight and grip it tight. Try not to close your eyes."

"I don't know—"

Keen didn't let her finish. "Ash, give me one of those 416s."

Roars joined the crack and thump of bullets assaulting the house. Deeper within the home, wood groaned and snapped followed by the heavy thud of feet on the hardwood floors.

In one fluid movement, Keen rolled to his knees and pointed a gun at the hallway, seemingly not hindered by his wounds. Two bears barreled into the room, blood matting their fur and rage filling their eyes.

"Thank fuck." His shoulders slumped. "Ash, to the left of the dishwasher, panel's on the right."

"How many guns are in this kitchen? And when did you install all of this?" Her eyes popped wide when yet another cache of weapons was revealed.

"A lot and when everyone was sleeping."

The crunch and crack of bone preceded the two bears shifting from two feet to four and she recalled seeing them around the house. They each sported several bullet holes, but the pain didn't seem to affect them. The moment they were back in human form, they were on the move, heading toward Ash.

The basement door swung wide and the males surrounding her tensed. Every gun in the room centered on the portal and the man in their sights.

"Wait! Dad, stay put!"

"What the hell?" Another barrage of bullets halted his words.

194

"Griss has come to visit his cousin." Keen slid a weapon over the glass strewn floor to her dad. "Use it." Keen turned his attention to her then. "Itana, you're staying here with Ash and your father. They'll cover the kitchen entrances. You two." He pointed at the other two guards, and Mia realized she didn't even know their names. They were heading into battle and she'd never... "One at the east end, other at the west. I'll take care of the front. Ty is on his way with a shit-ton of backup. We just have to stay alive and keep the Itana safe until then."

"But—"

"Go. I'll lay cover." Keen ignored her and rose to his knees, popping off a few bullets through the now missing window.

The rapid rain of fire ceased as he countered their attack. The two guards took their chance. Keeping low, they split off, heading in opposite directions as Keen ordered.

One raced to the left, his obvious injuries not slowing him. Blood coated his right leg, flowing from a wound in his thigh. The other headed right, mimicking his fellow bear's movements. Except an attacker chose that moment, that second, to sneak through the kitchen door. He slunk inside, gun poised and centered on one of her protectors.

Mia screamed, yelling a warning, but the stranger fired off two rounds, killing the male ready to die for her in less than a blink. It didn't matter that the interloper wasn't able to take another breath— her father and Keen took care of that—but one of her saviors was dead.

Gone.

In an instant.

"He killed him," the words were barely a whisper. "He killed him, Keen. He's gone."

"Mia." Keen gripped her shoulders. "*Mia.*" She blinked rapidly, tearing herself out of her daze, and focused on him. "You're not going to freak out on me, okay?"

She nodded.

He shook her. "I need the words. You're not gonna freak out."

"Right. No freaking out." Her heart raced, pounding and pushing against the walls of her chest in an effort to burst free.

"That's good. Ash, pick up the east." The crunch of booted feet against glass announced Ash's retreat, and Keen turned to her father. "Can you make it over here?"

Her dad didn't respond, but simply raced across the open expanse of the kitchen and dove behind the island. "I've got her. Go."

With that, Keen was gone, dashing toward the front of the house and leaving them alone.

"I'm scared." And she wasn't afraid to admit it.

"Point and shoot, remember that, little cub."

"Right. Right." She nodded, not truly believing in her ability to protect herself.

More pops, bangs, and cracks filled the air, the sounds bouncing off the walls. Suddenly roars joined in, the strike of flesh on flesh reaching them along with the snap of bone. Crap, crap, crap...

So focused on the sounds coming from the front of the house, neither of them noticed the new intruder. A rough, fur covered arm wrapped around her throat, yanking her away from her father and into the center of the kitchen. Mia screamed and clawed at her assailant, scratching and scraping the forearm that held her captive.

196

The rotting scent of sweat and blood clung to the male that clutched her, sinking into her pores and soaking her in the stench. His rancid breath fanned her face and invaded her nose.

"Got you."

Oh, God, no. Not Griss. She fought harder, wrenching against his ever tightening grasp. The press of his arm on her neck crushed her windpipe. Breathing became harder with each passing second. Soon she'd lose consciousness and drift in the horror of darkness.

Her father's roar came on the heels of Griss's words and then her focus was captured by the sight of Griss's arm rising, his hand clutching a gun pointed at her dad.

As if in slow motion she glimpsed the flex of muscles in the man's bicep, the shift of skin as the tightening rippled down his arm, the constriction of his hand on the handgun. The bullet left the muzzle in a flaring flash of light, singing across the room in a blurry zing.

When it slammed into her dad's chest, his skin reacted as if a pebble had struck the surface of a smooth pond. The ripples began at the very center and traveled outward, growing larger and larger. On its heels was an ever expanding blooming spot of blood, traveling through the cloth and soaking the fabric.

Her father's gaze met hers—fear, panic and pain tingeing his features—and then he slowly slumped sideways, body falling to the ground while his eyes fluttered closed.

No. No no no. Her frenzied attack on her captor increased, adrenaline and terror giving her strength. The pressure eased so she could breathe, which only served to give her more power. She struggled, twisting her body while kicking at Griss's legs. Mia dug her nails into his arm as hard as she could, and was rewarded with a snarl.

They approached the basement door, and he flung her down the steps. Her body slammed into stair after stair; shoulders, back, arms, and legs gouged by wood corners. She wrapped her arms around her head, hoping against hope she wouldn't break her neck or crush her skull. Staying conscious would be a very, very good thing.

Mia grunted when she finally landed on the bare concrete floor, body skidding until she collided with the cold bars of the cell.

Warm hands gripped her biceps and then slid over her body. She opened her eyes and met the guard's worried gaze.

"Itana?"

She wheezed, "Behind—"

Griss filled the man's body with bullets. The echoing sounds thundered off the brick walls, and she covered her ears to muffle the report.

The guard—she didn't even know his name—stumbled and then crumpled beside her. Oh God, blood flowed from his wounds and sunk into his clothing, bathing the fabric in red. Despite the pain ravaging her body, she reached for him, stretched her arm until she gripped one of his hands. Mia clutched him, tightening her hold and giving him whatever strength she possessed.

"Itana…" Blood gathered in his mouth and spilled past his lips, tiny air bubbles peppering the fluid.

"Shh… It's okay." She squeezed his hand and tears stung her eyes. He was dying for her. Right here, right now, his life was draining away. All because of her. "It's okay."

"Ita…" The light in his eyes dulled and then disappeared, his soul fleeing him as his last breath slipped from his lungs.

Eruptions, roars, and death from the continuing fight hovered above them, growing louder with each passing second, but her focus remained on the male beside her.

198

A rough hand collided with her cheek, sending her head rocking and face cracking against the concrete.

"You interfering, bitch!" Griss fisted her hair, dragging her to her feet. He stomped to the other side of the room and forced her to her knees. He shoved the muzzle of his gun into the underside of her chin. "Stay right fucking there. Move and you'll go back to Ty in fucking pieces."

Mia shuddered at the visual and bit her tongue. She knew she was dead no matter what and she wasn't about to listen to him. The moment his back was turned…

"Griss, what the hell are you doing?" the captured Itan roared.

"Going to the source, old man." The words were garbled by Griss's half shift, but his intent was clear. He centered his focus on Robert. "Why the hell do I need to *eventually* fucking inherit the title, huh? Fuck that. I handled the brat like you wanted. I'll take care of you, and Cutler is mine."

"No, that wasn't the plan, you ungrateful—"

The Itan didn't have a chance to finish. Shot after shot flew at the male and bullets tore holes into his frail, aged body. Surprise coated his features, and then nothing as blood fled his face and death overtook him.

Griss strode toward the dead guard at the base of the stairs and dug through his pockets, searching and then finally finding what he sought. The male palmed a set of keys and went to the cell's doors, trying one key after another until the familiar click of a disengaging lock sounded.

While he was distracted, Mia eased toward the staircase, dragging her body in slow, torturous flexes of muscle and skin grinding against concrete. The pain pierced her with every movement. She bit her tongue to keep screams at bay. She had to escape, get away from the madman that destroyed her home.

Griss swung the cell door wide and stomped to the prone Cutler Itan. He pressed his fingers against the man's neck. Mia fought to get to the steps. She sensed his rage, and knew she'd die at his hands if she didn't get away.

She crawled faster, scratching the smooth ground. She hurt everywhere, the entire expanse of her body throbbing with agonizing pain.

Then an earth-shaking roar battered the house, racing through the very foundation of the home and pulsing through her. It ached and rattled, but it was so very, very welcome.

Her Itan had come home.

"Fuck, no you don't. You're my ticket out of here." Clawed hands grabbed her, nails slicing into her skin until scraping against bone.

Mia screamed with the added pain. Her yell was answered by yet another roar from above. *Ty.*

"You bitch." The grasp tightened, stealing her breath.

He hauled her toward the steps. Her feet tangled with the leaden limbs of the dead guard, but Griss didn't stop. Her dragging weight forced his claws to dig higher along her biceps until her muscles were exposed from elbow to armpit. Blood flowed, rushing down her arms and leaving a ruby red river in its wake.

They emerged into the kitchen, glass and blood decorating the floor in a macabre mosaic of glittering color. But one person, one man-beast, captured her attention. Ty stood in the middle of the room, rage filling every inch of his heavily muscled, fur coated body. His blood-soaked clothes hung in tatters, barely clinging to his expanded body. Paws replaced hands and feet, while fangs and muzzle replaced a human mouth and teeth.

But his wounds drew her most. Large, gaping gashes and scrapes laid open, exposing the muscles of his body. Blood had dyed his clothing a deep red and she gasped when he swayed ever so slightly.

"Mine!" The roar, like the others, boomed through the home.

"You can have her as soon as you let me go. I'll fucking kill her if you don't." Griss's words filled her ear.

Even in his weakened state, Ty's bear wouldn't hear of it. "Mine. Die."

Griss laughed, the maniacal shriek bouncing off the bloody walls and glass-strewn floor. "Not until I'm out. I leave, and she lives. Otherwise, I'll gut her right fucking now." One clawed hand released her arm and moved to her stomach, the razor-sharp tips slicing easily through her shirt. "Back off."

Ty's gaze left hers for the briefest of moments, flicking to something above her and then focusing on Mia once again. That was her only warning, the only hint she received before the room exploded into action. Rough arms wrapped around her and Griss, breaking the hold the male had on her body. She was wrenched aside while Griss was shoved toward her crazed Itan.

The body that encased her was warm, familiar, and coated in as much blood as she was. She raised her gaze to look at her savior and met her father's concerned visage.

"Dad? You're okay?"

He managed a quick nod before the action in the center of the room drew them. The second she was free, Ty attacked, claws and teeth going after Griss with ferocious, deadly intensity. Her father pulled on her, tugged and yanked in an effort to leave, but she refused.

"No. I have to watch. I have to…"

Be there when he killed Griss?

Be there when he died?

No, Ty would win. Even beaten and damaged, he would destroy the inferior bear and then they could pick up the pieces of their lives, one by one.

Ty swiped at Griss, and the other bear countered, nails barely missing her Itan's already gash covered stomach. Ty responded with another, this time feinting with a half-assed attack on the man's stomach and then aiming for his neck. His nails grazed the insane Griss, sending rivulets of blood down his chest.

The men broke apart, easing away as they circled one another. Bodies crouched, fingers flexing, weight resting on the balls of their feet. They had eyes for each other and nothing else.

Movement near the doorway to the living room caught her attention, and she met Van's weary gaze. A bloodied Keen and Isaac soon crowded behind him. All four of the Abrams brothers were battered and wounded, but it was Ty they worried about.

She glared at the Abrams brothers. Ty was obviously severely injured and he wasn't healing as he should. "Why aren't you helping him?"

A snarl yanked her gaze back to the battling werebears just in time for her to see Ty land another strike. This time, the claws dug into Griss's chest, burrowing deep and exposing muscle and a hint of pale bone. Griss's answering roar of agony had her smiling on the inside. Good. The man should feel pain after the anguish he'd caused so many.

Her father whispered in her ear. "Be easy, little cub. They can't interfere. Griss has attacked Ty's clan and injured his Itana. This has turned into a challenge."

Griss swiped at Ty's arm, leaving a new furrow of torn flesh. Mia gasped and tugged against her father's hold. If no one else would help him, she would. His body couldn't take much more abuse. It already looked like he wore more blood than his body contained.

"Mia," her father snapped, but she didn't care.

"I have to get to Ty…"

Griss dragged his claws through Ty's jagged flesh.

"No." Her father gripped her hard, reminding her about her own injuries. "If you interfere, you both die. Both of you, do you hear me?" She didn't care and her father sensed that. He read her body language and posture with ease. "If you distract him and he falls, then you belong to Griss. The clan belongs to Griss. Do you understand? You need to stay strong for him. Support your Itan."

No. Just… *No.*

"Are you gonna stay put?"

All fight fled her. Every ounce of rage at Griss transformed to worry and fear. Not for herself, but for Ty, for Gigi, for the Abrams brothers, for the clan. What would happen to them if Ty fell beneath Griss's claws?

Mia nodded and stopped struggling. She would watch, she would support her Itan, she would be the Itana the clan deserved. Every twinge and throbbing ache ceased to matter, nothing existed in her world except Ty and his battle with Griss. She had to be strong. She could fall apart later.

Ty landed a blow, digging deep into Griss's shoulder and a rush of blood welled from the wound. Good.

The crazed bear attempted to return the strike, but Ty managed to stumble out of the way, easing just out of reach. Another strike. Another lurch. Ty tripped on a broken hunk of wood and caught himself on the kitchen table. His blood-coated palm slipped over the shined surface and a grunt escaped him. Hints of white bone were visible beneath all of the blood and gore and Mia ached for him. Tears stung her eyes, not from her own agony, but his.

Griss threw his head back and roared, the muscles of his neck straining with the action. The moment the sound left his lips, he leapt at Ty, flying through the air and straight for her Itan.

The two of them collided and fell to the glass covered ground in a tumbling mass of fur, fang, and claw. They rolled, one over the other, shifting and struggling until they finally collided with the wall.

Griss straddled Ty, his knees on either side of Ty's hips, and he attacked. He rained blows down on her Itan, claws and fists colliding with Ty's destroyed body. Gashes formed on gashes, one cut melding with another and Mia couldn't withhold her cry.

"Ty!" She fought her father, pulled and tugged against his hold. No, he wouldn't die, couldn't die. Not when she still had breath in her body.

Mia's father tightened his grip, the arm around her waist holding her fast. She struggled against him and ignored the pain of deep cuts and broken bones, ignored the agony that came with fighting her father's grasp.

Griss brought his fists down again and again… She sensed Ty's fatigue, saw the way each blow came closer to connecting fatally with his battered body.

"Ty!" Tears stung her eyes and trailed down her cheeks, the salty fluid adding to the wetness of her blood. Her Itan's gaze swung to hers, his focus entirely on her and she read his emotions in one sweep. Sorrow, heartbreak, love. "Ty," she whispered. "No." She fought her dad anew, scratching and clawing her father's arm in an effort to free herself. "No!"

The world moved in slow motion and she saw it then, saw the strike that would end her reason for breathing.

Griss lowered his arm, claws extended, nails glistening with Ty's blood. Light in the kitchen reflected off the sticky fluid. Tiny droplets dripped from the tips as they descended, those deadly talons aimed for her Itan's vulnerable neck. The strike sped closer and closer to Ty and she forced her eyes to remain centered on him, forced herself to hold his gaze to the very end. She prayed that he saw her love for him, prayed he realized that every bit of her soul belonged to him and him alone.

"Ty," she sobbed his name, arm outstretched and reaching for him.

Suddenly everything snapped into place. Ty broke from her gaze and captured Griss's arm before he could land the killing strike. He gripped the male's wrist, halting him in his tracks, holding him steady.

While the man fought Ty's immobilizing grasp, her Itan came at him with one great heaving blow. Ty sliced him, nails finding home in his enemy's throat. Each individual claw slipped through Griss's skin like butter, the flesh parting without protest.

Griss pushed away from Ty, clutching his neck in an attempt to stem the blood flow. But it was done and a matter of time now. Griss slipped, dropped to his knees, then slumped to the side, his massive body shuddering. Fur receded, bones snapped into human shape, and the bulged muscles lessened until he was in human form.

"No, you... can't... kill me." The words came with wheezing gasps.

"I did." Ty rolled to his feet and stood tall, staring down at the dying bear.

Pride and joy filled her. Her male would live and the one who threatened would be gone. He'd hurt so many in her new family that she didn't feel an ounce of sadness at his imminent death.

"I'm Itan. Can't... kill... Itan with no... heir..."

Ty dropped into a crouch. "You didn't give a fuck about that a second ago. Besides, if your guy had managed to kill Parker as you'd planned, I'd have a problem. But you hired shit people who couldn't fight worth a fuck." Her Itan reached for Griss, hands on both sides of his face. "I've got a cub, and you've got hell, asshole."

With those words, he yanked the man's head, the rapid movement followed by a low snap of bone. It was done, over, and if Ty was to be believed, Parker was fine.

Her Itan stared down at the dead body, his expression hidden from her by his lowered head, but she knew him. She could read him without difficulty and everything inside her ached for him. She didn't hesitate to shrug off her father's slackening hold and race across the broken remnants of their kitchen. Glass and wood dug into the bottoms of her feet, but she didn't care. She had to get to Ty.

Her movements drew his attention and then he was there, scooping her into his arms and holding her close, enveloping her in his embrace.

"Mia." A million emotions lived in that single word.

Mia wrapped her damaged body around him, disregarding the pain that accompanied the action and ignoring the gore that covered Ty. "Are you okay? Is it true?"

"I'll be fine, sweet cub, and so is Parker. We got him. We're all safe."

Tears filled her eyes, the sting nothing compared to what else filled her body. "Oh, Ty…" She snuggled close, blinking away the moisture. Movement across the kitchen caught her eye. Strangers, killers. Their coloring, and shapes of their half-shifted bodies, were nothing like the bears. She fought Ty's hold. "Ty!"

He tensed and looked over his shoulder, then relaxed. "Easy. They helped us. You're safe."

Safe… Gray eased into her vision, closing in on her, wrapping her in a painless embrace. "And Parker? He's okay?"

"I told you he was."

She looked to him and recognized the truth of his words. "Oh, okay."

Then darkness ruled her world.

chapter **sixteen**

Low whispers brought Mia around, the sweet, high-pitched words countered by a deep baritone.

"Now?" Sweet Parker. Joy filled her at hearing him and the knowledge that Ty spoke the truth washed over her. She didn't think he'd lied, not truly, but real evidence of Parker's survival comforted her.

"No, not now. Soon." Mia recognized the worry that filled Ty's voice.

"But, Pop…" Parker whined.

"Shh… She'll wake soon."

Parker's voice dropped lower until she could barely hear him. "It's been a week, Pop."

A week?

She remembered watching Ty fight, then Griss's death, the strangers lurking in the kitchen and finally passing out in Ty's arms… But a week?

Mia forced her eyes open, lifting the heavy lids with a deep groan, and gazed into the dim room. Immediately two sets of eyes focused on her. Joy etched Parker's face while worry and relief filled Ty's.

"Mim!" The cub's voice bolted through her head, and she winced.

"Shh... Quiet, okay?"

He nodded. "Quiet. Mim, you been sleeping a long time."

Mim? Pop?

"Yeah?" She cleared her throat. "You're okay?"

"Uh-huh," he nodded. "Uncle Griss stole me, and him and Sarah hurt me, but Pop saved me, and I'm all better." The childish grin she received had the residual lethargy drifting away.

"Good." Mia reached out and stroked his little hand. An unfamiliar heaviness weighed down her arm and she noticed the tubing taped to her forearm. An IV. She really had been out of it for a while. "Very, very good."

Ty rubbed his cheek along the top of the cub's head. "Go ask Gigi for a cookie, Parker. I need to talk to your mim for a little while." Parker dashed from the room. The moment he cleared the door, his voice rose in a bellow to Gigi.

Mia winced and pushed the ache aside. She was awake, and the people she loved were alive, including her father. She vaguely remembered him wrenching her from Griss's arms, so he had to be hanging around somewhere.

"Hey."

His anxious gaze remained centered on her. "Hey. How are you?"

"Tired. Achy. How is everyone? What happened?" She licked her dry lips and asked the question she didn't really want answered. "How hurt am I?"

Ty brushed a stray strand of hair from her forehead. "We can talk about it later. We've been waiting for you to wake up. There's no reason to—"

"What happened? What's wrong with me?" She wasn't about to be nudged aside, and there were too many questions pinging through her mind. Both of her arms were wrapped in bandages, it hurt to breathe, and one of her knees was encased in something.

Ty grimaced and pressed his lips together. "We can talk more when you're better."

Mia glared. True, she was plagued with fatigue and pain throbbed through her body, but it was nothing compared to not knowing. "Tell me, Ty."

So he did. Griss and Sarah working together was old news, but the assistance of the wolves and battling the hyenas was new. He still hadn't addressed her injuries.

"We now govern the hyena territory?" She raised her eyebrows.

"No, you and I plus Reid govern the territory."

Her eyebrows rose higher. "But bears and wolves hate each other."

Ty shrugged. "We're working it out."

But a new tension filled him. His muscles were taut, wound tight, and she waited to see if he'd snap.

"What else?"

He refused to meet her gaze, instead focusing on the wall on the opposite side of the room. "Sarah."

"What about her?"

"I had to…" He kept his attention averted, but reached out and twined their fingers together. "Challenges, fighting, that's one thing, but she didn't fight. It was," he shook his head. "She asked for mercy. The hyenas broke her. They raped and beat her. But Mia..." Ty sighed.

Mia shifted until her hand rested atop his and she rubbed her thumb over his skin, giving him comfort in the only way she could.

He turned his attention to their joined hands, staring intently at their woven fingers. "It took less than a second. One slice." Ty met her gaze, and she noticed a growing moisture in his eyes. "She was part of my clan."

She ignored the lingering pain and pushed herself up, shifting until she leaned against her Itan to comfort him as much as he would allow. "She asked. She knew what would happen if you brought her back and if they..." She thought of what the woman would have looked like by the time Ty arrived; battered, broken and raped. "If that's what they did, you were right to grant her mercy." She nuzzled him, reveling in his warmth and the scent of his skin. "What else happened?"

"Robert is dead."

Mia nodded. Yes, she remembered that. "And you..." She dug through her memories. "Killed Griss?"

"Yes."

"How many," she gulped, swallowing past the growing ball in her throat. "How many of ours did we lose?"

"Four. Two during our fight with the hyenas and the two guards here at the house. We still haven't found Martin, so five really."

Tears burned her eyes, the salty liquid stinging and then rolling down her cheeks. "Five?" Her voice cracked, and she shuddered. "You killed him too quickly. You should have let your brothers help. You could have tied him down and sliced him—"

"Mia," he cupped her cheek. "No more of this. No more details. Not today. You just woke up, Itana."

"Ty. I want the rest."

He sighed. "The Southeast Itan didn't arrive until the morning after." His gaze bore into hers. "Parker is ours now. At least until he's capable of being the Cutler Itan."

"Ours?" It was what she craved more than anything in the world, but she worried about whether he spoke the truth. "Really ours?"

"Yes, love, ours."

"But who's going to rule Cutl—"

"We *definitely* aren't going to worry about that until later." He rubbed his thumb across her cheekbone and she leaned into his touch. The stroke soothed her like nothing could, calming her in an instant. "Are you hungry?"

Mia took a minute to take stock of her body's needs. Her arms ached, but she recalled Griss's claws digging deep so it wasn't surprising. It hurt to breathe, every inhale and exhale causing a jolt of pain. She shifted her weight and realized that even more pain radiated from her right leg. But she had to remember her discomfort was inconsequential. She was alive while five of her clan weren't.

Her stomach growled, making its desire for food known. "Maybe a little?"

Ty dropped a kiss to her forehead. "Let me see what Gigi has for you. I'm sure she put something together and is waiting for a chance to take care of you."

He shifted away from her, his hand slowly losing touch with her cheek, and she grabbed his wrist. "Don't leave me alone."

Sadness, worry, and love filled his gaze. "Anything, love. Let me call Gigi."

213

Mia slumped against the pillows once again. Ty reached for the phone on the bedside table and a few button pushes later, he was giving directions to Gigi. He turned off the phone and placed it on its cradle before turning back to her.

"What else do you need?"

Ignoring the pain caused by the movement, she reached for his hand and twined their fingers together. "You. Just you."

A small smile banished some of the fatigue marring his face. He leaned toward her, lips pursed for a kiss, and she tilted back her head in invitation. A week. She'd been gone from him for a week, and she craved the intimacy. He drew closer and closer until mere inches separated them. Yes, they'd have this chaste brush of lips and when she was better they'd—

"None of that, now." Gigi bustled into the room carrying an overflowing tray and Parker skipped in her wake. His smile was infectious, and Mia couldn't help but answer it with one of her own. She was alive, those going after Parker were dead, and she had Ty at her side. Life was good. Perfect even. She just wondered what shoe would drop next.

Gigi nudged Ty aside and leaned over Mia, setting the heavy tray across her lap, its legs balancing on the bed. The sweet woman fussed over her, placing a napkin in her lap and silverware within reach.

"There you go. I expect you to eat most of that, missy. No skimping on meals. You've already lost enough weight as it is." Gigi clucked and then whirled on Ty. "No hanky-panky. The woman near bled to death, has a passel of broken ribs and a busted leg. She doesn't need any of that. I'll let you stay, but you keep those hands to yourself."

Mia smiled at the abashed expression Ty wore. The man probably hadn't been dressed down in years. She glanced at Parker, smiling even wider when she saw he had adopted Gigi's chiding look.

"Yes, Gigi."

The woman harrumphed and turned toward the door. "Come on, Parker. We'll let your Mim and Pop eat while we bake cookies."

"Chocolate chip with nuts and…" The excited boy's voice lessened as he followed Gigi from the room.

Ty tugged a chair to the bedside and reached for her fork. "You heard the woman, no hanky panky." He waggled his eyebrows. "At least not until I get you to eat something."

"I'm not feeling up to—"

"Hush." His eyes softened. "Itana, I'm happy you're alive and awake. I merely wanted to bring a smile to your face." He cupped her cheek. "You scared me. Isaac said you weren't waking up because of a head injury and there was nothing we could do. I can deal with a lot of things, my Itana, but losing you isn't one of them."

"I—" Her emotions were all over the place, bouncing from one to another and yet another. She ached for him, yet yearned to rest. Her mind was willing, but her body… not so much.

Ty speared a bite of potato salad. "Here, try this. You loved it on our picnic."

Yes, she had, but not nearly as much as she'd loved his touch and his masculine scent surrounding her. Mia obediently opened her mouth, taking the morsel and moaning as the flavors coated her tongue. Her stomach growled again, demanding more.

Ty obliged, feeding her morsel after morsel until half of the tray was emptied. She nibbled and snacked and moaned again and again as each new dish crossed her tongue. With each sound, his eyes darkened, his bear coming out to play. The scruff on his cheeks grew, showing her the beast lurked near the surface.

When her stomach was full and sated, she shook her head and slumped against the pillows. She yawned wide and sighed. "No more." She rubbed her stomach, noting there was less than before. A week of not eating had to have resulted in a heck of a weight loss if her once rounded abdomen was not so rounded any longer. "I'm full." He raised a single brow in disbelief. "No, I am. Promise." She yawned again. "Parker called us Mim and Pop?"

Ty blushed and shrugged. "I can't expect him to call us Mom and Dad—he has parents, even if they're not at his side any longer—but he wanted to call us something."

Mia smiled. "I like it."

"Good. You're really done?"

She leaned her head against the pillows and snuggled in. "Uh-huh. Can I get this off?" She raised her left arm to indicate her IV.

"Sure, I'll get Isaac." He lifted the tray from her lap and strode toward the door.

"Wait!" Her voice was hoarse, but still loud enough to have him halting in his tracks. "Don't leave me." She didn't want to be alone, not when her body was so vulnerable. "You can get Isaac later. Just don't leave me. Not yet."

Sadness filled his gaze. "Never, love. Let me put this outside for Gigi, and I'll stay as long as you want."

"With me?" Her heart thundered. "In bed? With me?"

He gripped the tray so hard his knuckles turned white, and fur slid over his forearms. "Mia, you don't understand what you're asking."

She needed him, though. She needed his touch, his nearness, his warmth and scent surrounding her. A week and her body craved him even if her sluggish mind had yet to catch up. It was an animalistic drive to have him close.

"Please?"

Ty felt like a sick fuck. He held a sleeping Mia in his arms, her body pressed tight against him and the remainder of her bandages scraping his skin. Her curves had been reduced during her coma, but that didn't make her any less attractive to him. It did, however, make the bear grumble and growl while it pushed at him to feed her more. His beast demanded Ty return her health so her skin glowed with life once again.

Easier said than done.

Especially when, by having her half-draped across him, he could think of nothing but his throbbing, aching cock. It pounded and pressed against the zipper of his jeans, fighting for release. It didn't help when she sighed and eased closer. Or when she nuzzled his neck and pressed soft kisses on the column of his throat before licking his skin. Her sounds dug into him, clawing and scraping at his control. Now that she was on the mend, his body seemed to take that as permission to lust after her. He really shouldn't have removed her IV. Without it, she was able to wrap her arms around him and snuggle even closer. She'd whimpered and moaned when getting into position, but then a soft hum came from her when she found a pose she liked.

Damn it, he needed to get his mind off of Mia and how beautiful she'd be bare and spread out before him.

Things had exploded immediately after the battle with Griss and his cohorts, and it'd only gotten worse as the wounded and dead were found. The tension was compounded by the presence of the Southeast Itan and his second-in-command. Especially considering the two bears were waiting to speak with Mia before making a ruling about Cutler. Parker's future was secured, but the Cutler clan was in limbo.

Plus, he'd claimed the hyena's town, Boyne Falls.

Then there was Isaac. His brother's face had been torn to shreds, the hyena's claws coated with poison, and instead of tending to himself, he'd cared for others. Which gave the toxins time to do their damage and scar him for life. Ty had sustained similar injuries—the lines still bright red as his body attempted to heal itself—but his scars were nothing like his brothers. Ty's were easily covered by clothing while Isaac's...

chapter **seventeen**

Mia knew there were secrets afoot. They lurked in the shadows and were hidden in horribly produced innocent expressions. If Gigi, Ty or her father thought they were being sly, they were lying to themselves.

She'd been awake from her coma for two days, and the time spent with her eyes open grew with each passing hour. First it'd been fifteen minutes, then an hour, and now she could stay conscious for as much as six hours straight. It wasn't just a desire to be pain free that motivated her to get better, but also the prospect of truly becoming Ty's Itana. Words were one thing, but consummating their joining would solidify her place in the clan.

When she'd questioned her father about her rapid healing, he reminded her that she was half bear. Even if she couldn't shift, a bit of a furball lurked inside her. Hadn't she ever thought it was odd that she never got sick as a child and her bruises typically disappeared in hours? No, she really hadn't. The only reason she'd taken so long to come out of her coma was due to the severity of her injuries. She'd lost a ton of blood and there had been swelling around her brain. Now that she was on the mend and eating well, her body was ready to get up and go.

Except everyone kept urging her to stay in bed.

"You need to rest, need time to heal and regain your strength."

"Aren't you tired?"

"Don't you want to go back to bed for a little longer? Oh, that's good, Mia, here I'll help you with the covers."

Then whoever happened to be shoving those words down her throat would urge her toward the bed before she got halfway to the door.

Well, she was done. She'd been sleeping next to Ty for two days—both of them fully clothed—and the man hadn't given her more than a chaste kiss on the forehead. He'd been trying to keep his battle wounds hidden from her, but she'd caught glimpses of them nonetheless. Every time she saw one of the bright red, jagged lines, her heart ached. He'd fought so very, very hard to get Parker back and he'd wear the evidence of his struggle for the rest of his life.

After a light brushing of his lips across her skin, he'd disappear for the morning, leaving her with her father. Don't get her wrong, she loved her dad. She just didn't love being kept in the dark.

Rising shouts would come through the door now and again, snarls and growls quickly following the sounds, but her father wouldn't let her get anywhere near the door.

"You didn't grow up with bears, little cub, this is how we deal with things," he'd say.

Uh-huh. And she had a bridge to sell.

Then there was the fact that her only visitors were Ty, Parker, her father, and Gigi, and every one of them kept shoving her away from the door and back into bed. Oh yeah, something stank in Grayslake, and it lurked somewhere in her house.

Mia lay on the edge of the massive king size bed while her father rested in a large chair by the bay window. He was engrossed in a paperback, attention completely focused on his book, and she knew it was her time to act.

Feigning a moan, Mia rolled to her side and tugged on her blankets, doing her best to appear restless. In a split second, her dad tossed the book aside and the rapid thump of his feet colliding with the hardwood floors announced his approach.

She hardly hurt anymore, her ribs only putting up a token protest to her movement and her leg was strong once again. Even the wounds on her arms were near fully healed. But she had to put on a good show.

"Mia."

"Oh, you're here." She let her head list from side to side. "I'm so hot, Daddy. Can you help me with these covers and maybe get me a wet washcloth?"

He paled and then went into action. "Of course, little cub."

Large, gentle hands tugged and pulled on the knotted blankets. Good, Phase One of Operation Free Mia was underway. Another few yanks and her legs were free.

"There you go, sweetheart. Let me go get you that cloth."

In a split second, she was staring at her father's back as he hustled his large bulk into the master bathroom. The instant he was no longer in sight, Mia leapt from the bed and bolted to the room's door. She slinked through the open portal and carefully eased it shut behind her. It'd only be a handful of seconds before her absence was discovered. Hopefully it'd give her enough time to find out what had her Itan in knots day in and day out.

Mia dashed down the hallway, keeping to the walls in an effort to hide in the shadows. She tiptoed over the carpet, sprinting forward and then pausing when a raucous yell from Ty's study split the silence.

It wasn't until she was halfway to her destination that her father's first call reached her. Her name was said tentatively with a hint of worry. She'd apologize later.

She padded another few feet to the study's closed door. A familiar cacophony of yells rolled over her. Yet again there was bellowing, growls, and snarls, all coming from within Ty's study. Voices raised, the tones unknown to her, but that didn't change her intention. Ty was in there, fighting and verbally battling with others within his private haven. Enough was enough.

Not bothering to knock or slow her stride, Mia wrenched open the door and marched into the room. She only had eyes from one man within the space and her gaze remained intent on him, on the blackness of his eyes and the dark brown fur that coated his skin. These strangers had pushed him to this, pushed him to nearly losing control.

She inhaled deep, drawing the scents of the room into her lungs. Ty had begun teaching her about clan scent as they lay cuddled in bed. He'd told her how each long-term member held similar flavors that lurked beneath their natural aroma. These two men, old, white haired and wrinkled, did not belong to her clan.

"Mia," Ty growled at her and she ignored him. With luck, he'd spank her later. She'd welcome anything other than tender, sweet touches at this point. She'd relish any stroke that ended with clothes being removed so she could explore his body. She wanted to kiss and lick every wound and thank him for enduring such pain to save Parker and her.

"Gentlemen." She didn't smile in welcome and didn't care that both of them looked affronted when she didn't bother.

She skirted Ty's desk and finally stopped when she stood beside him and leaned against his chair. Now that she'd managed a minor escape, fatigue pulled at her and urged her to lay the heck down. She probably should have limited her flee to freedom to the hallway.

In moments, her father stood in the doorway, the look of fear quickly turning into annoyance. "Mia."

Did everyone have to growl at her?

"So, this is the whelp," the man sitting on the right sneered at her, curling his upper lip and exposing yellowed fangs. "The one who has held up these proceedings. The one you want to tie yourself to and destroy your line."

Destroy? Proceedings?

"Mia, go back to our room. You need to rest."

Narrowing her eyes, she turned her head and glared at him. "I'm fine."

"Mia, little cub, let me get you back to bed."

"I'm. Fine." This time her glare was directed at her father.

"Good. If that's the case, we can resolve the pending matters and return to our own clans." The jerky man cut in. "Miss Baker—"

Ty interrupted him. "Abrams, and you will call her Itana."

The guy's face flushed a deep red. "She isn't—"

"You better think about what you're getting ready to say." Isaac's familiar timber echoed through the room, and she turned her attention to him.

She couldn't have suppressed her gasp had she tried. Isaac's face was dissected by a thick, angry line that ran from his hairline, across his nose, skirted his lip and then farther past his jaw. It continued down his neck to disappear beneath his taut shirt.

Ty had told her, warned her, of Isaac's wounds. He'd explained that his brother's were similar to his own though a little more harsh, but seeing them…

The man grimaced and then quirked his lips in a bastardized smile before returning his attention to the jerk. His expression hardened, causing the redness of his scar to flee and pale against his tanned skin. "She is Grayslake's Itana in everything but deed and all clans should respect her as such."

"Regardless of the title the Grayslake clan has decided to bestow upon her, she's still a half-breed whelp that will end your line!" The man's face reddened until it was a deep burgundy.

Mia hated him already. Frowning, she turned to Ty, doing her best to push away the dizziness that threatened. "What is he talking about?"

"Sit down before you fall down." Ty scowled at her and pushed his seat back. In one tug, she was pulled into his lap and positioned across his legs.

"But what—"

"Dumb girl. Claiming you as his Itana means his sons won't inherit. They have to be able to shift to become the Itan and with *you*," he spat the word, "that won't happen."

Mia looked tilted her head to the side, confusion filling her, and then looked to her father. "But I thought…"

The guy snorted. "That's the problem with women."

"Enough." The other old dude finally spoke, and that single word shut the jerk-esque male up. "Ty's claiming of Mia is not what we're here to discuss. His choice of Itana is an internal matter. We remain in Grayslake to make a ruling regarding Parker and the position of Cutler Itan."

That got her attention. She sat up straighter and stared at what seemed to be the calmer of the two strangers. "He stays and Cutler can run off and find someone else." She waved her hands toward the door. "There's your answer, so shoo."

"Whelp…"

224

Mia rolled her eyes. "What is with you and name calling? My father raised me better than that, didn't yours?"

The man growled, and Ty returned the sound, his overriding the older man's with ease. It bounced off the walls, echoing in the small space. "You will stop."

"Don't you understand what you're doing to your line with that-that—"

Mia had enough. She leaned forward and clutched the desk for balance. "You know what, you're an idiot and an ass—"

"Language."

"How did you get so old without knowing that if there's love between two people, if there's a true connection, then the couple can have children who shift?" Mia was done playing nice. She'd been polite through every ordeal, but this guy took the cake. "Are you ignorant on purpose or are you just prejudiced against anyone who's not full bear?"

"You don't know what you're talking about, little girl."

Fatigue or not, this guy was pissing her off. "Oh, hell no."

"Language."

She turned a bit of her anger on her father. "Really, Daddy? Really? He's being a penis head." Her dad's lips twitched as he fought a smile. Long ago they'd compromised on a few curses.

"Malcolm. That's enough." The nicer guy spoke, silencing the jerk-o-saurus rex. "The Itana is correct."

"But—"

"You live in a town that frowns on such unions, so you believe what you believe. Those of us who see beyond our own territories—and have our clans' best interests ruling our actions—know the truth.

225

Even full humans and bears can produce shifting children. It's just a matter of finding your other half."

"Ha!" She pointed at the annoying guy. "Take that!"

"Mia," Ty groaned and she allowed him to tug her back against his chest.

"He's a jerk. I can't help it."

"He is a jerk." The man's lips twitched. "And I'm Terrence Jensen, Southeast Itan." He rose and extended his hand in welcome.

Mia placed her palm in his, shaking it gently. "What town?"

Terrence shrugged. "Just the Southeast."

Ty whispered in her ear. "All of them."

"Whoa." She opened her eyes wide in shock.

"Quite. Itana, we were waiting for you to recover so we could discuss our plans for Cutler. Due to the multiple deaths in the family, Parker is the only remaining male of that line." His voice was grave and serious.

"He's staying," she blurted the words before she could think better of them. Yelling at old guys was one thing, yelling at the freakin' Southeast Itan was another and she waited for him to blow up at her.

"Yes, he is." He tilted his head in acknowledgement. Whew, no growlies. "At least until his twenty-fifth birthday when he's old enough to claim the position. However, that leaves the clan without a leader for twenty-one years."

Mia snorted. "Considering who they had, they're better off with no one at all."

Ty groaned, "Mia."

"Point taken. Which is why I've decided to appoint a guardian for the town."

"You can't have the Abrams brothers!"

Ty slapped his hand over her mouth and pulled until she was forced to lay her head against his shoulder. "I love you, but shut up."

She loved him too, damn it, but that wasn't how she was going to tell him. Instead of melting, she glared at him.

Slowly the light dawned in his eyes, realizing what he'd said. "Mia..."

She glared at him more, and he leaned forward to whisper in her ear. "We'll talk about it, but I do. More than anything, I do." He pressed a kiss to her temple and then turned his attention back to the men. "Apologies, Terrence. Please continue."

Terrence chuckled and shook his head. "Young love. I remember it well. My Itana," the man turned and looked to Malcolm, "my *human* Itana who bore me three *shifting* cubs, is the same way."

She really wished Ty would move his hand so she could stick out her tongue at Malcolm. Sadly, he did not.

"As for Cutler, it's been decided that Thomas Baker will be the guardian. He's expected to arrive in—"

Mia let loose a scream of denial, muffled by Ty's hand over her mouth.

"Shh..." Ty held her close. She shot an accusing glare at him, and he sighed. "Yes, I suspected, but Mia..."

"It's a good thing, Mia." Isaac interrupted his brother. "I'll go with him, and keep an eye on things while he puts the clan in order. We have no idea what he's walking into. I'm not just a pretty face," he grimaced. "I may not be the clan's enforcer or keeper, but I can destroy others just as well as I can heal them."

Mia whimpered. They were taking things away from her. She'd just found a family, someone to love her, and now they were disappearing.

"Aw, Itana," Isaac winced. "It really is a good thing. I'll watch your dad's back and I won't have to deal with anyone's pity. No one will know the old me." He rubbed his finger over his nose, tracing the jagged scar.

She whimpered again, but ceased her struggling and leaned into Ty.

"You okay?" He murmured, and she nodded. "All right. Terrence your decision has been handed down and witnessed by my Itana. We thank you for your visit. I'll have Gigi pack up your belongings and prepare Thomas for—"

"Wait a minute." Mia's father broke in. "I know you love my daughter, and your clan has welcomed her as its Itana, but there's one detail that hasn't been handled. I'm not dragging my ass to Cutler and dealing with those backwards idiots without making sure she's taken care of."

Mia tugged Ty's hand from her mouth. "Daddy, I can take care of myself."

"Uh-huh." He raised an eyebrow. "This is a father's prerogative." He turned his attention to Ty. "I've been lenient because she's been healing, but I'm not leaving this house until you and your bear have claimed her."

"Fuck." The word popped from her mouth before she could call it back.

"Language."

chapter **eighteen**

Two days later, Ty eased into bed beside still unclaimed Mia, curling his body around her, sheltering and protecting her. The bear demanded the closeness, urged him to cover her with their scent. It also urged him to tie them together, sink his cock and fangs into her and claim her for all to see.

The moment their skin touched, his dick hardened and lengthened, filling his soft shorts. When she'd first awoken from her coma, he was careful to keep his still raw wounds covered, but now he'd succumbed to her wheedling and went to bed shirtless. Because, apparently she slept better if she could reach his skin. *Right.* He'd still worn boxers or sleep pants to bed, unable to face the temptation of his bare shaft coming into contact with her body. If he felt the silken caress of his flesh against hers, he'd take her, strip her bare and then sink into her welcoming heat.

Mia sighed and relaxed further. His touch always soothed his fretful Itana. From the moment the Southeast Itan had made his pronouncement, she'd been on edge. Then again, so had he, but for an entirely different reason.

She wanted him and he wanted her, but he couldn't take advantage of her. Two days ago, after Terrence had made his declaration, Mia had practically fainted in his lap. Without waiting for the man's permission, he'd spirited his Itana away and back to his bedroom. Dealing with clan politics and Malcolm's venom had obviously been too much for her. Now he wouldn't make the mistake of stressing her again. He'd keep her calm while she continued to heal.

Making love—claiming her—definitely didn't fall into the "calm" category.

Mia wiggled her ass, pressing her plump globes against his cock. After almost a week post-coma, she'd regained a lot of the curves she'd lost and in all the right places. Her breasts were large and lush once again, her butt nicely rounded, and her hips had filled out. His love had returned to her curvaceous glory.

And she knew it. The last week and a half had been a battle day in and day out. His brother Van had fetched the remainder of her belongings from her grandfather's house. Now she had an abundance of clothing that hugged each and every curve.

"Mia." He gripped her hip, stilling her action. "Quit it."

"Ty," she sighed and wiggled away from him, turning over until they could gaze at one another. "The non-natives are getting restless." Which was true. Terrence, Malcolm, Thomas and Isaac were ready to get on their way. "And so am I. There's no reason we have to delay any longer."

She poked out her lower lip, and he ached to nip the tiny bit of flesh. He hadn't even granted himself that temptation since the fight with Griss. His lips had never strayed toward hers, and every kiss landed on her temple or cheek.

"I refuse—"

"To take advantage of me in my weakened state while I'm healing and blah, blah. I'll be honest, I tune you out when you start in with that. You sorta turn into the Charlie Brown teacher in my head." Mia wiggled closer until they were chest to chest. "Wah, wah-wah, wah-wah…"

They shared breaths, moist air bathing skin. Her scent surrounded him, crept into him, and sank into every blood cell. It was like she lived inside him, soothing and exciting his beast in equal measure. He craved her more than life, loved her more than anything, and his teeth ached to sink into her flesh.

Love. Fuck. Claim. Those words repeated in his mind over and over. It was a constant litany that quickened with each second he spent close to her. She leaned the tiniest bit forward, sending another wave of that sweet aroma toward him. Then she demolished him, destroyed his resolve, pushing him to the breaking point.

She kissed him.

Only a tiny brush of her lips against his, but it was enough to obliterate the restraining pen around his bear. The barb wire topped concrete block enclosure that kept the bear captive in his mind crumbled with the grazing kiss. His animal roared and broke free of its confines, shoving forward and filling Ty with one single thought: *mine*.

Without thinking, he rolled, pushing her to her back and then placing his body atop hers. He was careful to keep his weight from her body, but he needed the closeness and dominance that came from their position.

"Mine," he snarled. His gums ached as his fangs descended and pushed past the flesh. They emerged in preparation of what was to come. The bear wasn't taking any chances. The animal wanted Ty ready when it came time to bite Mia's shoulder. It still grumbled about their interrupted mating at the clan's gathering place.

Mia spread her legs, and he eased between them. With the juncture of her thighs exposed, the musky, heady scent of her arousal surrounded him, and his cock somehow hardened further. She cradled him perfectly, his dick aligning with her fragrant slit and he couldn't wait to possess her. Memories of the salty sweetness of her cream assaulted him. Those were quickly followed by thoughts of her slick sheath wrapped around his fingers, milking his digits.

She rocked against him, sliding her heat along his rock hard shaft, and he cursed the presence of his shorts. He wanted skin on skin, hands exploring, and mouths trailing in their wake. He'd seen pieces of his lush Itana, but he wanted her laid bare before him.

"Yours. Forever yours."

The words struck him, delved into his chest and wrapped around his heart. Emotions he'd been holding in check burst free and soared through his body. He met her gaze, taking in every detail of her expression and cataloging it. They'd only have one claiming, one chance to make it perfect and mind-blowing, and he didn't want to fuck it up. She was his. Forever his. Mia's eyes filled with so much love and need, the feelings bored into him and swept away the remnants of his hesitation.

"Make me yours, Ty. Not because they want you to, but because you can't live without me." Hope shone in her gaze.

"I can't, Itana." Emotion clogged his throat. "I could never live without you."

Here he was, big, bad Itan and yet he felt the sting of tears. He'd never dreamed he'd end up with a mating like his parent's, never imagined he could find someone who completed him, but he had.

As the words passed his lips, Ty lowered his head and pressed a gentle kiss to her mouth. His cock still pounded and throbbed in his boxers, demanding release, but he refused to be rushed by his bear or his body.

He traced the seam of her lips with his tongue, silently begging her to open for him. And then she did; she admitted him to a slice of heaven. He delved into her depths, tasted and explored every inch of her mouth. Her natural flavors, the sweet honeydew that seemed to invade her, burst across his taste buds. He moaned and pressed deeper, hunted more of her arousing essence.

All the while, Mia's hands explored him, sliding over his arms, clutching his shoulders and grasping his back. She clung to him, tiny human nails digging into his skin and his bear rumbled in approval. It wanted to carry their Itana's marks.

Mia sucked on his tongue, and he groaned, imagining her sucking his cock. Slick, hot and wet, it'd be heavenly as she pleasured him. And he imagined her pussy would be even better.

Easing their kiss, he pulled away from her all too tempting lips and moved back until he knelt between her spread thighs.

She'd worn enticing lingerie to bed every night after her father's demand. She had been trying to tempt him into breaking and tonight's outfit was no different. The silk and lace clung to her abundant curves. Her breasts spilled over the delicate cups meant to keep her flesh contained. Instead, it accentuated her lushness, tempting him with their inability to keep her mounds captured.

The smooth fabric that stretched across her stomach enhanced the dip of her waist and flare of her wide hips. The nightie rose high across her thighs, and when she spread her legs farther, the hem crept up more. Now her familiar, flimsy panties were revealed to him. She seemed to have a pair in every color, but one thing remained consistent: they revealed more than they hid.

The lace snaked its way over her hips, across the rounded mound of her stomach and then faded into a solid, slim panel of silk that hid her treasures from his gaze. The ruby fabric was darkened near her center. Her cream soaked the delicate weave and teased him with what it concealed.

His cock pulsed, anxious to be buried inside her clutching wetness.

Ty slid his hands along her knees, noting the smoothness of her skin beneath his calloused palms. A tremor danced through her body, and he immediately lifted his hands. "Are my palms too rough?"

Mia struck lightning fast, rising until she could grasp his wrists, and she forced his hands back to her thighs. "They're perfect." She eased his touch higher. "Now claim me already."

He chuckled and grinned at her, and a new wave of her arousal crept into him, making him need. But he forced himself to go slow, to take his time as he slid his palms along her sides and traced the curve of her hips. And he moved slower still when he got to her abundant breasts and cupped their heavy weight.

Mia squirmed, a blush stealing into her cheeks, and she tore her gaze from him. "Ty, don't."

He kneaded the plump mounds and rubbed his thumbs over her hardened nipples. "Don't what?"

"They're…" she waved her hands at her chest. "Big and saggy and there's stretch mar—"

Her words ended on a gasp and, from a human perspective, his actions could be frightening, but he didn't care. He had a point to prove. Ty easily transformed his index fingers from human to bear, gaining a razor sharp nail at the tip of each digit, and he sliced through the thin strap that held the top of her nightie in place.

The fabric fell away to reveal the pale, plump mounds he'd been dreaming about for weeks. The one time they'd been intimate, he hadn't had the opportunity to discover all of Mia's secrets, and now he had his chance. He sure as hell wasn't going to waste it.

He cupped her breasts once again, weighing them and enjoying the feel of her silken skin against his. "They're perfect."

Ignoring his pounding cock, he leaned toward the tempting treats. His bear urged him, nudged him closer to their Itana. Keeping his gaze on Mia, he opened his mouth and flicked his tongue out, tapping one of her stiff nipples.

"Oh."

He did it again, gauging her reaction, watching for any hint of pleasure or distaste. He found nothing but desire.

"Oh my."

This time, he captured the bud with his mouth, sucking the hardened nub deep and continued to torment her with his tongue. He flicked and sucked, smiling against her breasts and reveling in every gasp, mewl, and moan that left her lips. She writhed beneath him, arching her back and pressing herself deeper into his mouth. And he took whatever she gave. This was the Itana he craved, the one who demanded, took, and screamed her desires.

"Ty... You... Oh, shit..."

Ty smiled to himself. He really was doing a good job if his mate had begun cursing. He hoped to hear quite a few more before the night was through. With his free hand, he continued tormenting her nipple, plucking and pinching the bit of flesh. Listening to her sounds, he repeated what made her gasp, remembered what made her moan, and eased off when he didn't get the response he craved.

Mia ran her fingers through his hair, directing his movements, her grip trying to force him where she desired. And he'd listen... eventually. For the moment, he was having too much fun.

Releasing her nipple with a soft *pop*, he pulled back and blew warm air across the berry-hued nub, smiling when it pebbled and stiffened even more.

"Ty, if you don't fuck me right now..." Mia growled.

Raising his gaze back to her, he grinned. "You'll do what?"

Instead of answering, she poked out her lower lip and whined. "Please?"

"Please what?" He murmured the words against her breast, enjoying the way she trembled beneath him. The bear chuffed and growled at the delay, but it managed to be a little proud, as well. They made their mate shiver and shudder with desire. Them.

"Please make me yours."

"Gladly."

It took him moments to tear her nightie from her body, a few slices and yanks, and her panties soon suffered the same fate. Then she was completely bare before him.

"How did I get so lucky?"

She was glorious in her pale, abundantly curved glory. Mia squirmed beneath his gaze, face pinking. "Ty."

Still she was embarrassed. Shaking his head, he slipped his claws beneath the waist of his boxers and quirked a brow at her. "Ready?"

Need replaced the embarrassment in an instant, and she held out her hands. "Gimme."

So he gave her exactly what she wanted. One wrenching tug tore the thin cotton from his body and exposed him fully to her. His cock, hard and ready to burst, jutted from his groin. It practically had a mind of its own and seemed to reach for Mia's moist center.

Her eyes widened, passion rising higher in her gaze, and she licked her lips.

"See something you like, Itana?" Ty grasped his dick, wrapped his fingers around his width and stroked his length.

He slid his rough palm along his shaft, starting at the base and traveling to the tip. A droplet of pre-come dotted the end, and he spread the tiny bit over his cockhead. He pressed the pad of his thumb against his slit and moaned with the pleasure the move caused. His balls drew up tight against him, and he couldn't believe he was already so close to coming. Fuck… What she did to him…

Mia licked her lips, and he trembled, want and need warring within him. His bear shoved at him, demanded Ty slide deep into Mia and take what belonged to them.

Soon...

"So beautiful..." She whispered the words, but he had no trouble hearing her.

"No, Itana, you're the beautiful one. Now, let me worship you and show you just how gorgeous you are." Ty eased forward, intent on pushing into her welcoming warmth, but her outstretched arm forestalled him.

"Wait. Will you..." She blushed. He'd never get enough of those blushes. "You know," she gestured toward his cock. Specifically his hand stroking his cock. "Keep doing that?" She licked her lips. "It's just... wow."

Her desire for him had Ty doing as she asked. It had him fisting his cock a little tighter, sliding his hand along his shaft a little slower, and teasing himself just a little more.

"Like this, Itana?" He squeezed his length just below the head, and another pearl of pre-come escaped.

"Yeah, like that."

And then she did something that nearly broke his control. His sweet mate slid her hand down her stomach, through the shortly cropped curls at the apex of her thighs and a single slim finger slipped between her sex lips.

*

Mia wasn't sure what the hell had gotten into her—it sure as heck wasn't Ty—but watching Ty pleasure himself at her request aroused her more than anything before. So much that she couldn't resist the urge to touch herself, to rub her clit in time with him as he stroked his cock. The first touch sent a shockwave of need up her spine, and she moaned with the sensation.

Mia licked her lips. "Touch yourself just like that."

"You're killing me, Itana." He groaned but didn't stop.

"Then I'm killing us both." She spread her thighs wider, and smiled when his gaze seemed more intent as she was revealed to him.

She circled her clit with her finger, going round and round the bundle of nerves that gave her such snippets of ecstasy. She wasn't quite ready to come—she wanted to reach that pinnacle while he was inside her—but she could enjoy herself a little before the grand finale.

She ventured farther south, sliding through the abundant cream that always accompanied Ty's closeness. For weeks, her body had been reacting to his presence, and it seemed like she'd finally be rewarded with what she desired most. She circled her moist entrance, letting her finger tease the delicate tissues, and she tormented herself with what was to come.

Ty's gaze followed her movements, his entire focus on the hand between her thighs and cupping her pussy. "Is this where you want to be, Itan?"

"Yes." He stroked himself from root to tip and back again. "There."

Mia slid a finger into her pussy, enjoying the slight tease of her penetration. It wasn't nearly enough and nowhere close to what she craved, but it served her purpose: it drove Ty crazy.

"Tell me." She'd never been so bold, so demanding and assertive, before. But there was something about Ty—something about being in his presence—that made her that way. It was through his desire, the way he valued her in everyday life, and craved her with his every breath, that had her bursting from her shell. "Tell me what you'll do to me."

"*With* you," his attention drifted up her body until his focus settled on her face. "Not to you, Itana. With you." He licked his lips, and she followed his movement with her eyes. She wanted to kiss him again, be ravaged by his mouth as he filled her with his dick. "I'm going to fill you, consume you. I'll push my cock into your delicious pussy until you beg me to stop and then I'll give you a tiny bit more and you'll…"

Mia shuddered and pushed two fingers into her pussy, imagining it was his hardness. "I'll love it."

"You will. And then I'll make love to you."

Mia whimpered and whined. "I want to be fu—"

"No, it'll always be love, Itana. Soft and sweet or sweaty and rough, there is always love between us. Isn't there?" The deep black of his eyes seemed to darken inexplicably further.

"Always." Mia curled her fingers and found her G-spot with ease, rubbing the sensitive collection of nerves inside her. "*Fuck.*" She rocked her hips. "You'd be so deep, Ty. Right there…" She panted and trembled when another shot of pleasure assaulted her. "Right there…"

Instead of answering with words, Ty growled and then snarled. "Mia, you need to stop or be ready."

"Ready for what?" She retreated and thrust deep again, enjoying the combination of bliss from her own touch and the way sprinkles of brown fur now coated his chest.

"Me."

Mia reveled in the power she held. All her life, men had made her feel as if she weren't good enough. But this man, this *male*, was at the edge of his control and ready to shatter because of her.

Because she was beautiful to him.

Because he desired her.

Because she was, irrevocably, his.

She slipped her fingers free of her pussy and held them up. They glistened in the low light of the room, the moon's glow making them shine in the dimness. "Taste me." She kept the words low, not wanting to break the seductive spell they'd woven around each other. "Taste me, Ty. Am I ready?"

Ty struck lightning fast, enveloping her cream-coated fingers with his mouth and sucking on her digits. His tongue played over each one, suckling and licking as if she were coated in food and he were starving. Each pull went straight to her pussy, her cunt clenching every time he sucked on her fingers. She panted and trembled, shuddering with the sensations that threatened to overtake her.

He finally slipped them free of his mouth. Instead of releasing her, he twined their fingers together and leaned over her, pressing their conjoined hands to the soft mattress. Now his mouth hovered inches from hers, his lips almost within reach.

"You're ready."

"Then make me yours."

The last word had barely left her lips when suddenly he was there, the head of his cock sliding past her outer sex lips and then edging its way into her center. His girth did exactly as she'd imagined, stretching her and filling her until a slight burn sent a low pulse of bliss through her. Mia moaned and wrapped her legs around him, dug her heels into his ass and flexed in an effort to get more of him.

The jerk didn't budge. He did laugh, though. Double jerk.

Inch by inch, he slowly entered her. Ty slipped more and more of his cock into her pussy, the head of his dick caressing and sliding against her inner walls. He slipped in and then retreated, only to push deeper with his next gentle thrust.

Finally, fina-freakin-ly, his hips were snug against her, his dick fully embed within her sheath. "You're mine." He flexed his hips, rubbing against her clit, and she trembled. "All mine. Forever."

Mia gulped. Yup, this was it. This was the tipping point. If they continued, she'd forever-ever be his. She waited for the panic, the denials and screams that this whole thing was wrong... Only they didn't come. Nope, not at all. Instead, a sense of peace joined her desperate need for Ty.

"Yes." She raised her head and kissed him, licking at his lips. A hint of her own musk met her, the salty fluid still clinging to him. That tiny taste of the forbidden made her crave more. "Make me yours, Ty."

Ty kept hold of her hand, fingers still twined, while he pushed up and balanced his weight on his free hand.

And then he moved. It was a small flex of his hips at first; a slow, incremental withdrawal followed by an equally gentle thrust forward. Even as tiny as the movement was, it drove her wild. His veined cock caressed her from inside out, teasing her nerve endings, and a shudder of delight attacked her muscles. Then he did it again, torment combined with pleasure struck her, and she loved it.

With each renewed penetration, his pace increased, giving and taking more from her. She tilted her hips, rocking into each thrust and fighting to take him even deeper than before. Over and over his hot flesh slid into her, stroking her with his hard cock.

She clutched his hand, savoring the added connection to him, but she needed more. She rubbed his forearm, then bicep, and finally stopped her explorations at his shoulder. She seized him, digging her nails into his skin. The tighter she held him, the harder he plunged inside her. His thrusts came faster and fiercer with every passing second, their bodies meeting in a sweat slickened slap of skin against skin.

241

Each time their hips collided she was struck with passionate joy. Her pussy clenched and tightened around his invasion, fighting to keep him inside her. Yes, she wanted him deep and hard within her forever. The more he gave, the more she craved. She wanted him, all of him.

Letting her touch move on, she clutched the back of his neck and sank her fingers into his hair. She yanked on him, catching him by surprise, and forced him to lower over her.

Now he was a living, breathing, ecstasy-giving blanket. Even with his new position, his hips didn't slow. But the angle of his thrusts did.

"Oh, fuck, Ty!" His cockhead stroked her G-spot and his pelvis rubbed her pussy in the perfect way that had her clit singing.

"Is that it, Itana?"

She whimpered. The pleasure stole her voice, but she did manage to nod. She dropped her feet from his hips and planted them on the mattress, pushing against the soft surface so she could meet his thrusts.

"Did I find the spot?"

She nodded and, with her expression, begged him to give her more. He gave her a fierce, bed-shaking thrust that wrenched a scream from her chest. "Ty!"

"Scream for me, Itana. Tell them all you belong to me."

Then he made her do it again... and again... and again...

His pace never faltered, never slowed or deviated from the punishing, pleasurable rhythm he established: hard, fast, and deep.

His thrusts made her body sing and every retreat had her pussy screaming an objection. And all the while, their gazes remained intent on one another. She saw every emotion that flitted across his face. She saw the love that filled his eyes, and the soul-deep need that

242

the bear possessed. She noted his pleasure that grew and grew alongside the determination that she felt the same.

She hoped he saw the same thing when he stared at her.

Mia's pleasure continued to increase, his steady rhythm driving her higher and higher. Each flex gave her more morsels of bliss. The trembles of her impending orgasm wracked her, the sensations pinging through her body and setting her nerves alight with the pleasure. Her muscles twitched and jerked as each bit of heaven filled her.

"Ty… Close…" She gasped with a particularly fierce thrust.

"Let go. I'll catch you."

So she did. She let his thrusts, the meeting of their hips, propel her to the brink. She didn't fight the rising joy and merely allowed herself to be shoved over the edge. She flew, weightless as the pleasure swelled in a giant bubble. It carried her higher and higher, growing with every furious breath and then… it popped.

It shattered and every hoarded snippet of ecstasy exploded. She cried out as the tidal wave of enormous power overtook her and dragged her in its wake. Her pussy pulsed and squeezed Ty's cock, each involuntary motion simply adding to the bliss he gifted her. Wave after wave of rapture assaulted her, beat and pummeled her body with the overwhelming sensations.

She screamed and writhed beneath him, begging and babbling for more. It was too much and not enough and… Her body was no longer her own.

At that moment, it was his. Irrevocably his.

"Ty," she moaned with his next thrust and tilted her head to the side. "Claim me."

*

Ty nearly came, nearly lost it completely when she uttered those two words. His cock throbbed, balls ached, and bear roared. The beast urged him to do as she asked. It demanded he slide his fangs into the flesh of her shoulder and solidify their mating.

His. *Thrust.* His. *Withdraw.* His. *Thrust.*

Waiting a moment or two before ending this pleasurable torment wouldn't kill him. Mia clenched around his dick, her pussy milking him and practically begging for his cum. Okay, maybe it would kill him.

But still he continued. "Come for me again, Itana."

Mia sobbed and shook her head. She still convulsed, body twitching and shifting restlessly beneath him. He knew pleasure thrummed through her veins, and he wanted to add a little more before he caused her any pain. The ecstasy of her orgasm would overshadow any agony his bite produced.

Ty changed his angle, tilting his hips, and he lengthened his strokes. He spent a tiny bit more time snug against her, grinding his hips tightly to hers, and he was rewarded with a deep moan. Yes, that's what she needed.

He picked up a new pace that drove them both wild. Thrust, grind, withdraw, repeat. His balls slapped against the curve of her ass, and they silently begged for permission to come, to fill Mia and claim her from inside out.

"One more Mia and you're mine." Sweat dripped from his brow and landed on her glistening skin, painting her with his scent. Yes, he'd coat her in his aroma, cover every inch of her with his essence so everyone would know who she belonged to. *Yes...*

"I just need..." She tilted her head farther, exposing more of her tempting neck and shoulder.

His bear, pushed to the edge of his control, couldn't resist the temptation. He'd wanted to wait, wanted her to come all over his cock once again before he let himself go, but the beast wasn't having it. The animal burst from its confines and invaded his human body. It forced his head down, stretched Ty's jaws wide and then Mia's sweet blood coated his tongue.

Then… then she found her peak for a second time. The tremors of her body and the way her cunt milked his cock were unmistakable. Her screams of pleasure echoed around them, filling the room and joining the sounds of their bodies meeting.

Now it was his turn to lose control. Ty released the rough harness that kept his orgasm at bay and allowed himself to come. Immediately his cock and balls rejoiced, hurriedly reaching for the pinnacle and then falling over the edge.

Pleasure wrapped around his dick, his shaft hardening and seeming to grow within his Itana as pulse after pulse of ecstasy assaulted him. It encompassed his body, wrapping him in a tremulous blanket of bliss. Now both his body and his bear were soaring with the joy of release and claiming. Mia was theirs now, and no other could ever take her from him. He'd mated her, claimed her, in the way of his kind.

Mia whimpered, and he noted the trembles triggered by her orgasm eased, and Ty slowed his thrusts until he simply rested against her. He kept his softening cock inside her soaked pussy, not looking forward to separating from her body. It'd have to happen… eventually.

He slipped his fangs from her abused flesh and lapped at the wound, sealing the tears with his saliva. The berry sweetness of her blood coated his taste buds and his cock twitched in sparkling arousal. Shit, he couldn't go again. Not yet.

Another gentle lap and he finally looked at his handy work. The injury was red and agitated, but the outline of his bite was unmistakable. Any who laid eyes on his mark would know she was well and truly claimed—and loved—by her Itan. The more fierce the bite, the more emotion had overtaken the bear during their mating. And her mark was... He winced and realized that maybe he should have been a bit gentler. But she'd begged and squeezed and then the bear had...

Mia wiggled and moaned, and all bits of regret fell away under the pleasure she rekindled. Ty sighed. He had one last thing to do before he lost himself in her body once again.

Ty rolled away from her, causing her to whimper, and he could practically hear his cock whine along with her. He sighed. He rolled to his side and then kept going until he stood tall beside the bed. He strode around the furniture, and he caught her blinding smile. Hell, did his bare ass put that grin there or was it something else? He'd definitely have to investigate later.

It was another half-dozen steps to his destination, and he stopped by the double doors that separated his haven from the rest of the world. Resolve and determination filling him, he let his hands shift into his bear's claws. Reaching up, he dug his nails into one of the solid wood doors, nails sinking into the surface with ease, and wrenched the panel. It snapped from its hinges without protest, and he tossed the hunk of wood into the hallway.

Taking a deep breath, he released his bear's frustrated roar, shaking the floor and walls with his volume. He wanted everyone to listen, and listen good. "It's done. Now get the *fuck* outta my house!"

chapter **nineteen**

The bite on her neck ached, throbbing when she turned just right, or rather, wrong. But the pain didn't matter, not when she was truly the clan's Itana, and no one could do anything to remove her from the position. Well, they could kill her... She cut a narrow-eyed glance at Malcolm. She wouldn't put it past that asshole-ish bear.

Ty wrapped his warm arm around her waist and tugged her close, pulling on her until she was snuggled against him in the shelter of his body. "Quit growling at him."

That was about the time she realized she *had* been growling. Dang. Ever since she'd mated Ty two days ago, she'd exhibited more and more werebear traits. Growls, snarls, achy gums and hairy legs were the worst of her symptoms. The hairy legs pissed her off most.

Instead of responding to Ty's suggestion—she refused to be ordered around—she nuzzled his shoulder and drew in a lungful of his scent. His flavors never failed to calm her. The heated musk of man and the clean aroma of grass reminded her of spring days and the wicked nights they spent together before the final showdown with Griss.

She caught Malcolm glaring at the two of them and she growled in return; on purpose and everything.

"Mia…"

She huffed and turned her glare on Ty. "He started it."

"It doesn't matter. He's Terrence's second in command, even if he's an ass."

"Language," her father harrumphed.

Mia turned, slid from Ty's grasp, and faced her father. He had a worn bag slung over his shoulder and his suitcase, just as dinged and damaged, sitting at his feet. Tears burned her eyes, the reality of what was to come hitting home. A fist clenched her heart, squeezing tight until she thought she'd die on the spot.

"Dad," she whispered.

"Little cub." He dropped his duffle and opened his arms.

She didn't hesitate to wrench from Ty's grasp and launch herself at her father. As always, he caught her with ease, and the welcoming scent of home wrapped around her. Peace enveloped her, sinking into her soul. She pressed her cheek against his neck and squeezed a tiny bit harder, holding him closer.

"I don't want you to go. You can move to Grayslake and—"

He stroked her back, large, familiar hand soothing her as he had so many times in the past. "Hush."

Mia sobbed, she couldn't help it. Not when it seemed like half of her heart was being ripped from her chest. A gaping hole had lived in her soul before she'd met Ty, and for the first time, she'd felt whole. Now her father was being torn from her. Just when she'd found happiness, it was being stomped on by the Southeast Itan.

"But—"

Her father rubbed his cheek on the top of her head, his scruff dragging against the strands. He was marking her as his, something he'd done through her entire life. "Who's my best girl?"

She answered as she always did. "I'm your best girl."

He brushed his lips across her temple. "And a few hundred miles isn't gonna change that," he whispered against her skin. "You have your fated mate and that small cub to raise. And I expect to hear about a new grandchild on the way real soon."

Heat suffused her cheeks. "Dad."

He gave her one last kiss on her forehead. "Like the whole house hasn't heard you. Shit."

"Language." She smiled and squeezed him.

He harrumphed. "*Shoot.* I understood the first night, but I ended up at Van's last night just to get some sleep." He tightened his arms for a brief moment then released her and stepped back. "Now, call me as much as you want, and I'm only six hours away. Less if I fly."

Ty wrapped his arm around her waist, pulling her close once again. "Same goes for us. We know Cutler didn't treat your family well. If you have any problems…"

Isaac joined their group. The harsh scar that bisected his face no longer held the bright red hue of a new wound. His bear had obviously gone to work on fixing the gouge. Except there was only so much the animal could do when the cut was poisoned and the toxins were given a chance to dig their hooks into his cells. He smiled at her, the left side reaching its full height while the right sagged just a bit.

The realization he'd always be hindered by the wound cut her. She knew women. Most were always quick to judge based on appearances, and plenty would overlook Isaac Abrams. They didn't know what they'd be missing.

"Not worried about me, bro? I'm crushed." Isaac clutched his chest.

Ty snorted. "You'll get over it."

The two brothers joked with each other, trading barbs, and another pang struck her. She'd gotten used to the snarky exchanges and now there'd be one less... She sniffled and wiped away the tear that trailed down her cheek.

Her father took a deep breath, his nostrils flaring and then he released it on a slow exhale. He looked at her with a mixture of pity and pure joy. "Aw, Mia..."

"What?" She brushed aside another tear.

"You know." He raised a single brow.

"I have no idea what you're talking about." She furrowed her brow. Maybe he was going senile already.

He smiled wide, his attention shifting to her stomach and back to her face again. "None?"

"But it doesn't..." The conversation between Ty and Isaac became a low buzz in her mind, her brain focusing on the idea her father had planted in her head. "One time..."

"One?"

Her cheeks burned and she could only imagine how red her face was now. "Okay, but that's fast." She gazed at the curve of her stomach and ran her hand over the slight swell. Not that the swell was due to a baby or anything—chocolate really was her best friend—but could there be a little peanut in there? "Now is fast, right? It is fast. It seems fast. I mean, it takes lotsa times for *that*. You and Mom never had another cub, and you were together for years before... Well, before."

"You mother and I never..." This time it was her father's turn to flush pink.

Oh.

"But you were mated."

"And there are plenty of ways to love someone." He cleared his throat. "But that doesn't matter. Your scent is just a tiny bit different."

Different.

"Baby?" Ty squeezed her waist, and she turned her attention to her Itan.

"Yeah?"

"It's time for them to go."

"Go?" Her mind reeled. She wasn't ready for babies and diapers and... "We've only been mated for two days," she blurted out the words.

Ty raised his eyebrows. "And?"

"And," her father cut in. "I'll be seeing you two in just over seven months." His gaze was telling, his focus shifting from Ty to Mia's stomach and back again.

"Seven months?" she whispered.

"Seven months!" Ty's shout overrode her.

"It takes nine. I know about biology. I failed it a couple of times, but it takes nine." She was babbling, and she knew it, but couldn't seem to stop. "I can count. One, two, three... Nine!"

Her dad stepped forward and pressed a soft kiss to her cheek. "I know, little cub, I tutored you through every semester. But that doesn't change the fact that I'll be back in seven months. It's a werebear cub."

Dazed, she watched her father shake Ty's hand and then the brothers exchanged one of those manly, back pounding hugs. All three men smiled wide, joy and excitement filling every crease and line of their faces while she… freaked the hell out on the inside.

Like, freaked.

"Aw, little cub." Her dad's voice drew her attention. "I loved you with everything in me and you'll love this cub twice as much. You'll be fine."

"Fine," she whispered and nodded, not believing herself for a second. "Right, fine."

And that was the one word she kept repeating as her father and Isaac got into their SUV. And when they backed down the driveway. And she said it a few more times as Terrence and a still scowling Malcolm did the same. And for the last time when she finally stood alone on the front porch of her new home.

Mia stared at her stomach, rubbing the small swell and imagining the tiny life that was probably, maybe not—and wouldn't *maybe not* be awesome because she wasn't ready for a child—nestled in her womb. "Everything will be fine."

THE END

about celia kyle

Celia Kyle would like to rule the world and become a ninja. As a fallback, she's working on her writing career and giving readers stories that touch their hearts and *ahem* other places.

Visit her online at:
http://celiakyle.com
http://twitter.com/celiakyle
http://facebook.com/authorceliakyle

If you'd like to be notified of new releases AND get free eBooks, subscribe here: http://celiakyle.com/news

copyright

Summerhouse Publishing
2885 Sanford Ave SW #26314
Grandville, MI 49418
http://summerhousepublishing.com

Made in the USA
Lexington, KY
28 February 2019